What people are saying about …

heading home

"*Heading Home* is the delicious unfolding of A. J.'s tale. Our favorite firecracker of a girl with the fake Southern accent is coming into her own as an adult. Whether A. J. is seeking after God on starlit night, arguing with her Italian American family on the phone, or drifting out on the lake with the cowboy of her dreams, Riva takes us on a journey of hilarity, holiness, family fun, and true love. *Heading Home* made me feel like I came home."

Susanna Foth Aughtmon, author of *All I Need Is Jesus and a Good Pair of Jeans*

"Renée Riva's *Heading Home* is a touching, satisfying episode in the life of the irrepressible A. J. Degulio. Reader beware! Beginning this book near bedtime may result in daytime drowsiness!"

Sylvia Dorham, author and voice-over artist whose credits include Riva's *Saving Sailor*

"A sweet tale of true love, quirky characters, and a girl named A. J. you can't help but adore. Renée Riva is a gem of an author in Christian fiction. Everyone should have the chance to enjoy her wonderful stories, and *Heading Home* is a great addition. *Viva la famiglia!*"

C. J. Darlington, author of *Thicker than Blood* and cofounder of TitleTrakk.com

"Riva's warm, often humorous, and delightful story of first love, loyalties, and complicated promises offers readers a mix of faith and fun wrapped in fiction."

Gail Welborn, review in *Seattle Christian Book Review Examiner*

"Quirky characters and infectious humor!"

RT Book Reviews

"*Heading Home* wins a place on my bookshelves that house only titles I plan to read again and again. The humor, the pathos, and the believability of the characters and the plot make *Heading Home* an absolute delight—enjoyable and unforgettable. Renee deserves high praise for a book that will touch lives and teach tolerance while adhering to strong Christian beliefs."

Colleen L. Reece, author of 140+ "Books You Can Trust," six million copies sold

heading home

heading home

a novel

renée riva

David C Cook®

transforming lives together

HEADING HOME
Published by David C. Cook
4050 Lee Vance View
Colorado Springs, CO 80918 U.S.A.

David C. Cook Distribution Canada
55 Woodslee Avenue, Paris, Ontario, Canada N3L 3E5

David C. Cook U.K., Kingsway Communications
Eastbourne, East Sussex BN23 6NT, England

David C. Cook and the graphic circle C logo
are registered trademarks of Cook Communications Ministries.

The Web site addresses recommended throughout this book are offered as a
resource to you. These Web sites are not intended in any way to be or imply an
endorsement on the part of David C. Cook, nor do we vouch for their content.

This story is a work of fiction. All characters and events are the product of the author's
imagination. Any resemblance to any person, living or dead, is coincidental.

Photo of elephant in AfterWords courtesy of Wendie L. Wendt.

LCCN 2010920348
ISBN 978-1-4347-6776-9
eISBN 978-0-7814-0438-9

© 2010 Renée Riva
Published in association with the literary agency of Alive
Communications, Inc., 7680 Goddard Street, Suite 200, Colorado
Springs, CO 80920. www.alivecommunications.com

The Team: Don Pape, Jamie Chavez, Amy Kiechlin,
Sarah Schultz, Jaci Schneider, Karen Athen
Cover Design: Jason Gabbert, The DesignWorks Group
Cover Photos: Shutterstock, royalty-free

Printed in the United States of America
First Edition 2010

1 2 3 4 5 6 7 8 9 10

012710

For my Mom –
And in loving memory of my Dad –
Who gave us a place called home

Acknowledgments

Once upon a time, there was a quirky little kid with a big dream. And now that I'm big, I realize what a gift it is to be living that dream, doing what I love most. Writing. I also realize that it takes a village to raise a writer and launch a book. I would like to take this opportunity to thank my village:

Beth Jusino for taking on this quirky writer. Don Pape for taking on my quirky stories. Jamie Chavez, Jaci Schneider, Sandi Winn, and Sylvia Durham for helping me to write a little less quirky. The amazing team at David C. Cook for getting my books into print and out to readers.

My people: Linda Henning, my lifelong friend and veterinarian consultant. JoAnn, my wild and adventurous traveling companion. Pat Kunzl, Fan of the Year. Tisha Bryan and her class of kids, for praying for my books. My dear Greek friends, the Tahopoulos family, for your help with words, wisdom, and traditions. You are the real deal, and I'll miss you. My church family and all of your adorable children. Seraphim A. Dunaway, for your love of writing, heroic saints, and noble characters. May you grow up to be one of them. My endorsers, for saying nice things about my books. The folks at the Desert Gold Motel, where my stories came to life. And my faithful friends and readers who allow me to keep writing.

Especially Bear, my big hunk husband … I'm at a loss of words with gratitude. Enjoy it while you can! Mom, for raising this quirky kid and not squelching my creativity. *Mia famiglia,* it's always about *you,* isn't it?

Thank you, all, for being part of my village and for helping this kid's dream to come true. God bless you, everyone.

Glory to You, Lord Jesus Christ. At the end of the day, it is really all about You.

From a crumbling castle in the hills of Tuscany ...

In the fall of 1968, when I was ten years old, our family moved to an old castle in Tuscany, Italy. My one regret was that I had to leave my dog, Sailor, behind. My sole comfort was that my friend Danny agreed to keep him for me until I could return someday. *Someday* turned into eight years.

We wrote letters frequently on behalf of Sailor. Every once in a while we would remember to mention his name....

> November 27, 1974
>
> Dear Danny,
>
> How's Sailor? Here's my school photo of me at sixteen. I can't believe I've been here for six years! I'm still planning to come to Indian Island when I turn eighteen, to attend veterinary school. Be sure and reserve Papoose for me to rent for the summer. Only two more years until I get to see Sailor again.
>
> How are you? Are you a pastor yet? Besides a vet, I'm kind of thinking of being a nun. Then I could help starving animals and people. I wrote Sister Abigail about it. She said I could probably do both.

Write back, please.

Yours truly,

A. J.

December 13, 1974
Dear A. J.,

Sailor really liked your school photo. You sure don't look ten years old anymore. Sailor is very glad you're coming back. He wants you to be sure to call me as soon as you get here. Things are going well for me. I'm now the youth pastor at Squawkomish Baptist.

I was walking through Saddlemyer's Dime Store when I saw this snow globe. For some reason it reminded me of you. Merry Christmas!

Hurry home—Sailor misses you,

Danny

Arrivederci, Roma!
July 13, 1976

"Surprise!"

My carry-on bag nearly drops from my hands as loud, smiling faces suddenly spring up out of nowhere. A mix of birthday balloons and banners with "GO WSU COUGARS" fills the already-crowded waiting area at my departure gate in the Rome International Airport.

"Happy birthday and *arrivederci,* kiddo!" Mama yells, accompanied by that confident gleam of victory, confirming that she has successfully pulled off the surprise party of the century. Who but my mother would stage a going away–birthday party in the middle of a busy airport?

This is the day that I have been longing for for eight years ... my return to Indian Island, my childhood haven. I'm only hours away from being reunited with my best friend, Danny, and my faithful dog, Sailor, and looking ahead to a hopeful future in veterinary medicine.

"Now boarding flight 49 to New York." As the announcement comes over the intercom, I am suddenly surrounded and smothered with hugs and kisses from Mama, Daddy, my sister, my brothers, aunts, uncles, cousins, courtesy cousins, and best friends Bianca and Dominic.

Inching my way through the boarding line, my last hug comes from Dominic, my closest male companion of the past four years. "*Ciao,* Angelina." He smiles and kisses my cheek. "I'm going to miss you."

I return Dominic's kiss. "*Ciao, amico mio.*"

At my parting gate I wave good-bye to all I love, then turn and walk down the Jetway toward home … half a world away.

❧ 1 ❧
Return to Indian Island
July 1976

The rowboat smashes into the dock with a thud. A startled mallard plunges into the lake and paddles quickly away.

"I'm home!" I yell at the top of my lungs. I've waited eight long years to hear myself say those two words again. Stepping onto the shores of Indian Island is like stepping back in time. Hidden among the trees in the Pitchy Pine Forest, little Papoose awaits its family's return. Voices and laughter still echo from its walls: Mama, Daddy, Adriana, J. R., Dino, and Benji. The faint squeak of a hamster wheel drifts from the shed like a sad melody, carrying the memory of Ruby Jean.

Running toward the cabin, the words ring over and over in my head, *I'm home! I'm home!* I whisper it this time, just to hear myself say it again. Feeling quite smug that I still have the key, I let myself in, relishing the thought that no one else knows I'm here. I'd debated over clanging the bell on the main shore, knowing the mini tug would have come for me, but I wanted my reunion to happen right here, on my old, beloved island.

When I enter the cabin, I'm relieved to find everything in Papoose the same as when we'd left, as though no one has taken our place. My eyes dart to the phone number of Big Chief, still tacked to the wall above the phone. I've played this moment in my mind so many times.

Lord, help me to pull this off. Dialing the number, my hands begin to shake. The old, familiar ring blares in my ear....

"Hello?"

It's Danny. That same Southern voice that made my heart skip a beat the first time I ever heard it is making it pound now. "Well, howdy on ya!" I bellow, in the best Southern drawl I can muster—not easy, after speaking Italian for the past eight years.

There's a long pause. "Howdy yourself. May I ask who's callin'?"

"You can ask all ya want, but I ain't gonna tell ya. I'm frankly more in'erested in that log cabin you've got over yonder from your place a piece. Any chance it might be up for rent this summer?"

There is no way Danny would even think of being stuck on an island with some kook. He'd rather leave Papoose empty than have to deal with a nutty neighbor.

"Who *is* this?" He sounds more curious than annoyed.

"Well, who in the Sam Hill do ya think it is?"

"Um, I have no idea, but in answer to your first question, I don't rent that cabin out. I have a family I keep it reserved for ... for whenever she ... *they* come back."

I can't stand it any longer. "Well, Danny boy, it just breaks my li'l heart that you don't recognize a true Southern belle when you hear one." *That'll get his wheels turning.*

"... No way ... A. J.? Is that you?"

"*Bingo!* Race you to Juniper Beach—and bring my dog!" I slam down the receiver and dart out the screen door so fast it nearly flies off its hinges.

I'm whippin' down that old Pitchy Pine Trail faster than a baby jackrabbit. The first thing I see when I reach Juniper Beach is my big old dog.

"Sailor!" I cry, with tears streaming down my face. Sailor comes barreling down the beach, twice as fat and half as fast as when we parted. He pounces on me so hard I nearly fall over. I bury my face in his fur and sob like the day I found him on death row. When I look up, I see Danny walking toward me real slow, as though he doesn't want to intrude on my reunion with Sailor.

Wiping away my tears, my eyes come to focus on the face I've so longed to see—besides Sailor's. *Oh … my … gosh.* This is *not* the Danny I remember. Before me stands a towering six-foot-somethin' sandy-blond, sun-bronzed cowboy—a perfect cross between the Duke and Little Joe Cartwright. When we're within arms' reach of each other, we both just stop. Eight years is a long time—from saying good-bye as kids to saying hello as adults.

"Hey, A. J.," Danny says, real tender.

No one has *ever* said my name the way Danny says my name … with the most beautiful Southern accent I've ever heard in my entire life. I stand still, just staring at him … and I have only one thing to say. "Can you ride a horse?"

Danny looks taken aback and amused at the same time. "Did you just ask me if I can ride a horse?"

(Daddy once told me, "A. J., when you find your cowboy, make sure he can actually ride a horse. Any man can put on the hat and the boots and call himself a cowboy, but only a real man can actually ride the horse.")

"Um … never mind," I answer. "But can you?"

"Ride a horse?"

I nod. "Uh-huh."

Now he's grinning, like he just realized I must be the same quirky kid he knew before. Not bothering to ask why, he just answers the question. "Yeah, A. J., I can ride a horse."

"Oh. Okay."

"Is that good?"

"Yeah. That's good." *That's real good.*

Now Danny's looking at me with those blue, blue eyes that always made me feel like he could see right into the depths of my soul. Is this really my childhood friend? Our nearly four-year age difference that once posed such a gap between us seems strangely insignificant now.

Danny sticks his hands in his pockets. His expression suggests that maybe he's thinking the same thing. I wonder if he still sees me as the same freckle-faced kid with the fake Southern accent who could squirt half the lake between her two front teeth. At least I've grown into my teeth now and speak Italian instead of Southern.

So here we are face-to-face, after all these years, in a standoff, wondering how we're going to fill this awkward moment. In the midst of our dilemma, Sailor charges up from the water and takes a flying leap right for me. I'm shoved headlong into Danny and fall to the sand in his arms.

He smiles down at me then glances over at Sailor. "Good boy," he whispers. "It only took me eight years to teach him that trick." He laughs while gently brushing sand from my face. His eyes linger for a moment as though he's contemplating something, then he glances down the shoreline. "So … how would you like to go out on the water?"

"Drifting?" I've dreamed of nothing else since I left the island.

"Drifting it is. I'll launch the boat." He helps me up then heads toward the old dinghy resting on shore. Wedged deep in sand and beach grass, it doesn't look like it's moved since I left. I watch Danny grab hold of the bow and hoist it from the shore to the water as though it weighs nearly nothing. With a shove, he launches it into the bay. "Your ship awaits you," he calls down the beach to me. Sailor lops along the shoreline and leaps into the boat, barely clearing the oarlock. The old dog just ain't what he used to be, but he obviously still loves to drift.

Sailor takes the front seat with his nose to the wind, resembling a hairy bow ornament. I take the middle seat, Danny takes the stern. The sun is slowly sinking behind the hills, casting an orange glow over Indian Lake. I arrange myself in drift mode: lying on my back across the seat, eyes to the sky, feet hanging over the side of the boat. Danny follows suit, clasping his hands behind his head. I breathe in the sweet, warm summer air. "I'm home," I whisper, glancing over at Danny.

He returns my smile. "Welcome home, A. J."

A gentle breeze ruffles up Sailor's fur as he turns his nose to catch the scent in the wind. I'm so happy to be back with my dog. My eyes shift from Sailor to Danny. I cannot get over that this is really Danny Morgan.

He looks over and catches me staring.

"You've gotten taller, haven't you?" I say, trying to cover myself.

"Maybe a few inches."

"Maybe a few feet! What did they feed you on that farm, Miracle-Gro?"

"Grits." He smiles. "Lots of grits."

Grits look good on you. "So, do you miss your farm life?"

"Sometimes. But I'm pretty excited about my plans for the island."

"Plans?"

He glances around like he's about to divulge a secret he doesn't want anyone else to hear. "You tell me your plans first, then I'll tell you mine."

"Okay. Well ... for starters, my veterinary courses start up in September, and will probably take me ... about the rest of my life to complete."

"Washington State University?"

"Yep. Go Cougs!"

"But you're staying on the island, right?"

"Right. Grandma's letting me use her car. The campus isn't that far, really—takes me less than a half hour each way. It'll cost a lot less to live here and commute than if I live on campus. As long as your new plans don't include upping the rent on me."

Danny smiles. "I can probably swing you a pretty good deal— like rent free, if I can get you to help me with my plans." His smile turns to a grin.

"*Really?* You may have yourself a deal! I couldn't bear the thought of giving up the island to live in a dorm. Besides, they don't allow dogs in the dorms." Sailor perks up at the word *dogs* and wags his tail. "Wait—maybe you'd better tell me what your plans are first."

"*Well* ... I'm thinkin' of turning the island into a summer camp."

"A summer camp? On the island?" I swing my feet back in the boat and sit up, facing Danny.

"There are a lot of kids around here with nothing to do in the summer," Danny says. "I'd like to offer them a place to go. My dream is to eventually work here full-time. Summer camps all summer, weekend retreats fall and winter."

"What happened to becoming a preacher?"

"I can still preach to the kids at camp, but as far as becoming a full-time pastor for a church, my heart's turning more toward a summer camp on this island."

"And what will you do on your summer camp island?"

"Well," Danny swings his legs into the boat and sits up too. His eyes light up like a little kid talking about his birthday plans. "Every time I get out on the lake to go fishin', I look back at the island and picture the whole setup. Big Chief was first built as a hunting lodge, you know, so it's definitely big enough for the camp headquarters."

That explains all those deer and moose heads hanging on the walls, anyway.

"The dining area could probably handle enough tables for a mess hall, and that old stone fireplace would be a perfect gathering place. Then I'll need to insulate the other two cabins to withstand the winters. That way we can rent the camp out for weekend retreats during the rest of the year to keep a cash flow coming in."

"Who would be renting it?"

"Churches and social groups are always looking for peaceful getaways for their retreats. What could be more peaceful than this?" Danny looks around like he is the proud owner of the best island in the world. I happen to agree with him on that. "We could pull in business from Coeur d'Alene to Moscow along the Idaho border and from Spokane on the Washington side."

He keeps saying we.

"Then, I thought Pocahontas could be the bunkhouse—should be able to fit about a dozen bunks upstairs and another dozen down—around fifty campers total—counselors included. Girls upstairs, boys downstairs, with no common access. And Papoose … I'd like to keep Papoose for the local residents." He smiles over at me. And he still has the bluest eyes I have ever seen. *Sigh.*

He continues, "Then, out in the Pitchy Pine Forest, over by your cemetery, I'd have archery.…"

"Hold on. You can't have a bunch of kids stomping through my critter cemetery chasing after arrows. Those are sacred burial grounds."

Danny looks at me. "I hadn't thought about that. Now that's something new to consider. That might weird out a few of the parents if their kids come home talkin' about running through a critter cemetery."

"There is nothing weird whatsoever about people burying their pets."

"Pets, yeah. But bugs, lizards, mice, and rats may be a different story."

"Who's going to know what's buried there if they don't dig 'em up? Besides, after eight years there's probably not much left of them."

"Okay, fine. I'll put a locked gate on it. We'll just tell the campers we have a few of our dead relatives buried in there. It wouldn't be camp without the makin's for a few spooky stories." Danny laughs.

"So anyway, as I was explaining, the best part is down at Juniper Beach. Get this: swimming, fishing, and sailing on the lake, with campfires and stargazing on the beach at night. And then ... in the clearing over by the chapel, behind your critter cemetery, I'd build a corral for my ponies."

"What ponies?"

"The ones I'm hoping to buy at the spring auction in time for the official camp opening next summer."

"And how do you plan to get your ponies out to the island?"

Danny looks at me like it's the most obvious thing in the world. "On the tugboat."

"Ah, the tugboat—of course."

"By the way, I'm hosting about ten Sunday-school kids for an overnight campout this Friday. I thought it might be a good opportunity to get a feel for what I'm in for on a small scale. My assistant youth leader offered to help with the girls if I need her, but, now that you're here, I thought I'd offer the job to you first. Any chance you'd be willing to help with the girl campers?"

Looking back at the island, I'm trying to envision this quiet island retreat swarming with rowdy little campers. "Uh, sure, I'll help." I get the feeling I may soon be living a reenactment of the Swiss Family Robinson. "So have you thought of a name for your camp yet?"

"Not yet. Any ideas?"

"Hmm, how about Camp Down Yonder?" I offer up in a nice Southern drawl. "Or maybe Camp Dan Yonder, after you."

Danny looks subtly amused. "You makin' fun of my camp?"

"No, sir, just thinkin' it's a fine name for an Okie to call his summa' camp."

He just stares at me, as though strongly considering throwing me overboard. Then something in his demeanor changes. "So, besides WSU this fall, what are your plans for next summer?"

"I'm considering some opportunities in ... charity work. I'm not sure yet if, or where, that will happen."

"Hmm." He looks away for a moment, then looks back at me with *those eyes*. "Well, if you decide to stick around here for the summer, would you ... consider being ... my wrangler—for the ponies, I mean?"

His eyes are so penetrating, I can't look away.

"Um ..."

"I'll throw a hamster in on the deal if you stay."

"I'd ... love to be your wrangler—I mean, the ponies' wrangler—if I stick around."

❦ 2 ❦
Promises to Keep

Danny stops by just as I'm untying the skiff from the dock. "Where're you off to?"

"I'm heading downlake to spend the afternoon with Sister Abigail."

"Again? Didn't you spend the afternoon with her yesterday?"

"As a matter of fact, I did." *And the day before that too.*

Danny looks concerned. "Wanna lift there on the tug?"

"No, no. I'm fine with the skiff, but thanks." I fire up the motor.

"Are you sure you'll be okay out there with that little boat? It's looking kinda stormy."

"What? I can't hear you over the motor." *Well—barely.* I'm afraid that if he keeps me talking, I'll end up saying too much.

"Don't blow away again," he yells. "I've already had to save you once."

I turn the throttle down to a low idle. "Don't worry. I'm wind-proof now. I weigh too much to blow away."

"I doubt that. You don't look any bigger than when you blew away the first time."

"Thanks." *I think.* I guess that means I'm not a cow. "Could you do me a favor?"

"Name it."

"Could you take Sailor back to Big Chief with you so he doesn't sit at the end of the dock and howl all day? He gets crazy every time I leave without him. He probably thinks I won't be back for another eight years."

"I know how he feels." Danny gives the skiff a shove off. He still has a crinkle in his forehead. "Stop by Big Chief when you get back so I know you're okay. The church ladies loaded me up with a bunch of campfire treats and craft projects for the kids' retreat. We can look through everything when you get back. I'll build a fire in case it rains. I'll even roast you a hot dog...."

I put the motor in gear and give him a thumbs-up as I head out.

※

The return trip to the island turns into twenty minutes of whipping wind and pelting rain, making for one soggy boat ride. These summer storms always throw me. Who thinks about carrying a poncho around in July? By the time I reach the island, I'm drenched to the bone. Danny's previous offer of a warm fire and hot dogs sounds really good right now. I must be starving: I'm not real fond of hot dogs.

I show up on Danny's doorstep under an enormous umbrella.

"I hope that's you under there, A. J.," Danny says, peeking under my dripping dome. "Nice to see you made it back."

Sailor is equally happy to see me. He obviously decided to spend the afternoon here, once he realized it was either Danny or no one. A blast of heat greets me when I step inside the door. I'm drawn to the fire like a wet moth to a warm flame. Nothing can beat a crackling fire on a stormy night—especially seated on a gigantic sheepskin rug.

"Whoa. They must grow monster sheep where you come from."

Danny's busy stabbing hot dogs with skewers, but looks over at me and grins. "That's actually four sheep you're sittin' on there, darlin'," he says, with an exaggerated drawl.

"Oh." I peek on the underside of the rug, and sure enough, there they are, all stitched together. "Well, who's counting, anyway?"

The rain is coming down in sheets, pounding against the windows. The wind is howling through the branches overhead. Summer thunderstorms still stir up fear in me. Bad memories. "Are you sure those trees are secure up there and won't come smashing through the roof?"

"Don't worry, A. J., if I see one comin' through, I'll throw myself over you and save you."

"Really? Can we do a practice drill?" *I cannot believe I said that!* My face is so red I can feel it, and it's *not* from the fire. "Um, I didn't really say that. I mean … I didn't mean to say it … like that." I'm too embarrassed to even look at him. Instead, I stare into the fire, hoping he'll think my burning face is a reflection of the flames in the fireplace. From the corner of my eye I see a pointed stick slowly coming toward me. It stops right in front of me. I glance over cautiously. Our eyes meet. "Are you going to skewer me for saying that?"

"You know, they used to stone women like you." Danny laughs and reaches for the Ball Park franks. "So, Jezebel, one hot dog or two?"

"One, please." I think my body's gone into shock eating the way I have since I've been back from Italy. I was so used to eating vegetables, olives, pasta with herbs, everything fresh from either the garden or the daily trip to market. "You wouldn't have anything remotely healthy to go with that, would you—you know, something green, maybe?"

"I do. How about some pickle relish?" Danny goes to the kitchen.

"*Pickle relish?* I hardly think that qualifies as vegetables."

"Sure it does." He returns with a big canning jar of relish. "Fresh from the garden—my grandpa canned this stuff by the gallons. It keeps for years." He stares at the jar.

"I'm sorry. I didn't mean to remind you...."

Danny looks at me. "It's okay, I like to remember him. I just miss ..." He looks away, and sighs. "It's been three years, but this island is just not the same without him."

I take the jar and gently set it on the counter.

Danny pulls a chair up to the fire and starts to roast the hot dogs. The first one's a casualty and goes to Sailor.

"So, how are things back in Oklahoma? What's your brother doing now?"

"Jason pretty much runs the farm now. Daddy's retired for the most part, except for helping Jason out now and then."

"Is Jason married?"

"Engaged."

"To ...?"

"Cindy."

"And Cindy is ...?"

"A girl."

"You don't have a lot to say about Cindy, do you?"

"Well, um ... it's an interesting match."

"As in ...?" What is it with guys? Getting a complete sentence out of them is like pulling teeth.

"As in, Jason is a farmer, and Cindy is really into … Amway. They seem very … different from one another."

"Is she pretty?"

"Y-eah, in a calculated sort of way."

"Describe *calculated* pretty."

"A Barbie doll in a suit."

"Nice metaphor. And your concern is?"

Danny rotates the hot dog, looking regretful for even bringing up the topic with me. "I'm a little concerned for Jason, especially if he wants a family—Cindy's not exactly the motherly type."

"What makes you say that?"

"I don't know, it's just hard to picture someone being good with children if they show no interest or compassion for baby farm animals.… You know, A. J., I probably shouldn't be discussing Cindy like this."

"Too late. You just crossed the line with me on that one. If you think you can make a statement about baby farm animals and not finish it … I don't think so." I cross my arms and sit back. "What did Miss Amway do to the animals?"

Danny tries to offer me a hot dog instead.

I don't budge. I just raise my eyebrows like Mama does when she's waiting for an answer and isn't going anywhere until she gets it.

"Okay. She refused to help raise five baby ducks when her French poodle killed the mother."

Oh–oh–oh–please. That does it right there—and a poodle, no less! "I never want to meet her. I think Jason might be better off raising ducks than marrying Cindy."

"Hey look, I'm sorry, I didn't mean to put Cindy down or say things about animals that would upset you."

I realize he never meant to tell me any of it to begin with. Women are cursed with the gumption to gossip. "Don't worry, I'll get over it, as long as she never shows up on the island."

Danny holds up a perfectly roasted hot dog and offers it to me.

"Nice job. I always get those big black bubbles in mine when I do it." After heaping on the relish, I dive right in. "Wow. This is the best hot dog I've ever tasted."

"I'd say that's probably the best relish you've ever tasted."

"No, really. I love the relish, but this is really a great tasting dog."

"You must be starving."

We think alike.

Danny wants to know if I'm still writing novels.

"As a matter of fact, I just started *Treasure in a Bottle* as a tribute to returning to the island."

"So what's it about?"

"Well, there's this girl, Emma, who comes back to live on the island she grew up on when she was young, and there's this guy, Pierre, who was her best friend who still lives there...." *Oh, great—is this too obvious or what?* "Anyway, Pierre finds out that Emma was already engaged to some other guy, named Johnny. So Pierre disappears with a broken heart. Then Emma realizes she really loved Pierre more than Johnny, but it's too late—Pierre is nowhere to be found. One day Emma finds a bottle washed up on the beach with a ring inside and a note that says, 'If you ever decide to marry me, this is for you.' Emma has to spend the rest of the story trying to find Pierre, who, it turns out, is living on a small island just a canoe's throw away from her island."

Danny laughs. "A canoe's *throw?*"

"Okay, a canoe's *row.* Whatever. Anyway, Emma rows over to the other island, finds Pierre living in a thatched-roof tiki hut, and they end up getting married. Ta-da!"

By the time Danny's finished his second dog, I'm only half-way through my first. He moves on to dessert and says he's going to toast me the perfect marshmallow. He's such a gentleman. This seems the perfect moment to talk to him about the struggle raging in my soul. If anyone could understand this spiritual dilemma I'm in, I'm pretty sure it would be Danny. I finally crack. I can't keep it in any longer.

"I've been visiting with Sister Abigail, my old catechism teacher."

"Yeah, I kind of caught that."

"She's been helping me with some tough decisions that I've wanted to talk to you about, but I wasn't sure how to explain it all to you."

"Don't tell me—you're engaged to a guy named Johnny?"

I wish it were that easy. "Actually ... I'm thinking of ... of ... of joining the Sisters of Our Lady of the Lake."

Danny's skewer drops on the rug, gooey marshmallow and all. "*W-hat* did you say?"

I stare at the gooey marshmallow mashed into the rug. "You know how much I loved the Franciscan sisters in Italy, right? After living almost next door to them for eight years, we were practically family. They took me under their wings—even let me help write and direct the Christmas and Easter plays that the orphanage put on for the church. Anyway, Sister Abigail has agreed to help me figure out if I might want to serve God as a vocation...." I babble on like a telemarketer during the dinner hour. "We've been talking about maybe having me stay at one of the monasteries for part of next summer to see if the sisterhood is something I should pursue … or … not.…"

Danny's staring into the fire.

"They're having an inquirer's retreat that she suggested I go on next weekend."

When I've finish rambling, he looks at me. "Are you talkin' *nun* here, A. J.?"

"Um … kind of."

He exhales. "How can you *kind of* be a nun?"

"Well, I don't mean I would be *kind of* a nun. I mean, I'm *kind of* considering being a sister."

"What's the difference?"

"Well, a nun takes permanent vows and stays cloistered in the monastery, but a sister takes temporary vows and can do charity or mission work out in the community."

"Temporary, as in summer break, or what?"

"No, as in year by year. I would have to do local charity work during the school year and limit any mission work to the summer."

He stares at me dead on. "You're *serious,* aren't you?"

"Is there … something wrong with me taking this seriously?"

"I'm not sure how to answer that." He's staring at me like a wounded deer that's come face-to-face with the hunter who just shot him. "… I guess I just thought …" He turns away.

"Tell me."

"I just never expected … I mean, it's a noble calling and all, but … I think I'd rather hear that you're engaged to a guy named Johnny."

"I don't know anyone named Johnny."

"Okay, Dominic, then. I could at least compete with that—but *joining a convent?* Look, A. J., I understand wanting to serve God and all. But ... what happened to becoming a *vet*—didn't you just enroll in school for fall?"

"I *am* going to go to school. They actually want sisters to go to college. They want smart sisters."

"Smart sisters?" Danny runs his hands through his hair. "Whoa ... I'm sorry—but help me out here. You're planning to go to vet school *and* become a sister? Are you planning to feed starving people *and animals* in India, or what?"

"It all depends where I'm most needed when I decide to take my vows."

The crinkle in Danny's forehead deepens. "What kind of vows are we talkin' about?"

"Poverty, obedience, and ... well, chastity."

Danny's chair slides back from the fire. He stands up. He paces around the room a few times, then walks back over and looks me straight in the eye. "Correct me if I'm wrong, but doesn't sisterhood translate into *singlehood?*"

"Only if I take vows. I said I'm just *thinking* about it. It's really no different than you thinking of becoming a pastor."

"No *different? A. J.!*" He takes a deep breath. "A. J.," he repeats, quieter, "pastors can marry and have families ... unlike nuns, who can't do *either*. What about ..." He looks away, then back at me as his eyes search mine. "What about ... *us?*"

I can barely look at him. "We can still be *us*. At least until I take my vows—I mean, *if* I take my vows."

Danny says nothing, just stares at me like I just finished him off with my last shot.

"Am I wrong for wanting to serve God?"

He drops his hands in defeat. "No, A. J. There's nothing wrong with … that. If you want to be a sister, then you go be a sister." He turns and walks out the front door, leaving me to myself—in his house.

3

Camp Wannacomeback

I like to rise with the sun, facing east, with my window shade up. The best part of my morning is feeling the first ray of sunlight on my eyelids—before my mind has time to register any of the blunders going on in my life—like how I've just crushed the heart of the only man I've ever loved. Now that I've had my moment of bliss shattered by that recollection, I wish I could just lie here all day. But alas, life must go on....

"Aaggghhh!" I bolt upright in bed with a near coronary. Two eyes are peering through the window at me from beneath a bright feathered headband. As quick as he popped up, the little Indian pops back down and disappears. Funny, I haven't noticed any little people running around the island recently.

While I'm throwing on my overalls, it dawns on me. Campers. The Sunday-school campers. Tonight's the campout. And I volunteered to help out. But that was when Danny was still speaking to me—before I dashed all hope of ever being his pony wrangler.

I trudge my way over to the designated sleeping dorm in Pocahontas, wondering why on earth this kid is here so early. A young woman is out on the porch, sweeping up the summer's accumulation of pine needles. Must be the Indian brave's mother. "Good morning!" I call out, approaching the cabin.

"Oh, hello." She stops sweeping. "You must be A. J."

"Uh, yes … I am." *How did you know that?*

"Danny has told us all about you. The kids are sure looking forward to meeting 'the nice, funny animal-lover on the island.'"

"Ah." *That must have been before "nun" was added to my profile.* I peer around. "Where are the kids?"

"Oh, they aren't coming until this afternoon. I came early to help set up. By the way, I'm Jamie, the camp cook."

"Great. It's nice of you to volunteer."

"Well, I'm not that noble, really. I'm actually here because of my son, who is running around out there somewhere. I'm sure he'll pop up sooner or later."

"As a matter of fact, I think he already has. If he's the one in the Indian feathers, I caught a quick peek at him this morning."

"That's my Jordy. He's so excited to be here. He'll be the youngest one in the group—first grader. It's his first camping experience, which is one reason I thought I'd help out. I wasn't sure I wanted to set him loose on Danny without backup reinforcements—he can be a bit of a handful."

Kinda got that feeling. "Well, speaking of Danny, I should probably go find out what I need to do to help set up."

"All right." She smiles and resumes sweeping. "Looking forward to working with you. I'm sure this will be an unforgettable experience for all of us."

You can count on it. "I'll catch you a little later." I scuttle back down the stairs and continue on to Big Chief to check in with my boss—if he's still talking to me.

"Ahoy, ahoy, ahoy!" A loud voice shatters the silence of the peaceful morning sunrise. My eyes shift to the dock. Little Jordy is perched in the captain's chair of the tug, barking out orders to Danny while he unloads the camp supplies. "Me big chief, you kemosthabe—unload those tomahawks, now!"

"Ahoy!" I yell back, sounding much more enthused than I feel.

Danny glances up, pauses briefly, then continues unloading boxes.

"Move it, kemosthabe, no sthlowing down for the Indian princeth!" Jordy bellows.

Danny unloads the last box as I step onto the dock.

"Mornin', kemosthabe," I tease. Can't help adding a subtle smirk.

"Mornin', princeth," he replies, with a perfect lisp, then grabs a box and starts for the cabin.

"Want a hand?"

"Grab a box if you like," he says, without looking at me.

I grab the box of food and start up the ramp behind him.

When we reach the cabin, Danny gestures for me to set the box on the table.

"I'm guessing you'll still need help with the campers?"

He stops and looks at me, finally. "Actually, a couple of youth leaders volunteered to come help. I wasn't sure you were … still interested."

"Oh. Is there … something else I could do?"

He looks around. "Well, I could probably use some help with camp crafts."

"What crafts would I be doing?"

Danny slides one of the boxes in front of me. "They're all in here. These are the nylon cords for lanyards. You've already seen the supplies for buddy burners—everything comes with a set of instructions. Go ahead and set things out if you'd like to see what all is in there."

"What time are the kids showing up?"

"After lunch—around two o'clock. My helpers should be here around one." He turns to go.

"Wait … do I get to pick a camp name? In Bluebirds, all of our counselors had pretend names and dressed up in fun outfits."

"Go ahead, whatever you want." He walks away.

Okay. I will.

❧

One o'clock sharp, I'm arranging the crafts on the outdoor picnic table in front of Big Chief. I am now a camp pixie named Sprite. It's the best thing I could come up with from rummaging through the old hope chest at Papoose. An old green belted mini shift and a pair of red and white-striped tights. After adding a pair of wings cut from cardboard and covered in glitter, I'm ready to fly.

A loud boat engine cuts into the afternoon calm. A racy red jet boat speeds toward the island. When it pulls up to the dock, a dark Indian princess, wearing a buckskin dress, moccasins, and braids, hops out.

This is Danny's assistant leader?

Danny is right there to tie off the boat and help with her giant rolling suitcase.

Geez, what'd you bring in there, your own tepee?

The two of them sit on the dock together until it's time for Danny to go pick up the campers on the mainland. She's older than I thought she'd be—looks about Danny's age … twenty-one- or -two-ish. She climbs aboard the tug to go with him. I realize this is only a working relationship, but I wasn't expecting his assistant to look so … well, anyway, they should really have a chaperone—so the kids don't get the wrong idea. Where's that Jordy kid when I need him?

I'm sorting out strands of nylon for the lanyard project absentmindedly, wondering who this little Indian squaw is. When I finally focus in on what I'm doing, I realize I've grouped the most horrid color combinations together: orange and red, pink and green, blue and yellow. *Eww.* Start over.

By the time I've rearranged the color combos, the tug is chugging its way back to the island. When it's close enough to make out who's who, I notice the Indian squaw is in *my* chair. At least they have a boatload of kids with them this time. Danny should not be left alone with someone like her. He's too naive to know the games women like her can play. It's the same old "let me be your Indian princess camp helper" game. *I'm on to you, little squaw.* Someone needs to look out for him!

The minute the boat docks, nine kids in feather headdresses hop onto the dock. With Jordy, it makes ten little Indians. I finally get the connection: Indian Island, Indian headdresses, Indian princess … and one camp pixie. I flutter my way down to meet the campers, while keeping an eye on the princess.

Danny splits the kids into two groups, "Okay, braves over here with me and squaws over there with Pocahontas."

Pocahontas? That's original—named after our sleeping dorm.

Danny turns and sees me coming. "Oh, and this is our crafts director.…"

"Sprite," I reply.

"*Sprite?*" Pocahontas says. "You mean like the pop?"

"No … Sprite, like a pixie."

"Oh, I get it. You're a Pixy Stick."

"No, I'm a *fairy.*" I shoot a glance to Danny, hoping he's picking up her slow uptake, but he's too immersed in his campers. I make my way over to greet the squaws, who are all smiles—except for one. A little redhead with enough freckles to play connect the dots for life and the biggest scowl I've ever seen on a kid at camp. She looks as though she's carrying the weight of the world on a pair of twelve-year-old shoulders.

Danny pulls me aside. "Hey, I need you to do me a favor. Pocahontas is going to have her hands full with the girls' group, but there's one squaw who needs one-on-one supervision. Her family's going through a rough time right now. Do you think you could take her … under your wing, so to speak?"

I glance back at my wings. "Um, s-sure, I guess so."

"Thanks. Consider it charity work."

"Is that a dig?"

"Nope." He swallows hard and looks away. "She's the one standing alone over there. The redhead. I'll let you introduce yourself."

No problem. I straighten up my wings and head for the challenge. "Hi there," I say, in my happy voice. "What's your name?"

She glares at me. "I'm not allowed to tell strangers my name."

Right. "Well, I'm Sprite."

She eyes me with suspicion. "What are you supposed to be, a flying candy cane or Peter Pan?"

"Neither, actually."

"Well, whatever you are, you look kind of dumb mixed in with the Indian theme."

Charming kid. "Come on, I'll show you to our cabin. You get to be my roommate."

"Lucky me," she mumbles.

I grab her sleeping bag and lead her up the ramp to the trail. Turning back, I can hear all of the other girls giggling away with Pocahontas, the way little squaws at camp are supposed to.

"Do we have to wear these dorky feather headbands? The church lady wouldn't let me on the boat until I put it on."

"Hmm. Well, we do need something for fire starter to get the camp-fire going," I say, jokingly.

She doesn't smile. "I think I'd rather watch your costume go up in flames."

I eventually get a name out of this kid.

Stormy.

⁂

With matches in hand and a little kindling in my carryall, Stormy and I arrive at the fire circle to get the campfire ablaze before the rest of the tribe joins us for camp songs and the big hot-dog roast. "How about if you gather up some driftwood and help me get the fire going?" I ask, *nicely.*

Stormy drags her feet along in the sand, reluctantly picking up random sticks and driftwood. Meanwhile, I drop my carryall of kin-dling on the sand and sort out the best fodder for fire starter. After lighting a piece of straw, I begin to feed my smallest sticks to the min-iscule flame.

"That's not how you light a fire, ya know."

I swing around to find Stormy standing over me, giving me a pathetic look.

"Is that so? You think you can do better?"

"Well, duh. Anybody could do a better job than that."

"Listen up, *Stormy,* how about you get down here and show me how it's done?"

"No problem. Move over, *Peter Pan.*" Stormy moves right in, as though this is her life's calling. She forms a little A-frame stick formation, stuffs it with kindling, and lights it. The campfire is ablaze within minutes.

"Nice work," I comment. "Where'd you learn to build a fire like that?"

"My dad."

"Really? Does your family do much camping?"

"Used to ... before my dad got too sick." Stormy digs her bare feet into the sand and draws around them with a stick.

I take off my fairy slippers and dig my feet into the sand too. "Your dad is sick?"

She nods. "Leukemia."

"Leukemia?"

She nods again and begins to flick sand all over with her stick. "He used to be in remission, and lived at home, but not anymore. Now he has to live in a hospital." She starts stabbing the sand. "And my mom had to go to work to help pay for it. And now she works"—stab-stab-stab—"*all the time.*"

I look over and nod. "I'm sorry."

Stormy picks up a rock from where she's sitting and hurls it into the water. I do the same.

She reaches for a bigger rock and tosses it.

I reach for an even bigger one—which barely makes it to the water. Stormy scans the beach then runs over and grabs a boulder. Charging down to the shore, she hurls it into the water and watches it make a big splash.

No longer able to hold back a smile, I stroll to the water's edge, grab an enormous boulder, and chuck it into the water.

Stormy darts down the beach, giggling her head off, and tries to lift a stone slab, but can't get it to budge. I run to her side and together we lift the monster slab and plunge it into the waves, laughing hysterically.

Drenched from the splash, and doubled over in laughter, Stormy reaches under the water, grabs a handful of wet sand and milfoil weed, and hurls it right at me. It splatters all over my pixie dress, which she finds unbearably funny. I reach in with two hands and return the gesture. Stormy looks like something exploded in her face. I laugh so hard my sides begin to ache. The two of us are covered in mud and milfoil.

Glancing back toward the fire, I suddenly realize we have an audience. The entire tribe, including Chief Danny and the Indian princess, are watching in amazement. Danny looks amused, Pocahontas looks horrified, and the campers look thoroughly intrigued. Without a moment's hesitation, the other nine little Indians, with Jordy in the lead, charge to the water, chanting the hand-over-the-mouth Indian battle cry, "Wa-wa-wa-wa-wa!"

While the mud and milfoil wars are raging from one end of Juniper Beach to the other, I snag the chance to retreat gracefully. I stroll past Danny and *her*, holding my muddy milfoiled head high. "Cover my camper for me, will you? I'm going to go change into something more comfortable."

Danny gives me a slight smile and a nod.

Compete with that, Pocahontas.

4

A Cowgirl and Indians

I return to the beach dressed as a cowgirl. In other words, a perfect complement to Danny, who just naturally looks more like a cowboy than an Indian chief. It's now the Wild West against Apache Junction. I'm giving Pocahontas a run for her money with my pink cowgirl boots and matching hat. I came across the ensemble at the New to You thrift shop following the pony wrangler discussion with Danny. Impulse buy. It's not often you find Western attire in pink. And for a kids' pony camp, what could be cuter?

Neither Danny nor I thought this camp theme through much prior to the campers coming. The Indian theme may be winning for now, but not for long. Just wait until those ponies arrive in spring. This island will be the Wild West through and through. And there will be no need for anyone to be running around in moccasins and a Cherokee buckskin dress at the A. J. Corral. Second thought, knowing my luck, we'll end up with a corral full of spotted pinto ponies, and Pocahontas will show up in her buckskin mukluk boots.

It appears the mud and milfoil wars on Juniper Beach have come to a truce. The little Indians, caked in muck from head to toe, are marching back to their cabins with Danny's helpers, Todd and

Pocahontas. Danny's staying back to tend to the fire. I mosey on over and take a seat on the log next to him.

"A cowgirl named Sprite?" Danny comments. "It's original, anyway."

"Sorry, I don't have a spare Cheyenne buckskin jumper around to wear. Besides, there are already *two* Pocahontases on this island— your assistant, and the cabin." Emphasis on *two,* as in *unoriginal.*

"I think the wrangler outfit suits you better, anyway."

Because I look more like a cowhand than a princess? "So, how long have you and Pocahontas been working together?"

"Just brought her on board. It sounded like you might have other plans in the works." Danny throws another log on the fire, causing sparks to fly.

I detect a hint of repressed frustration.

"Nice job on the fire," he says.

"Thanks, but the fire-builder badge would have to go to Stormy." Danny looks at me. "*Really?* Well, the friend-of-Stormy badge would go to you. She's been a real challenge for us all year. You're the only one who's been able to break through her shell."

While I'm pondering that thought, the whole tribe shows up around the fire pit, looking more like scrubbed-up cherubs than wild Indians.

Stormy pulls up next to me. "You looked better covered in mud," she says, but this time it's said with a smile.

"Thanks. I think I liked you better with green milfoil hair."

"Me too." She laughs.

Danny looks over and smiles, but is quickly interrupted by Pocahontas, who has changed into an elaborately beaded, fringed gown. She scoots in next to Danny.

Stormy doesn't miss a thing. "What's up with the fringy getup—
is this the Navaho Academy Awards Night?"

I can't help my sudden outburst of laughter.

Danny shoots me a glare.

I can't believe he's defending her.

Pocahontas slips a beaded Indian necklace around Danny's neck as
a "peace offering," which is probably some secret symbolism for Indian
women to stake a claim on their men. Little Jordy jumps on Danny's
back, grabs hold of the necklace like it's a pair of reins, and pulls back
so hard the strand breaks. Bright little beads fly in all directions.

Jordy's mom looks up from the table where she's setting out the
hot-dog fixin's. "Jordy Tyler Jacobs, you hustle over here, right now!"

I give her a reassuring smile. "Kids will be kids!" No need to
get worked up over a few silly beads. Still smiling, I glance over at
Danny, who does not return my smile.

While Danny and Pocahontas are busy helping the bigger kids
whittle points on their roasting sticks, I start everyone in a round of
"Michael, Row Your Boat Ashore." Jordy's favorite part is belting out
"Oh Michael!" before each chorus. By the tenth round or so, we've
all had enough of Michael rowing his boat.

"Anyone have a request for the next song?"

"'Barges,' can we sing 'Barges'?" Stormy asks.

"How do you know that song?"

"Girl Scouts."

"Barges" … my favorite campfire song. "Can you help me teach it
to the kids?"

"Sure." Stormy jumps right in: "Out of my window looking in
the night, I can see the barges' flickering light…."

I'm fine until we come to the chorus: "Barges, I would like to go with you, I would like to sail the oceans blue. Barges, have you treasures in your hold, do you fight with pirates brave and bold?"

Like déjà vu, I'm ten years old again, out on the lake drifting … when daydreams of being rescued by handsome rogue pirates filled my mind. Then, one day, it became more than just a daydream. Sailor and I were alone on the island. We went drifting in a windstorm. We blew downlake. Nobody knew we were missing—but Danny came. He rescued me on the high sea. He wrapped me in his warm jacket, took me home, and built a fire for me. From that moment on he was my hero—my true-life pirate. I've never forgotten.

I glance over at Danny. He's staring back at me. I feel like he knows exactly what I'm thinking about. *Do you remember?* I ask with my eyes.

He returns my smile, but his eyes are sad. He looks away.

Jamie gives the signal that the dinner fixin's are ready to go. Hot dogs are loaded onto the ends of sticks and thrust into the flames by eager campers. An organized assortment of buns, chips, coleslaw, and relish is hit by a ten-kid tornado, sweeping through the line, rearranging everything. Faces that started out as clean canvases are now smeared with a colorful array of ketchup, mustard, and pickle relish, looking like little Picassos. A camp cookout at its finest.

Loaded down with food, I bravely make my way toward Danny, hoping to sit by him for the fireside festivities. Pocahontas shuffles past me in the "fringy getup," nearly bumping me into the fire pit with her swinging hips. She plops her beaded behind down next to Danny and quickly engages him in a little powwow of her own.

"I saved you a seat, Sprite!" Stormy calls to me from across the fire pit.

It's nice to feel wanted by *someone* around here.

As the night rolls on, the stars come out and the singing and laughter die down. Danny takes the stage in front of the fire. Holding up a beautiful, big picture Bible, he announces that we need to come up with a good name for our camp. "The camper who comes up with the winning name will win the picture Bible for keeps." He opens the prize Bible to a story on King David and draws the kids into a discussion. "Anyone know what it means to be a girl or boy after God's own heart?"

"I know, I know!" A little blond camper waves her hands impatiently, bouncing up and down on her log.

"Nikki?" Danny replies.

"I think it means that since God's heart is big enough to love everybody in the whole world, that we should all grow hearts like His."

Oh, sweet.

"How about you, Sammy? What do you think?"

Sammy is Jordy's neighbor. Jordy's mom invited him along for the campout. She mentioned his family life is a little on the rough side, and thought it might do him some good to get away for some fun with nice kids.

"I think that was a pretty stupid thing to say, coming from a stupid girl. I don't even believe in God."

"Well, then, you'll probably go to hell," Jordy informs him, matter of fact.

"Jordy!" his mother exclaims.

Jordy's mom volunteers to take the younger group back to the bunkhouse for the night. She probably figures Sammy will have less chance of offending anyone else, and Jordy will have less chance of offending Sammy.

Danny and Pocahontas regroup with the older kids. Meanwhile, Stormy is busy looking at constellations with me. "So how do those stars just go on and on and on, forever and ever?" she wants to know.

Funny. "I wondered that same thing when I was around your age."

"You did?"

"Yep. I was right here on this beach, with that same pair of binoculars, looking at infinity."

Shifting my eyes to Danny, I realize he's listening attentively to our conversation. "A wise woman once said, 'God didn't give us minds that are able to understand everything. That's part of the mystery. Now, you can drive yourself crazy trying to understand something you were never meant to figure out down here, or you can just trust Him until He's ready to let you in on it. Until then, just enjoy the mystery.'"

"Wow." Stormy thinks about that for a minute. "That's a good way to look at it. Who said that?"

"Danny's grandmother, shortly before she went to heaven."

I look at Danny. He's looking back at me. Neither one of us seems compelled to look away.

"Danny, come do a rain dance with us!" Pocahontas hops up and falls in line behind the little rainmakers circling the campfire. "C'mon, Danny!"

Danny blinks. The moment is lost.

One of the other campers comes over to join Stormy in stargazing. "Can I watch the stars with you?"

Stormy looks surprised. "S-sure. You want to take a look through the binoculars?"

"Yeah!" The little camper named Dora takes the binoculars. "Can you show me where the Little Dipper is?"

The two of them pass the binoculars back and forth, pointing out new discoveries for nearly an hour. After they've exhausted the entire galaxy, Stormy lays her head on my shoulder and eventually starts to nod off. Dora then lays her head on Stormy's shoulder and does the same. When I'm about to nod off myself, Pocahontas comes over and sits down beside me. "Hey, Sprite, looks like you have a couple of sleepy campers on your hands."

"More like on my shoulder," I reply.

Pocahontas laughs, exposing a beautiful smile. "Would you like me to take both girls back with my group to the sleeping dorm?"

"Well, I thought Stormy was going to be sleeping in my cabin, but …" I nudge Stormy. "Hey, kiddo, did you want to sleep at Papoose with me, or at Pocahontas with the other girls?"

Stormy blinks awake and peers around. Dora stirs as well. "I'd like to sleep with the other kids," Stormy says.

Part of me feels sad that she won't be joining me, but the bigger part of me is happy for her. She wants to be included. "Okay, but I'll have to get your overnight things from Papoose." I start to get up.

"I'll take her by to grab her stuff," Pocahontas says to me.

"Oh, great, thanks." Not only is she gorgeous, she's even nice. *Dang it.*

Stormy leans over and gives me a hug. "'Night, Sprite."

"Sweet dreams, Stormy." I watch her walk away with Pocahontas and her squaws.

Danny's junior helper, Todd, volunteers to take the boys back to the dorm, following Pocahontas. This leaves me and Danny sitting across the fire from each other, staring at one another. I notice Danny's wearing his cowboy boots, which he wasn't wearing earlier. He even has his Stetson hat beside him.

I feel awkward just sitting here. "Hi, cowboy."

"Hey, cowgirl," he nods back. He reaches for his hat and starts to get up.

No, don't go. "How was your first day at camp?"

"Camp was good." He looks over at me. "And you?"

"Good. I think Stormy had a good day too."

"I'd say so. I'd say you have a way with kids like Stormy. You'd make one heck of a summer camp counselor." His eyes bore into mine through the flames. He places his Stetson on his head. "'Night," he says, tips his hat, and walks away.

Saturday morning Indian Island is brought to life bright and early by the sound of an out-of-tune bugle. Ten tired Indians beat a path to Big Chief for a bowl of camp mush and hot cocoa. Following breakfast, Danny gives a Bible lesson around the big stone fireplace in the gathering room. The campers seem a bit more subdued today, which is a good thing, considering they've worn the camp staff out.

"Okay, campers," Danny announces, "this is your last day at camp so let's make some memories!"

"Last day?" Sammy yells. "But I don't wanna go home, and when I get home, I know I'll just wanna come back—so can't we just stay here?"

"Sorry, buddy, but hopefully we'll have another camp this summer if you really wanna come back."

"Hey," Stormy says, "I think Sammy just came up with a good name for this camp—Camp Wannacomeback!"

Danny and I look at each other.

"I think we have a winner for naming the camp!" Danny announces. "All in favor of Camp Wannacomeback, give an Indian war cry."

"Wa-wa-wa-wa-wa-wa-wa-wa!"

I grab the picture Bible from the fireplace mantel, have all of the campers sign it, then hand it to Danny.

"Sammy, we'd like to honor you as the official name-giver of Camp Wannacomeback. And if you ever do come back, you will find a big *Welcome to Camp Wannacomeback* sign hanging down at the boat dock." He presents the Bible to Sammy.

"Wow. I've never won *anything* in my life. There must really be a God after all!"

"There is, Sammy. You'll learn all about Him in that book."

I lean over towards Stormy. "That was nice of you to give the credit for the camp name to Sammy," I whisper.

Stormy blushes. "I wanted him to win."

❧

Once everyone settles down, Danny explains the different stations we've set up around the island with camp activities. "Arts and crafts

will be here at Big Chief with Sprite. Swimming will be at Juniper
Beach with Todd. Fishing will leave from Juniper Beach with me.
And beading will be down on the dock with Pocahontas."

Three little beaders and Pocahontas head down to the dock in
front of my crafts table. "Okay, Stormy, what's your first choice?"

"Well, it sure as heck isn't beading."

"Okay, how about making a lanyard with my group?"

"Actually, I think I'll go fishing."

"Oh. Well, okay. Hope you catch a shark."

"Ha! There are no sharks in here—it's fresh water."

"But you just never know, do ya? You're fishing with the best.
Danny knows his hooks—tell him you want to try for a shark."

Stormy laughs. "Okay, I will. Have fun making your dumb
lanyards."

"I will, thanks."

❧

A dozen lanyards later, while I'm packing up my supplies, Stormy
arrives back at my table.

"How was the shark fishing?"

"Great, but I had to release it. Danny said you don't like to kill
fish and it was too big to fit in the bathtub, so we had to let it go."

"Is that so? What else did Danny tell you?"

"Oh, just not to mention the fish I caught after that, which was
just the right size, so he bashed it over and over in the head about
five times with a hammer and tossed it in a bucket for me to take
home for dinner."

Thanks. "Anything else?"

"Um … well, he asked what I liked best about camp so far, and I told him I liked you the best."

O-h-h-h, sweet. Sigh. "So, what did Danny say to that?"

"He said, 'Oh, you too, huh?' Then I asked him if you were his girlfriend."

"And …?" *What, what, what?*

"He said, last he checked you weren't real interested. So I told him maybe he should ask you again."

"And?"

"That's when he asked me if I knew how it felt when a girl like you says no to a guy like him. I said no, I didn't."

"What did he say to that?"

"He didn't say anything. He just pointed to the fish in the bucket."

5
Berry Pickin'

First thing Monday morning I'm off to visit Grandma Angelina. She's been living in our house in town while we've been in Italy. Just when I reach the entrance to our home, the front door suddenly swings open. "My Angelina!" I'm instantly engulfed in a pair of big, soft arms. "Come in, come in, letsa have coffee," she says in her endearing Italian accent. She steers me to the small kitchen table. "Sit, sit," she says. Then she sets out a small plate of her homemade cookies. "Eat, eat." When it comes to Italian women, anything having to do with hospitality is repeated twice—especially when they're trying to feed you—so you have to watch it or you'll eat twice as much as you should.

We spend the morning gabbing and dunking *biscotti* in tall mugs of sweet coffee. After catching up on the latest family gossip from Italy, Grandma fills me in on the neighbors. Miss Peepers is still the faithful neighborhood spy. My childhood friend Dorie, from across the street, is off studying art in Spain. That's about it for the neighborhood news. Grandma wants to know what I'm writing now.

I reveal the new novel synopsis to her, *Treasure in a Bottle.* Grandma is my biggest fan when it comes to my stories. She faithfully sent writing magazines to Italy every few months to encourage me. She's convinced I'll be a famous writer one day.

"That's a nice story," she says. "Tell me what happens at the end."

Grandma loves my twisted plots and has to know how they're going to end before anyone else finds out.

I suddenly notice the time. "Whoa! Time for Mass. Did you want to join me?"

Grandma sighs. "These old ankles of mine aren't doing so good this morning. I think I'd better stay home this time."

Since Grandma seldom drives anymore and prefers to just walk to the corner grocer, she's given me full use of Stewie, her 1960 Studebaker. She's having me keep it at the main shore landing so I can get back and forth to see her, and eventually back and forth from school come fall. According to Grandma, little Stewie runs like a top and is small enough to dodge in and out of tight spots around town. Of course, when you live in a two-stoplight town, there's not a lot of dodging going on. The little Studebaker reminds me of those comical windup toys.

"You light a candle for me," Grandma says. "I'll just take a short rest while you're gone."

I feel bad leaving her behind, but, for her sake, it's probably best. I haven't had much practice driving yet.

Puttering down Main Street in this red and white jalopy draws some interested stares from the town folk. *Hi, y'all. I'm A. J., just rolling through town inside a peppermint twist.* It reminds me of the looks

I got with Daddy when practice-driving the old Fiat in the hills of Tuscany. Of course that drew looks of panic rather than curiosity—people fearing for their lives. A sudden pang of loneliness comes over me and I find myself missing my family and relatives. Going from being surrounded by lots of family to being alone is quite a change. I used to wish I were an only child—now I'm starting to appreciate belonging to a big family. Especially when they're gone.

Pulling up to the curb in front of Our Lady of the Lake, I notice Danny's Jeep parked across the street in front of the Baptist church. I'm tempted to slip inside to see if he's preaching today. He preaches a lot in August. That's when the head pastor goes fishing. It's probably not the best time to pop in unexpectedly, all things considered. I think I'll pass.

The minute that Mass lets out, I make my way over to Stewie, while keeping an eye on the dispersing crowd across the street. Danny's propped against the back door of the church, chatting with folks on their way out to the parking lot. It doesn't surprise me that the majority of those stopping to talk are young, attractive females. I mean, he's looking pretty sharp in his black cords and white shirt.

I catch a glimpse of Pocahontas, working her way to the front of the line to see the "pastor." Danny glances in my direction when he hears Stewie rumble to life—but then he sees *her*. She smiles at him. He smiles back … a *big* smile. She accompanies him across the parking lot to his Jeep, flinging her long hair behind her. It's all wavy from having been in braids all weekend.

Sinking down, I duck behind my steering wheel. I'm not sure why I'm trying to hide—it's not as if Danny doesn't know I'm here. It's pretty obvious when you're driving a car like this.

Danny walks around to the passenger's side of his Jeep, opens the door, and helps Pocahontas in. Glancing briefly in my direction, he hops into the driver's seat. They pull out of the parking lot and head toward town. *Do I follow them?* How immature to even think that.

Jerking my steering wheel to the right, I step on the gas and speed through downtown Squawkomish. I am on their bumper in a New York minute and keep right on their tail until they run a yellow light, leaving me behind in a cloud of humiliating dust.

This is pathetic. I'm going home to my island.

There's something very consoling about changing out of a dress and back into a pair of comfy, worn-out overalls. I need my comfort clothes to recover from my botched stalking attempt. I was really only looking out for Danny's welfare. Women like *her* are notorious for manipulating good-hearted hunks … er, men. She may be nice, but then it may just be an act so Danny will think she's nice—until she snags him. It's not often you find a really gorgeous girl who's sincerely nice. Adriana has told me all about the malicious things that beautiful women are capable of. I just don't want to see Danny get hurt … any more than I've already hurt him myself.

I have to remind myself that Danny is a grown man and if he is not capable of seeing through shallow women by now, it's not my problem. Grabbing the old tin bucket off the kitchen counter, I start for the door. Darned if it's not the same old berry-stained bucket I used for blackberry picking as a kid. "C'mon, Sailor boy, race you to the berry bushes." The two of us barge our way past each other out the door.

Meandering along the Pitchy Pine Trail, I reminisce about warm summer afternoons picking berries with Mama. She always told me, "The best berries are the ones closest to the sun, kiddo." I'd charge ahead up the bank to stake our berry claim for the day. "C'mon up here, Mama—there's jumbo berries on the cliff over yonder."

"If you don't cut that Southern babble this instant, Angelina, I will toss you off of that cliff over yonder … into the bay down yonder!"

Sure do miss those days.

❧

The bushes closest to the sun are those on the cliff above Danny's boat dock—the exact place I first saw the Morgan family step foot on this island.

Marching my way up the steep path, I spot our old berry patch along the edge of the cliff. Ripe, juicy berries hanging from heavy clusters in full sunlight—just like Mama said. "This is it, Sailor: our favorite old berry patch." Grabbing the biggest berries first, I begin filling my bucket. "One for the bucket, one for me …" Sailor snatches up the ones that fall to the ground. He's the only dog in the world I've ever known to eat blackberries.

Working my way along the edge of the cliff, I notice a row-boat—*my* dinghy—making its way toward the cove below. I push back the vines obstructing my view. It's *her!* Pocahontas—in the din-ghy with Danny! What is *she* doing back on my island?

Danny rows the boat directly below my cliff, giving me a perfect bird's-eye view of the two of them. It reminds me of the days I used to sit up here and spy on all of Danny's relatives, taking notes for my *Island Review* newspaper. I highly doubt these two will be doing anything noteworthy. Just in case, time to nix the pie-pickin' plan for the sake of staying hidden. My bucket's nearly full anyway.

From this viewpoint, Pocahontas appears to be doing all the talking while Danny's rowing. She sure talks a lot. I hope Danny's bored out of his mind. I thought I was the only one he had the patience to listen to for that long. Apparently not. He's probably wishing he had someone more interesting along for the ride—me, for instance. It could have been me, *would* have been me, had I not mentioned wanting to join a convent. Maybe I should have waited to tell him; then I would be the one down there blabbing my head off instead of *her.*

While I'm trying to convince myself that they are nothing more than friends, darned if she doesn't move in right next to Danny. Danny appears to be baiting a fishhook, but it looks to me like she's trying to do more than just fish. Is she *kissing* him?

How dare she! How dare *he!* How dare he replace me like that—and so soon! The boat is drifting sideways so I can only see them from the back. This girl is way too close. And Danny isn't exactly shoving her off of his seat. I can't watch this. I grab my bucket to leave, but suddenly, as though my arm is not connected to the rest of my body, a force beyond my control takes over and hurls the bucket forward. While I'm still gripping the handle, the blackberries go flying … down … down … down, splattering on impact all over Danny and his Indian princess.

For a split second, I feel a great sense of elation, followed by a sudden wave of horror, followed by another wave of remorse. This must be the same range of emotions bomber pilots experience when they hit their targets dead on. Elation ... horror ... remorse.

Reality sets in. I have to get out of here! It will be only too obvious to Danny—I'm the only one living on the island besides him. I take off running for Papoose with Sailor on my heels, my berry bucket swinging wildly back and forth.

Running back through the Pitchy Pine Forest, one thought plays through my mind, over and over: *I cannot believe ... absolutely, cannot believe ... I could do such a thing!* This involuntary arm action has happened only one other time in my life, with a chocolate éclair and Annalisa Tartini in Italy. And, well ... turning out of the parking lot at church today ... okay, three times.

Bursting through the cabin door, I plunk the empty berry can on the counter, then sink my sorry behind into the overstuffed chair to wallow in my guilt and shame. Outside, a boat motor roars to life, then gets quieter in the distance between the island and the main shore. *The little blackberry tart must be on her way home to lick her wounds.* For some reason, that doesn't bother me as much as it should. Jealousy is an ugly black dog. *Angelina Juliana Degulio, you have got to get a grip on yourself and grow up. Lord, have mercy on me, a sinner. Don't let Danny know it was me.*

Bam-bam-bam! The pounding on my front door causes me to jump out of my skin. *Oh boy—I'm going down.*

"It's open," I call out casually, in an attempt to appear as a vision of calm. My show of mock serenity lasts only until Danny presents himself directly in front of me, covered in blackberry pulp. I want so badly to laugh my head off, and I would, if Danny weren't glaring down at me with dagger eyes.

"You want to tell me what this is all about, A. J.?" He does not sound amused.

"What?" I give the innocent route my best shot.

"That's good, A. J.—a nun who pelts people with blackberries, then lies about it. I can see you're gonna be a real asset to the church." Not only is his blond hair streaked purple, but he has berry splotches all over his face and white T-shirt as well. "I s'pose that berry-stained bucket on your counter isn't yours either?"

"For your information, I happen to be in pursuit of becoming a sister, not a saint."

"Oh, forgive me, *Sister Angelina*," he says coolly, "or would that be *Sister A. J.?* Tell me, is there a new order at the convent for sister spies?"

"Hey—I was just trying to pick some berries to make you a pie. I'm sorry they happened to spill on you and your little friend when you were making a public display of your affection for one another. It didn't take you long to forget about me, did it? Did you ask her if she wanted to be your pony wrangler? You probably threw a hamster in with the deal too."

Danny's expression turns to hurt. "That's really low, A. J." His piercing blue eyes convict me to my core. "You are the only one I've ever bared my heart to, or hoped to share my life with. But in light of your future plans, you needn't concern yourself with what I do, or who I'm with."

Danny turns and walks to the door while pulling off his ruined T-shirt. He stops and turns back, bearing an uncanny resemblance

to the statue of David—with jeans and a tan. "Here," he tosses me
his shirt. "I probably won't be needin' this. Remember me as the guy
with the trashed shirt … and heart."

Sinking deeper into my chair, I look down at the shirt heaped in
my lap. I've never felt so low in my life.

❧

It takes me all week to muster up the nerve to face Danny again.
With over a month left until school starts, there is no way I can go
that long without talking. One of us is going to have to make the
first move—and chances are, it won't be Danny. I finally force myself
to go see him. Sailor and I show up on his doorstep just as he's finishing his dinner—alone. I hold a blackberry pie out to him when
he opens the door. My rather lame attempt at a peace offering. He
doesn't reach for it. His recent encounter with blackberries may have
something to do with his apprehension.

"What's up?" he asks, in a guarded tone.

"May I … come in for a minute?"

Danny looks around as though looking for a reason to say no.
I get the feeling he's just not up for dealing with me right now. He
holds the screen door open for me, then goes over to the couch and
sits down.

I swing by the kitchen to drop off my pie. "I made you that pie
after all."

"Y-eah … caught that. Thanks." He casts a leery glance in my
direction. "It's not gonna suddenly erupt or anything, is it?" he asks
dryly.

"No, my blackberry bombing days are over. I'll just set it here on the counter for you." I join him in the living room and seat myself across the room from him on the other couch. "Oh, hey, I bleached your T-shirt for you." I look at the wrinkled-up wad in my hand, realize I've been clutching it like a security blanket. "Here." I toss it over to him.

He sets it aside. "Thanks." He's staring at me, waiting for me to say whatever it is I came to say. I can't even look him in the eye.

Staring at the floor, I stumble my way through an apology. "I-I don't know how to say this very well, but … I'm s-sorry for acting the way I did the other day with the blackberries. Please apologize to your … *friend* for me. I'm not sure what got into me." I look up at him. "Danny … whether or not you believe me, you mean more to me than … What I mean is, this decision I'm trying to make has nothing to do with me rejecting you. It's about keeping a promise."

"A promise? To who?"

I take a deep breath and look him in the eye. "God."

"God?"

I nod.

"What kind of promise?"

"It's … personal."

Danny cocks his head to one side, like he's wondering if this is where the conversation ends.

I glance down at my feet. "I made the promise when I was fourteen years old. I've never told anyone else. Not even the sisters."

He cocks his head to the other side.

"Okay. I'll tell you. Remember four years ago, when I wrote you about Benji falling off the roof of the villa and having to go to the hospital?"

Danny nods. "I remember."

"There was a point where it looked like Benji wasn't going to … make it. They brought us into this small room, where the doctor told us how bad it was. We were all scared. Even Mama and Daddy were scared. That night, when I was alone … I got on my knees, and I promised God that if He would save Benji, I would serve Him with my life—like the sisters, and—"

"And Benji lived," Danny finishes the sentence for me.

I nod. "The doctors said it was a miracle."

Danny leans back, releasing a long, heavy sigh. "Well, that explains a lot."

"In what way?"

"Why I've felt crazy ever since you've come back."

This time it's my turn to look puzzled.

He looks at me so intensely I'm just dying inside. "A. J., we've shared so much of our lives with each other—our childhood, our faith, our dreams, *a dog.* I felt like I knew you. I just couldn't figure out why, when you were in Italy, I felt like we were growing closer—you know—going somewhere together, but now that you're here … you seem a million miles away." His eyes sadden. "I guess I just always believed you … were the one. At least now I know the reason you're dumping me."

"Danny, I'm not—" I can't even say Danny and dumping in the same sentence.

He saves me from having to. "A. J., don't. How you decide to work this out is between you and God. From my standpoint, I've never felt that serving God had to be exclusive to other commitments in life. But, if you feel God is taking you down a road that doesn't include me … I will never try to come between you and God." With a soul-piercing glance, he gets up, then walks out the back door.

I'm getting used to letting myself out.

※

On the walk back to my cabin, I stop by my old critter cemetery, where all of my former pets and animals have long been buried. I was almost afraid to see what shape it was all in now, it's been so long since I've been here to care for it. What meets my eyes is completely unexpected. Not only is the little cemetery still intact and beautifully maintained, it's enclosed with a little white fence and has a border of wildflowers along the inside. In the middle of my cemetery stands a tiny marble headstone that has replaced my old wooden marker. I slowly approach and read the inscription:

In Loving Memory of Ruby Jean
A most beloved hamster
August 1968

Tears roll down my face. There's even a small gate where my sign hangs from an arched trellis covered in wild roses:

Welcome to A. J.'s Critter Cemetery
Death with Dignity for Dead Animals

Saint Francis is still standing faithfully on guard duty at the entrance.

"Danny." He did all of this for *me*. Why does he have to make this so hard for me? If only he were a jerk, it would be so much easier. But how can I say no to God? Animals were enough to care about as a child. But after working with the nuns and kids at the orphanage, I realized that people are God's true passion—His pride and joy—the apple of His eye. And He's calling me to serve them.

Turning to go, I spot something hidden in the trees. I make my way along a rock-laid path that leads to a tiny log chapel with one stained-glass window and a small steeple. Inside the one-room chapel, a candelabrum stands on an old wood table. It's covered in melted waxes of all colors, apparent that many candles have burned here. Danny's sanctuary. I kneel, and my tears continue to fall.

✾ 6 ✾
The Last Dance

"Angelina!" Grandma Angelina calls to me from the peony patch. She grows the biggest pink peonies I've ever seen. She's fun to watch out in the garden, singing away in her calf-length dress, thick stockings, and stumpy high heels. How she gardens in heels is beyond me. I have never once in my life seen either of my Italian grandmothers in a pair of pants.

Grandma finishes cutting her bouquet, then hails me toward the back door. "Letsa have coffee." Pushing loose strands of silver hair under her scarf, she ushers me inside, slips her bouquet into a vase of water, and goes to light the burner.

Over our usual Folgers and *biscotti,* Grandma Angelina gets right to the heart of the matter. "What's going on with that nice Morgan boy? I haven't heard much about him lately."

I fill Grandma in on everything about me and Danny, from the time she brought me his snow globe in Italy, until now. The snow globe was the turning point from "friends" to "something more." We realized that absence really does make the heart grow fonder when you're soul mates who share the same hopes and dreams … well, *shared,* anyway.

Then I blurt out the bit about my considering joining the Sisters of Our Lady of the Lake. Moreover, I go so far as to ask what she thinks of the whole idea. I can always trust the Italian women in my life to be straight up with me.

"I think it's nuts," she says.

"What's so nuts about wanting to serve God?"

"Well, let me get this straight." She rolls up what's left of her jacket sleeves and blows a wild wisp of hair from her face. "You're telling me that you broka the boy's heart and told him you want to join a convent?"

"Might. I said I *might* want to join a convent."

"And he wanted you to help him run a summer camp on the island?"

"Right."

"And he wanted a future and a family with you someday, something you would no longer be able to do if you follow through on these vows?"

"… Right."

She dunks her *biscotti* in her coffee and shakes her head. "*Mamma mia,* Angelina." She looks me right in the eye. "Let me put it to you like this. I know Danny Morgan better than you think I do. I'mma old, but I'mma pretty smart for an old gal. If you have a man like Danny Morgan, who loves God, loves you, and is interested in serving God with you, then all I can say is: Angelina Degulio, what'sa matter you?"

"But, I made a promise—and it would show God that I'm willing to sacrifice all of that to serve Him."

"It might also mean that you'll end up sacrificing the very thing God most wanted you to have. You think God expects you to sacrifice love in order to give love?" She takes another bite while shaking her head. "Not just anyone can be a nun. It may be God's will to keep you *out* of the convent!"

Thanks for the vote of confidence.

"You know, you'll never have coffee and *biscotti* with your granddaughter if you take those vows."

"Why not?"

"Because you can't have grandchildren unless you have children of your own."

"Oh, right."

"Just think if I, or your own mama, made that decision. You and your brothers and sister wouldn't be here. Look at the heritage God gave to all of us because we believed in family and were faithful to keep the family together. You are part of a legacy that took generations to build. It's now up to you to pass that blessing on to the next generation. Families like ours are few and far between, and not something to take lightly."

"Don't you think God calls some women to serve single?"

"I *know* there are women God calls to serve single—but you are probably not one of them. I know you, Angelina. You were always such a gushy little kid, saving everything on earth. You couldn't even watch me kill a spider without crying. I can't imagine you going through life without having someone of your own to love, and children of your own to gush over. Besides that, there are very few truly good men out there. Sure, you'd be better off single than with the wrong man, but if you have someone like Danny Morgan waiting for you, I sure wouldn't give him up so easily. He reminds me a lot of your grandfather. I wouldn't trade the years I had with your grandfather for anything."

"You must think a lot of Danny Morgan."

"Yes, I do, and I'll tell you what else—who do you think has been checking in on me the whole time you've been away in Italy? He's helped me with mowing, and moving things, and picking up groceries whenever I need something if he's going to town. He's a fine young man. That Danny Morgan is going to go places in life, and if I were you, I'd sure want to be the one going with him."

"I do want to, Grandma. Or did, anyway. The problem is … I made a promise when Benji got hurt that if God let him live, I would serve Him my whole life, like the sisters at the convent."

"Hold on there." Grandma pushes her coffee mug out of the way. "Did you promise to *be* a nun, or to serve Him *like* the nuns?"

"What's the difference?"

"The rest of your life is the difference. God sees the intent of your heart—He isn't going to send you to hell over a technicality." Grandma lines up her coffee mug, cream pitcher, and sugar bowl like she's getting her ducks in a row. "Now you listen to me, Angelina, you don't have to join a convent to serve God. You marry a good man and the two of you can serve God together. Trust me, if you don't see what you're giving up, someone else will. And by then it will be too late."

"I know. I just want to know what God really wants me to do. I'll think about what you've said while I'm at the retreat, I promise." *There I go again—making more promises.*

❧

On my way out of town, I pull Stewie into Saddlemyer's Dime Store to pick up a few essentials for the retreat: Life Savers, chewing gum, a spiral notebook, and toothpaste. I know the sisters are not into vanity, but I certainly hope they're still permitted to brush their teeth. I can think of nothing worse than waking up in the morning when your teeth feel like they're wearing fuzzy little sweaters, and not being able to brush.

J. D. Saddlemyer's was a pretty hoppin' place back in the sixties, especially for the country-western crowd. Back then, J. D.'s three kids, Eddie, Alexandra, and Alec, got to work at the soda fountain counter. I was so jealous. I always dreamt of pulling that handle on the soda fountain, making root beer floats for everybody, but we moved to Italy before I ever got my chance.

I'm singing along to "Save the Last Dance for Me," working my way down the toothpaste aisle, torn between Pearl Drops and Pepsodent. When I look up, I find myself face-to-face with Danny Morgan. I'm holding Pearl Drops in one hand and Pepsodent in the other, frozen in place. We both just stand here staring at each other. "So, what's up?" he says.

"I'm on my way to Peaceful Pines," I mutter. "The, uh, retreat."

Danny nods.

I glance at my hands. "I need some toothpaste."

He nods again.

"Are you … looking for something?"

"You."

"Me?"

"Yeah, you." His eyes melt right into mine. "May I … have this dance?" he asks, softly.

I look around. "Here?"

"Yeah."

"Uh … okay." I lift my arms, still clutching the toothpaste.

Danny gently removes the toothpaste from my hands, sets it on the shelf, and takes my hands in his. He never once takes his eyes off mine. We're dancing through the aisles of the dime store to the words *Darlin', save the last dance for me,* but the only thing I can hear is everything my grandma said to me a half hour ago.

As the song comes to an end, Danny gently lets go of my hands. "Thanks," he whispers, then turns and walks out the door.

I'm left standing alone in aisle three. I'm so dazed, I leave the store without buying anything I came for. I pull out on the highway and head away from Squawkomish, feeling like Danny Morgan just walked out of my life … for good.

7
Peaceful Pines

After two hours of puttering up the mountain pass, Stewie finally rolls into Peaceful Pines Retreat Center. I feel like I'm in the Swiss Alps, half expecting Heidi to come yodeling around the corner with a flock of goats. Rather than goats, a cluster of nuns come flowing by in their habits.

I climb out of Stewie and fall in line behind them. They, at least, seem to know where they're going. I trail along on their heels, meandering along pine-scented pathways until I find myself on the front steps of a magnificent old wooden lodge. Pine, I presume. The lobby is filled with women; those wearing habits behind the registration desks, and those not wearing habits waiting in line.

When I reach the front of the line, I'm handed a registration packet with my room number and schedule for the weekend. "Oh, what about my room key?" I ask the sister.

"We have no need for locks here, dear," she says, with a kind smile. "We've all taken vows of poverty."

I laugh, assuming she's making a joke. *Um, okay, guess not.* I head straight for my car and lock up everything but my car keys and overnight bag, then walk back toward the lodge. You never know what kind of deranged characters might be lurking up in these hills just waiting to prey on innocent, unsuspecting victims. Another book begging to be written. *The Peaceful Pines Predator,* nominated for Year's Best Suspense Thriller, written by A. J. Degulio.

According to the schedule, the evening session starts right after dinner, which allows me time to swing by my room first.

The old pine lodge has a dozen rooms on each floor. The sisters are all rooming on the first floor. My room is on the second floor with the other inquirers. Observing the sisters below, I suddenly picture myself thirty years from now wearing a habit, looking equally as kind, contented, holy … single…. A vision of Danny suddenly pops into my head. With *her.* Pocahontas. Panic follows. On the verge of making a run for my car, I'm halted by the photo display on the knotty pine walls in the hallway. Framed photographs of sisters doing charity work all over the world.

My eyes are suddenly drawn to an old convent, looking much like the convent we lived by in Tuscany. How I miss those beautiful Franciscan nuns! I picture them now working the gardens. Memories of Sister Aggie and the Reverend Mother come to mind: cantering through the Tuscan hills on horseback at dusk, their long habits flowing behind. Their kind, gentle smiles, shining eyes filled with joy, and that spirit of love always pouring from their hearts—my earthly guardian angels. *Okay, okay, I remember why I'm here….*

Arriving at room 203, I find out I have a roommate waiting for me.

"You must be my new roomie," she says cheerfully.

"I'm A. J. Well, actually, my formal name is Angelina."

"Angelina—like an angel," she says. "I'm Ruth." She gives me a warm hug. "Welcome."

Ruth has a sweet face and long, dark hair that falls in soft curls down her back. The first thing I wonder is if she'll have to cut them all off once she takes her vows. Will I have to cut my own hair? I like it longish. Scoping out the room, I set my overnight bag on the unclaimed bed.

"What part of the formation process are you interested in—aspirancy or postulants?" Ruth asks.

What or what? "Um, I thought this was just an inquirer's weekend. Am I at the wrong retreat?"

"Oh, no, you're at the right place. It's just that some of us already know that we want to take vows." She sits down on the bed across from me, so I take a seat on mine as well. "Do you know anything about the formation process, or is that what you came here to find out?"

"Um … I think that's why I'm here. I'm just kind of looking into the idea of maybe staying at a monastery next summer … to see if this sisterhood thing is something I should maybe consider for my future."

"Oh. Sorry if I seem nosy. I just love hearing how other women come to find their calling. Do you mind if I ask what brought you to consider the consecrated life?"

Oh, man. "Well, I lived near a convent in Italy, and I spent a lot of time with the sisters at a local orphanage. I always felt inspired by the sisters and am wondering if maybe it's my calling too. I really don't know much about any part of the process yet."

Ruth pulls her long curls into a ponytail and flings it behind her. "Don't worry, they'll explain the whole formation process this weekend, but I've already learned a lot about it from my aunt—she's been a nun since she was my age. She's my inspiration. Anyway, she told me that aspirancy is the next step, where you stay at one of the convents for six weeks to further discern your call. Then you become a postulant. After that, you go through the novitiate period, then the period of temporary vows, and finally, solemn vows."

"Wow." *I think I need a translator.* "Are you already planning to go that far?"

Ruth smiles. "I hope so. I've wanted to be a sister since I was a little girl. My aunt was always filling my head with great stories of charity, like the work of Mother Teresa. My dream was to one day join a charity with my aunt—maybe even the one in India with the Sisters of Charity. It's still my dream." She lets out a small sigh. "I really want to work with the babies and orphans."

Babies? I thought Mother Teresa only worked with old people who were dying. I love babies too. Maybe these Indian babies would make up for the ones I won't be having myself. Maybe I could be a grandmother to them when they grow up. We could have *biscotti* and Folgers coffee together. It might not be as bad as Grandma Angelina thinks it will be.

"Shall we walk to dinner?" Ruth asks. "It's probably time."

"Sure."

She takes my arm, like a long-lost friend, and walks me to dinner. "Oh, Angelina, I'm so glad you're here."

Is she for real? Are there really people this nice in the world? People who pretend to be that nice but really aren't are so annoying. But I believe she's sincere. I doubt if I could ever be that nice—even if I become a nun.

Ruth seats us at a table with six other women, introducing me first, then herself. "How about if we go around the table and introduce ourselves?" she suggests. I finally discover through introductions that Ruth was here at the last inquiry weekend and was asked back to help the new people to feel comfortable. It must be her gift.

While waiting for dinner to be served, Ruth asks everyone to share when we first felt God's calling on our lives. Beginning with me. *Great.*

"Well … um, I think that my first calling was to care for orphaned and dead animals. I actually made a small critter cemetery … on my island … and I saved Sailor—that's my dog—from death row.…" The weird glances are starting up. "… *but,* I'm not sure if that is still my calling, which is why I'm here—to try and figure it out."

When the food arrives, I comment on the nice appetizer and joke about saving room for the filet mignon. After more strange looks, Ruth explains to me that one aspect of this weekend includes a partial fast. Apparently, this was not an appetizer. All we get for dinner is bread, fruit, and water. It's something about keeping the focus off of our needs and more on spiritual matters. Personally, I can think much clearer on a full stomach; otherwise, food is the only thing I think about. I decide to keep my idea of making a late-night run to the nearest town with a McDonald's to myself.

❧

After our so-called dinner, we're ushered into the chapel where the evening is led by Reverend Mother Mary O'Brien and the Sisters of

Our Lady of the Lake. Sister Abigail is also attending to help us with our questions about the formation process, the religious community, and belonging to the sisterhood.

Someone's hand is up, waving wildly, while the Reverend Mother is trying to talk. It finally distracts her enough that she can't go on with what she's trying to say. "Question, dear?"

"Yes, Mother. What if I want to take eternal vows now and skip the simple vows? I already know that I want to live in the convent and was hoping to move in as soon as possible."

I'm trying my hardest not to laugh as I glance over at Ruth. "What a nut," I whisper. "They're going to tell her she needs to pray for patience right off the bat!"

"I know how she feels," Ruth whispers back, *nicely.* "I feel the same way about going to India."

Okay. I think this all takes a little more holiness than I will ever have. I admit it, Mother Teresa I am not. Although, Mother Teresa was the inspiration behind my critter cemetery. She opened the doors of dignity for humanity, I opened my critter cemetery for the animal kingdom. Mother Teresa covered the dying destitute, I covered the dead animals. We're actually not a bad team. Key word: *team.* Reminds me of what Grandma Angelina said about serving God with someone, rather than alone. Like maybe at a Christian summer camp … as a pony wrangler …

The chapel is beautifully lit with candles aglow against dark, rich woods that make up the altar and pews. Candles have always had a calming affect on me. After feeling more than a bit displaced, their soft glow is helping me to settle in a little. As a choir of sisters begins to sing a beautiful hymn, my mind drifts off with the melody …

back to aisle three at Saddlemyer's … dancing with Danny along the shelves of toothpaste....

"Welcome, ladies...."

Back to reality.

The sisters share their testimonies of how they came to fulfill their calling at Our Lady of the Lake. Each story makes my heart beat a little stronger, encouraging me to keep pursuing this higher path. These are the women who put into words and actions that yearning deep in my soul that calls me to something greater than myself and gives reason and purpose to my existence. My heart is saying, *A. J., you can become one of these women.* My mind argues back, *These are the kind of women who always put you to shame.* And while it appears that most of the girls here have their minds entirely on heavenly things, in between each of my noble thoughts, I keep thinking about how good a juicy burger sounds right now. I cannot seem to keep my mind tracking in the same direction for very long. Probably from a protein deficiency. I just flip-flop back and forth between aspirations of the consecrated life in the convent, to McDonald's, to a life with the man I love on Indian Island. I think I'm going to be schizophrenic by the time I leave here. My heart says: *No, I'm not.* My mind says: *Yes, I am.*

After concluding with the question-and-answer time, we get to meet one-on-one with the sisters to discuss any personal fears or concerns we might have. *Might* have? This could take all night. Sister Abigail has to go over and over the same things with me until she's blue in the face.

"No, Angelina, the Lord will not intentionally place you in the worst place on earth—only the place that's best for you."

"Yes, some places may have running water."

"I'm sorry, I can't recall the longest I've gone without a shower."

"No, I've never had to eat grub worms to survive."

"I don't believe that animals have an eternal soul, but this I know: If the Creator of the universe wants to surprise us by having our pets meet us in heaven—He is certainly capable of doing so."

By the time I return to my room, Ruth is waiting on her bed. She has such a radiance about her, she's actually glowing. Then I realize she's sitting in front of her night-light. "So, how did your time go with Sister Abigail?" she asks.

"Well, she had to listen to a lot of fears and concerns, but I think I feel pretty good about things now. She said that when we go to the altar and seek God's will for our lives, He may not tell us our big life plan, but He has a way of letting our hearts know at least the next thing to do."

Ruth nods solemnly. "Oh yes, I agree."

"How about you—did you get to meet with Sister Marguerite?"

"I did. I got to hear all about India. She even worked with the babies herself. She says they are always praying for sisters to come to India."

"India—wow." I can't bring myself to really think in that direction. "I think I'd like to teach catechism to start with, maybe in Squawkomish. Sister Abigail says she can mentor me if I want to help teach with her. I have to stay in the area anyway for school, so I probably won't be going to India for a while." *Lord willing.*

I lay awake listening to all of Ruth's future hopes and dreams until the mandatory lights-out bell rings at eleven p.m. By two a.m., I'm still lying here wide awake, with my stomach roaring, thinking how discouraging it is to listen to someone else's entire life plan when I don't even know where I want to go *tomorrow*. Wait—I take that back. I know exactly where I'd like to go tomorrow. To the Golden Arches—as in burgers and fries, not heaven. Not a real holy thought to fall asleep on either. Talk about weird dreams: Mother Teresa and me feeding starving dogs in India, and Ruth with her long curls being cut off. It's a relief to wake up and see that Ruth's curls are still intact. And I'm not in India.

Today we are being asked to spend time in complete solitude and journal our thoughts and insights. I don't have a problem with this, except that my journal pages remain empty—apart from some random doodling. I have got to find a place besides my room where I can be completely alone—somewhere out in nature. It's my only hope for hearing from God.

We all meet for a silent lunch in the dining hall. I can see that the pages in Ruth's journal are filled up. Lunch turns out to be a cup of broth, a side of green beans, and a slice of bread. Ruth continues to write left-handed while eating right-handed. A truly gifted soul.

Here is my journal:

Day 2. We had our rations cut again. Breakfast was a bowl of oatmeal.
Random doodles:
Mrs. Daniel Jackson Morgan

Angelina Juliana Morgan

Daniel & Angelina Morgan

Mr. and Mrs. Morgan

Hold on ...

Mr. and Dr. Morgan

Doctor Angelina Juliana Morgan: Veterinarian Extraordinaire

Desperate to hear from God, I know exactly where I need to go. The moment lunch is over, I slip out the back door and hightail it for the mountaintop. Mountaintops have a way of helping me feel one step closer to God—one foot on earth, and one foot in heaven.

Looking down from the meadow along the ridge, I have a sudden urge to break into the chorus from *The Sound of Music*. It's the only way I can think of to release all of this inner tension. In my best Julie Andrews voice, I belt out, "The hills are alive with the sound of m-u-u-u-sic...." I spin around and sing till I'm so dizzy I fall over in a soft patch of wildflowers. If Danny could see me now, he'd probably thank God for saving him from a lifetime with a nutcase.

Now I'm just lying here in the grass ... waiting, waiting, waiting ... to hear from God. My head is still spinning and I'm looking up at the clouds, trying to imagine what God might want to say to me right now. The first thought that comes to mind is, *A. J., fasting and spinning is probably not a good combination.* I feel sick.

It's getting dark. I'm still lying here, staring at stars now instead of clouds. I've already missed dinner, but then, what's to miss? I think we're supposed to be in the chapel by now, but I've decided I'm not moving until I hear from God.

It's starting to rain. Still waiting … waiting … waiting …

8
midnight Revelations

It's midnight. I'm standing in the pouring rain, drenched to the bone. A faint light is slowly making its way toward me in the distance. He must have heard me and he's coming for me. The light comes closer and closer, brighter and brighter, until it's shining on my face. He's finally here. It's Danny.

"A. J.? Is that you?" Danny jumps from the tugboat to the landing on the shore of Indian Lake. He tries to shield his face from the whipping rain with the collar of his jacket. His eyes dart from me to my duffle bag. He ties off the boat, then focuses on me. "I heard the bell clanging but thought it was a prank—I almost didn't come. What in the world are you doin' here in the middle of the night?"

I can't answer. I just stand here dripping.

Danny covers the distance between us in a few strides. He pulls off his jean jacket and wraps it around me. "A. J.—*what happened?*"

I can do little more than shrug my shoulders. Sailor's playing shipmate, barking his head off from the bow of the boat—too old to make the jump, but letting me know he's happy to have me home again. *Home.* That thought alone brings on the tears. "I'm n–not going to be a s-sister," I sob.

"What? Did they *kick you out?*"

I shake my head and cry even harder. "I r-ran away."

"You ran away—from a *church retreat?*"

I nod.

"Why?"

"Because ... my grandma was right."

"Right about what?"

"About *everything*. About you, and me, and life, and serving God, and Folgers coffee and *biscotti* with grandchildren." Now I'm really sobbing.

"Hey, c'mere." Danny gently pulls me in, wrapping his strong arms around me. The rain's pouring down on us, but he just holds me close while I sob it all out. "It's all gonna be okay," he whispers with that voice that just soothes my soul.

Sailor's pacing anxiously on the deck of the tug, hoping for some action. When I finally look up, Danny wipes away my tears, then holds me at arm's length. He tries to catch my eyes with his. "You want to talk about it?"

I nod.

"Let's get you outta the rain first." He grabs my duffle bag with one hand, drapes his other arm around me, and guides me over to the tug. "C'mon, we'll go sit in the cabin with the heater on and talk, okay?"

"'Kay," I sniffle, and trudge along beside him.

Danny tosses my bag in first, helps me aboard, and leads me into the cabin. He settles me into the captain's chair, then reaches around me, starts the engine, flips on the heater, lights the lantern, swings my captain's chair around to face him, and sits facing me in the first mate's chair. He focuses in on me until he can capture my eyes in the soft glow of the lantern, smiles gently, and says, "Talk to me."

I wipe my eyes with my sleeve, take a deep breath, and start talking. "Well … I went to my retreat at the Peaceful Pines. Everything was peaceful and piney—just like the name. And holy. The sisters, the chapel, the candles, all holy—except me. Even my roommate was holy. She knew exactly what she was supposed to do with her life. And the more excited everyone else got about their calling, the more confused I got about mine. I couldn't even handle the fasting without complaining. How would that look in Bangladesh?

"So there I was, hiding out on the mountain alone, after everyone else had gone into chapel. I was just lying there waiting to hear from God."

"What were you waiting to hear?"

"Whether or not to pursue the consecrated life of the convent. We were supposed to go out alone to count the cost, then return to the chapel and lay anything down at the altar that we felt we were still struggling to give up—hopes, dreams, whatever. The Reverend Mother said that once you lay them down, if God gives you peace over them, you can continue to move forward. So I stayed out there the entire afternoon and half the night. Instead of returning to the chapel, I kneeled on that mountain and made it my altar.

"I prayed, 'God, show me what I need to lay down.' And He showed me. Instead of peace, I envisioned myself on the island, going for a walk in the dark by your cabin, and inside the bright yellow windows I could see you. You were eating by the fire, and there was an empty chair across from you, but then *she* walked over and sat down. It was a horrid feeling. I suddenly realized that one day you'll get married—to *someone else,* and I'll have to spend the rest of my life looking in those windows at you and *her,* thinking *that could have been me.* But instead, I'd have to walk home alone, back to my lonely cabin, and sleep in my cold, lonely bed, all by myself, night after night…. You know what I mean?"

Danny's eyebrows raise slightly. "Oh yeah, I know what you mean. *All too well,*" he mutters.

"Then I had to lay down the chance of ever having my own babies. I have always wanted a house full of Southern-speaking babies. Even before I knew you I was secretly planning to raise my babies speaking Southern. I even made up my own Southern accent. Then God brought you to the island. I was only ten years old, but I knew you were my secret gift from God. For someday—"

"You *did?*"

"From the day I met you—you were mine. And I never told a soul. I tried to give you back to God on the mountain, but He wouldn't take you from my heart. And every time I tried to lay those babies down, they just kept crawling off the altar."

"*Good babies,*" Danny whispers.

"So I asked God, 'What should I do?' I don't know if it was in the wind outside or just in my head, but I'm pretty sure I heard 'A. J., go home.' And then it hit me, and I just knew—*home,* home is where my calling is, right here on Indian Island, helping you run your camp, maybe even for the rest of my life …" I have to look down for this part, "with you…."

A slight smile appears on Danny's face. His eyes look misty in the soft light.

"So, how on earth could I lay all of that down to go to India with Ruth?"

"You can't," he whispers.

"You're right. *I can't.* And I thought of how you've always been there for me. How you taught me about infinity and pondered the mysteries of God with me and took care of Sailor for me—for *eight years,* and sent me the snow globe that calmed my spirit, and made me a beautiful garden, and fenced in my critter cemetery ..."

"You noticed."

"... and how much I hurt you, and how if I didn't snap out of it, you would marry Pocahontas, or *whoever,* and it would be too late for me, and I would miss my true calling in life.

"Well, the next thing I knew, I was running down that mountain, back to my room to grab my overnight bag and tell Ruth that I just got my calling and was heading home, and that's when I found it."

"Found what?"

"This." I hold up my hand with a ruby ring. "When I tossed my toothbrush into my vanity case, I noticed the little velvet box tucked in the side pocket. That's when I found the ring and realized you must have snuck it in my beauty case when I was inside Saddlemyer's. I figured you got the idea from my novel *Treasure in a Bottle* ... you know, 'If you ever decide to marry me, this is for you'? I figured it must be a promise ring since it was a ruby instead of a diamond. So I came flying home to tell you how sorry I am and ask if you'll please forgive me, and tell you that, yes, I will promise myself to you!"

Danny stares at me and blinks. "Um ... can I think about this for a second?" He looks up toward heaven, shakes his head, and laughs, like God is playing a joke on him. He looks back down at me. "Um, A. J., I didn't put that ring in there."

"*What?*"

"That's ... not my ring."

"You mean this isn't from you?"

Danny shakes his head, looking as confused as I feel. "Can I see it for a minute?"

Feeling like an absolute idiot, I slide the ring off of my finger and hand it over.

The lights begin to come on in Danny's eyes. "That vanity case—where did you get that?"

"It was on the old bureau at Papoose."

Danny nods. "This was my grandmother's promise ring. I remember her showing it to me before. She said my grandpa gave her a ruby promise ring because the color reminded him of her name, Scarlett. She must have kept it stored in that case."

"Oh." *Take me now, Lord!* I just accepted a promise ring from someone who never asked me to be promised to him.

Danny stands up and looks down at me. He has one hand on his hip and runs his other hand through his hair. A smile slowly crosses his face.

"You think this is funny?"

"Yeah. I do."

Now he's grinning. He probably thinks I deserve this for everything I've put him through. "Well, then, I guess this probably means that you really don't want to be promised to me," I mutter.

"Is that a promise proposal?" he asks wryly.

"What do you mean, 'Is that a promise proposal?'"

"I mean, are you asking me to promise myself to you?"

"Of course I'm not asking you to promise yourself to me!"

"Well, isn't asking me if I don't want to be promised to you indirectly the same as asking if I do want to be promised to you?"

Oh, brother. "I don't know, maybe. Kind of. Sorta."

"Well, in that case, yes, A. J., I would love to be promised to you."

"You would?"

"I would. Thanks for asking. But, you know, I can't help feelin' like maybe you just want me because I'm Southern. You know how some guys say they love a girl because she's beautiful, but it's not really love at all? Well, I'm kinda wondering if maybe what you think is love is nothing more than *Southern infatuation.* It's a real problem for us guys in the South—you know, bein' used for our Southern accents." He shrugs. "What the heck, I think I'm okay with that."

"You are?"

He leans down, gripping the arms of my chair, and in a low voice, says, "I am. But if you *ever* leave me like that again … there will be no Southern boy waitin' for you, sister."

He straightens up, takes me by the hand, and leads me out to the boat deck. The rain has let up and the clouds are moving swiftly across the dark sky in front of a bright full moon. Danny turns to face me. He takes hold of my jacket collar with both hands, like he's about to shake me to pieces for all I've put him through. Instead, he pulls me close until our foreheads touch. "A. J. Degulio," he says, "I can't imagine going through life with anyone but you. I would love to be promised to you." Then he kisses me so tenderly it would put Little Joe Cartwright to shame.

❧ 9 ❧
Sailing Lessons

I wake up with the morning sun, realizing two things. One, I missed church. Slept right through both the first and second Mass. And two, instead of packing for India, I am promised to Danny Morgan and staying right here on this island where I belong. Danny's even letting me wear his grandma's ruby ring until he can buy me one. I've spent the entire morning lying here on the bed staring at it.

I'm pulled out of my daze by a rap on the door. "A. J., you home?" Danny sticks his head in the screen door. I'd propped open the main door earlier to let the sunshine in, then climbed back under my blanket to watch how the sunlight reflects off of the ruby ring onto the cabin walls.

"You're still in bed? What a bum!"

"I take it you went to church already?"

"I did. I thought about stopping by to see if you wanted to go, but I had a feeling you might not be up. I couldn't believe what time it was when you finally stopped talking and let me go home." He laughs. "Good thing I wasn't preachin' today."

"Well, I *was* up early." *Long enough to open the front door. I just didn't stay up.* "What are you up to now?"

"I just came by to make sure I didn't just dream that you ran away from a church retreat in the middle of the night to tell me you wanted to marry me."

Okay, that sounds pretty embarrassing when you put it like that. "That wasn't a marriage proposal—it was a promise proposal."

"Well, isn't a promise proposal indirectly like a marriage proposal, being that the promise eventually leads to marriage?"

Uggghhh! It's too early for this. "Um, I'll own up to that if you'll promise never to repeat it to anyone else for as long as you live."

Danny smiles. "I wouldn't share those sacred words with anyone but you, A. J. And since you're not joining the convent today, would you like to do something together?"

"Yeah, maybe. Like what?"

"I was wondering if you'd like to go sailin' with me?"

"Sailing? In what?"

"A sailboat."

"You don't have a sailboat."

"I do now. Found it at the church rummage sale last weekend."

"Really? Do you know how to sail?"

"Nope. I thought maybe we could learn together. I'm sure it's a lot like drifting, but with a sail. It sounded like something you might like so I bought it, hopin' you might come back someday and sail with me."

"What if I didn't?"

"Then I guess I'd be sailin' solo."

"Or sailin' with Sailor, or sailin' with Sally … or Susie …"

"I don't think so. I wouldn't want to risk ruining the sails with berry stains."

"Good point. Okay, go get your sailboat set to sail, and I'll slip over with Sailor 'soon as I'm in my sailin' suit."

Danny walks to the door, then turns and stands in the doorway just looking back at me.

"What? What are you staring at?" I ask.

"Just you."

"Why?"

"Because I can." He smiles, and leaves.

Right when I pull my sailing shirt over my head, the phone rings, making me jump.

"Hello?"

"A. J., is that you?"

"Yes, Mama, it's me—who else would it be?" She still asks every time she calls.

I can hear her yelling for Daddy to pick up the other phone. He comes on the line. "Hey, *ficcucia,* is that you?" He always calls me little fig.

"Hi, Daddy! How is everybody?" I first have to establish that nothing's wrong.

"We're great! Boys are great, Nonna still can't stand me, Adriana's happy modeling—life as usual. How's everything on the island?"

Mama cuts in, "When is school starting? And how's Sailor? Have you seen Danny lately—tell him to give his mama a big *buongiorno* from me."

"Sailor's fine, school starts next month, and yes, I've seen Danny—we're going sailing today."

"Sailing? In what?"

"A sailboat. Danny bought one at a garage sale."

"Do either of you know how to sail?"

"Not really, but I'm sure we'll figure it out. Hey, what are the boys and Adriana up to?"

"The boys are keeping busy with the villa remodels," Mama informs me, "and Dino found himself a cute little Italian girl he's been spending a lot of time with. Adriana came to visit last weekend with Pip the Mighty Mutt."

"Looks great," Daddy adds. "So does your sister." He laughs.

"Hey," Mama cuts in, "what's this nonsense about you thinking of joining the convent?"

"Oh, you've talked to Grandma?"

"Thought we'd better ask you ourselves. I told your grandma, 'Not unless they allow dogs in convents these days,' because you went home to be a vet, not a nun. So where'd she get that crazy notion?"

"Um, I just thought maybe I should be doing something more holy and noble on the side … but I think I'm over it now."

"A. J.," Mama says, "raising a family is the most noble thing you could ever do, and don't worry about becoming holy. Your children will make you holy, whether you like it or not."

"You mean to say that I made you holy, Mama?"

"Yes, I have you to thank for my sainthood status. Especially for having to put up with your fake Southern accent all those years. I can't wait for the day that you have a quirky Southern-speaking kid of your own."

What she doesn't know is that's my dream. But we won't be discussing that right now. "So are you planning a trip back here anytime soon?"

"We'll just have to see how things go. For now we're too booked up to get away," Daddy says. "We sure miss you. Maybe if things slow down in the winter, we could try and plan a visit. Christmas on the island might be fun."

"Oh, do come for the holidays—I miss all of you. How's Nonna doing?"

"Healthy as an ox, and still nutty as a fruitcake."

"Sonny …" Mama cuts in. Mama always uses her warning tone when Daddy makes comments about her mother. She agrees with him most of the time, but still, it's her mother. "Well, kiddo, we'd better scoot. Long distance, you know?"

"Love and miss you, Fig," Daddy says.

"Me too. *Arrivederci.*"

"*Arrivederci,* kiddo!" Mama yells.

Now I miss them more than ever.

Sailing. I've never gone sailing before. Surprising, considering that it must be much like drifting, only with more wind. I wonder if it's as easy as it looks. I mean, how hard could it be to sit on the deck of a boat while the wind pushes it around? Hopefully Danny knows more about it than I do. I'm wearing my blue and white striped shirt, white shorts, and a pair of white Keds, just to look the part. Sailor's wearing a blue and white bandanna, looking equally impressive. If nothing else, we'll at least appear as if we know what we're doing.

"Ahoy, mates!" Danny yells as we approach the dock.

I burst out laughing. "*That's* your sailboat?"

"What? You got a problem with my boat?" Danny's standing in what looks like a tub toy with a piece of bright yellow fabric flapping in the wind.

I'm laughing so hard I can barely answer. I had pictured this big old pirate ship, like the *Buccaneer* at the Grand Old Sea Palace where we vacationed every summer on the Riviera. Instead, I'm looking at something the size of my dinghy, with a single sail. "Where's my pirate ship?" I finally yell back.

"Hey, what did you expect for fifty bucks? I'll make you a deal. If you decide you like sailin', I'll build you a pirate ship."

"Deal!"

Danny holds out his hand and helps me aboard. There's barely enough room for all three of us once Sailor climbs in. Danny and I sit together on the little bench seat by the rudder. I know what a rudder is, but that's about the extent of it.

Danny glances around, looking rather proud of his new vessel. "It's really not a bad little boat."

I look around at all twelve feet of it. "Yeah, it is kinda cute." It's all wood and could look real nice with a fresh coat of varnish. The once-bright yellow sail is faded and frayed. "So, do you know how to drive this thing?"

"We'll see, won't we?" Danny shoves us off from the dock, and we sit here going nowhere. "I think we have to figure out which way the wind's blowin' and adjust the sail to catch it."

"Yeah, I hear that's the idea, anyway." There's a very slight breeze, so we tinker with the sail, trying to get it to catch the wind, but it just keeps flapping around. "Do you think we need to wear our life jackets out here?" We both laugh because we are still going absolutely nowhere, fast.

After ten minutes of nothing, the sail finally catches a breeze. Danny breaks out in a sailor's song:

"Her flag was three colors, her masthead was low,

"Hey-ho blow the man down,

"She was round in the corner and buff in the bow,

"Give me some time to blow the man down."

We're actually *sailing,* slowly, but sailing. Even Sailor's excited. He's sitting up straight, nose to the wind, living up to his name, and looking very dignified in his bandanna.

Clipping along at a nice pace, we pick up speed the farther out we go. Danny's holding the rudder with one hand and my hand with the other. We all deserve to be on a picture postcard. "This is great! I can't believe I've never tried this before." The minute I say that, the wind shifts and our sail goes flat. "Hey, what's the deal? I was just getting the hang of this." The waves are picking up whitecaps, so there's obviously wind out here. We just haven't caught it.

"I think we need to readjust our sail." Danny lets go of my hand and starts to mess around with the sail again. It suddenly fills up like a parachute and we go shooting off in another direction.

"Whoa, that works!" I grab ahold of the boat rim. We're skipping across the lake so fast I feel like we're in a fast-motion cartoon. Fortunately, there's nothing to crash into. "Tweak the sail, Danny, maybe it'll slow us down."

Danny shifts the mast. The little seacraft spins completely the other direction, then flips over, sending us flying into the water.

We're out in the middle of the lake with an upside-down sailboat, a dog, and life jackets floating by. "Grab the life jackets!" Danny yells. "We might need 'em after all."

I swim after the two life jackets before they get away. Danny's working on flipping the boat upright. My tennies pop off my feet as soon as I start to kick. Meanwhile, Sailor is swimming after me, trying to save me, but nearly drowning me in the effort. I round up both of my shoes and the life jackets and swim back to help Danny. Righting a sailboat is not as easy as flipping a dinghy back over, mainly because there's a sail to deal with. It takes both of us to flip it upright. "Holy cow, it's full of water!"

"The bailing can!" Danny yells. "I have to go after it or we'll never make it back." He reaches under the water, pulls off his tennis shoes, tosses them into the boat, then goes after the can before it sinks.

When he returns, the two of us get on either side of the boat and hoist ourselves in at the same time. After we roll into the boat, Danny pulls Sailor back in. We're lying here looking like we've just survived the ultimate shipwreck. Danny and I look at each other and start laughing. "Think we'd qualify for the America's Cup?" he says. We're up to our necks in water, laughing too hard to bail. Danny tosses me a life jacket. "Here, you might need this after all."

"Thanks," I say, dumping a bucket of water on him.

"What's that for?"

"For trying to tell me this is just like drifting with wind. This is like race-car driving on water! Drifting is dry and relaxing. Sailing is ... *wet*."

I dump more water on Danny to prove my point, and accidentally bonk him on the head with the can.

"Give me that." Danny grabs the can from me. "You're dangerous with that thing." He starts to bail. "Now that you've acquired such a fondness for sailing, are you ready for your pirate ship?"

"I would *love* to have a pirate ship—once you take sailing lessons."

"Once *I* take sailing lessons? What about *you?*"

"I plan to lie on the deck with Sailor while you pirate us around the lake."

"Is that so?"

"Yep. You can be my pirate, and I'll be your wench."

"My *wench?*" Danny laughs. "Well, in that case, have you ever been kissed by a pirate before?" Danny drapes his wet arm around my shoulder.

"Hold on there, Bluebeard. Maybe this would be a good time to bring up the matter of your other wench first."

"My *other* wench?" Danny's obviously taken aback. He thinks a minute. "Oh, *her?* Are you talkin' about the wench in my rowboat?"

"Yep, her … aka Pocahontas."

I detect a hint of amusement in Danny's eyes. "That was Wendy. Wendy wasn't my wench."

"Well, if Wendy wasn't your wench, why was Wendy with you?"

"Well, what wooked wike Wendy was my wench wasn't weally the way it was."

Oh brother. "You're obviously more amused by this than I am."

"Sorry." He's trying his best to rein in his grin. "Nothing happened in the rowboat."

"If that was nothing, then why did it appear as though she was mauling you? And I didn't exactly see you fighting her off."

"As soon as she showed up next to me on the boat seat, I started baiting a fishhook with a worm. I figured that would keep a little distance between us. It was actually working … until the worm fell off."

I eye him doubtfully.

Danny cracks a smile. "I knew you were watchin' from up on that cliff. Sailor was a dead giveaway. It was nice to know you were jealous."

"Ha! Me, jealous of some Hiawatha wannabe? I was *not* jealous."

"Yeah, I think ya were. Jealous enough to part with your berries."

"Freak accident."

Danny laughs. "Right. Hey, look, if it makes you feel any better, your timing was perfect—the air raid came right after the worm fell off the hook."

"So, you weren't really mad at me when you came over to Papoose and chewed me out?"

"I was upset that you dumped me, but, I gotta admit, the blackberry massacre was pretty classic. Touching, really." His smile breaks into a huge grin. "You have no idea how hard I laughed after I left you lookin' all remorseful sittin' at your cabin. The memory of you up on that cliff, hurlin' berries—then playing innocent …" He shakes his head. "Only you would try to pull that off, A. J."

"Yeah, well, my memories aren't quite as humorous as yours seem to be. I'm still stuck with the *memowies* of the *wicked wittle wench* in my head."

"I guess that's the price you pay for leavin' your man."

"I didn't *leave* you. I just placed you on hold."

"Yeah, indefinitely. Next time, at least place me on layaway with a deposit, so I know you'll be coming back to pick me up."

We're drifting at a dead-man's pace in the middle of Indian Lake, inching our way toward home. Danny says he thinks he can help me get over "the *memowies* of the *wicked wittle wench*" by the time we reach the island.

"Oh, really, how?"

"C'mere, I'll show ya...."

From now on whenever the image of Danny and *her* pops into my head, it will quickly be replaced with the memory of being kissed by a pirate in a boatful of water on Indian Lake.

"So, have you forgotten yet?" Danny asks every so often.

"Um ... almost, but not quite."

It is a long trip home, but by the time we get there, I've pretty much forgotten all about ... what's-her-face.

❧ 10 ❧
Legacy of Love

On my way out the door from visiting Grandma, I check the mail-box and find a letter from Bianca—which I stash in my pocket to savor—and something from WSU. Glancing down at my fall schedule, a familiar wave of back-to-school blues rolls over me. This was always the time of year we had to leave the island and go back to school. Even though it's still a week away, once you have that school schedule in your hand, summer feels as good as gone. I have to remind myself that this time I'm going to school for something I want to learn about. Healing critters. No more math story problems asking what time the trains leave and arrive in Timbuktu. Instead it will be: How many milligrams of sulfadi-methoxine would you give a hamster weighing two ounces? *Very little.* I close the mailbox and head back to the front porch to read my letter from Bianca.

Tucked inside is a photo of Bianca and Dario ... *together.* That makes me smile. *So, you finally got your guy.* Bianca has had a crush on Dario since the day he and Dominic plopped them-selves down at our lunch table in the Macchiavelli High cafeteria, shocking us to death and winning us the envy of every girl in the school. Bianca finally grew into the French beauty Mama always said she'd be. She was well on her way in high school and at the tail end of her awkward stage. Most French beauties are like that—late bloomers.

According to the letter, the romance began on a day trip to Florence, which ended with a kiss on the River Arno. After two pages of the dramatic love story, she writes, "By the way, Dominic has been sulking ever since you left Tuscany. He told me to say, '*Buongiorno* to Angelina the heartbreaker.' He tells everyone you left for some Yankee cowboy. You know that he was in love with you, don't you?"

Yeah, I kinda knew. Sigh. I tuck the photo and letter back into the envelope and head back to the island, determined to enjoy the tail end of summer while it lasts.

Returning to Papoose, there's a note attached to my front door. *Meet me at Juniper Beach for a swim. Danny.* Opening the screen door, a blast of hot air greets me. The thought of diving under cool waves on Juniper Beach sounds *really* good right now. Sailor must have followed Danny, he's nowhere around. Reminding myself that it's still summer and hotter than blazes out, I throw on my swimsuit and cover-up, grab a towel, and head back out the door to Juniper Beach.

Sailor catches my scent and comes to greet me before I even make it through the trail. His fur is still wet from the lake. Of course, he waits until he's right next to me to shake. "Hey, thanks. You probably think that's funny, don't you?"

He shakes again for good measure.

Danny's knee-deep in the water, tinkering around with some dive gear he has loaded in the skiff. He looks like Sandy, Bud's older brother on *Flipper.* They were always out on the water with their dive masks, swimming around with their dolphin. Bud was kind of a dork, but Sandy was a cutie.

I wade in to meet Danny and get a big wet bear hug in return. "Between you and Sailor, who needs to go swimming?" I check out the gear in the boat. "Been diving already?"

"Yeah, a little. Remember Jordy's little camp buddy, Sammy, who came up with the name Camp Wannacomeback?"

"Sure, I remember Sammy."

"Well, I brought him out for the afternoon to go diving with me."

"Find anything?"

"A few things. He went home with a couple of old bottles. I found this old anchor that might come in handy for that pirate ship I plan to build you." He lifts up the rusty chain that's already attached to the bow of the boat.

"Isn't that kind of putting the anchor before the ship?"

He smiles. "Sometimes that's what it takes to motivate someone. Hey, aren't you hot?"

"I'm roasting." I scoop up a handful of cool water and trickle it down my arms.

"Here, let me help ya." Danny scoops me up and tosses me into the waves.

Sailor plunges in after me and starts swimming circles around me, splashing water in my face with his paws.

What is with guys, anyway? *I was real happy just wading, thank you all very much.*

Danny reaches for my hand and reels me back in before Sailor has a chance to drown me in his heroic attempt to save me.

Safely back in shallow waters, I help run interference for a school of minnows being chased down by a sunfish. Someone has to look out for the little guys.

"Hey, when you're done saving minnows, how would you like to boat over to Flip's Fish-n-Chips and grab a bite to eat?"

"Something about that sounds a bit ironic.... When I'm done rescuing fish, we'll head over and *eat* fish."

"Sounds good to me." Danny pulls the skiff closer to shore.

I grab my towel and my cover-up and climb aboard. Sailor gets in line, hoping someone's going to hoist him into the boat to join us, but he gets vetoed by Danny. "Sorry, boy, not this trip. There's something unappetizing about a big, wet, drooling dog in a small boat when you're trying to enjoy a meal."

We can still hear him howling halfway down the lake.

When we reach Flip's boat dock, I stay in the skiff while Danny goes to order our meal. Watching him walk over to the fish bar, I think of how close I came to losing him forever. I look down at my ring, glad that it's me who will be joining him for dinner. I'd hate to imagine someone else eating fish with him.

This just in on the six o'clock news: Sister Angelina Juliana Degulio of Our Lady of the Lake was taken into custody at Flip's Fish-n-Chips today for pelting a young couple in a skiff with a deluxe fish basket. The young female victim is recovering from a minor concussion at Squawkomish General Hospital, after being struck in the head by a flying bass. Sister Angelina, wearing a nun's habit at the time, was heard yelling, "Watch out for flying fish!"

"What are you thinkin' about?"

"Huh?"

Danny's standing on the dock holding our Cokes. "You have that mischievous look in your eye and a smirk on your face to go with it. What's goin' on in that little head of yours?"

"Oh—nothing."

"Yeah, I'm not buying it. Must be a doozer." He hands me the pop and goes back for the fish.

☙

Danny drives us out a ways and cuts the motor. He asks a blessing over our fish baskets and raises a toast to the sunset just beginning to set, casting a warm glow over the water. We set the fish baskets on the middle seat for our table.

"Okay, I have good news and bad news," Danny announces.

"Oh, yeah? What's the good news?"

He takes a bite of fish and keeps me guessing until he's done with half of his basket.

"Just tell me!"

"Um … okay. The good news is: There's a Christian summer camp down South with the same concept I have in mind for Indian Island. They've accepted my application to attend their Camp Directors' Conference. It's a training course on how to run a Christian youth camp."

"*Really?*"

"Really."

"That's great! So your camp might start to take shape by next summer? Grandma Angelina was right."

"How's that?"

"Well, besides thinking the world of you, she said you'd be going places in life."

"Your grandma said that?"

"Yeah. She also said that I'd be a fool not to be going with you."

"Smart woman, your grandma."

"So what's the bad news?"

"Well, the first place I'm goin' happens to be in Kentucky. One week of hands-on learning while camp is in session, followed by a week of workshops."

"You're leaving me for *two weeks?*"

"Yeah, looks that way."

"But I just got you *back!*"

"No, *I* just got *you* back."

"Oh. Yeah. Well, same difference. When do you leave?"

"Next week."

"Dang. I mean, the part about you being gone. But I'm really happy for you being able to go—I think."

"Thanks. Me too." Danny reaches over and takes my hand. "You still like that ring?"

"I *love* this ring."

"I'm glad you'll have something to remember me with—in case you feel like running off to join the circus or something while I'm away."

"*Danny.* I'm not going anywhere—just school. What could possibly happen in two weeks at WSU? Wait. Don't answer that."

"I'm thinking of lookin' for a ring while I'm in Kentucky. Can you give me an idea of what you'd like?"

I look down at the antique ruby and gold ring. "I really like this ring. It's special knowing this belonged to a couple who loved each other for a lifetime. Know what I mean?"

"So—you'd rather have this ring?"

I hold my hand up to the sunset, where the ruby reflects the last rays of daylight. "This represents true love. It's a legacy. Maybe we can pass it on the same way someday."

Danny looks at me tenderly. "Can we seal this deal before you change your mind?" Without waiting for me to answer, he leans across the seat and kisses me. "It's a done deal," he whispers. "The ring is all yours. And so am I."

Once the sun has gone down, we drift along beneath the stars. In the dead silence Danny suddenly says, "As long as we're on this topic ..."

"What topic?"

"Our future."

"We are?"

"We are now."

"Oh. Okay." I sit back and brace myself.

"Have you considered the fact that you're Catholic and I'm Baptist?"

"Um, I'm aware of that, yes. Have I considered how we're going to resolve that? No, not really."

"Well ... I've been thinkin', how about if we start by visiting each other's churches?" Danny suggests.

"That's a start, anyway."

✺

Island Journal: Danny brought up the topic of "religion."
After changing my plans about being a sister, I figured I'd
have to become a Baptist if Danny was going to be a preacher.
But with Danny looking into the possibility of becoming an
independent camp director, I'm feeling less pressure to have to
become a Baptist. Since neither of us are seriously considering
becoming clergy or living in a convent, I think now we are on
equal ground for deciding together how we'd like to worship
God as a couple. Being that both denominations are grounded
in Jesus, I can't imagine they could be that different from one
another. So, God, this one is up to You.

✺

Sunday morning Danny picks me up at my dock for church. My first
visit to the Baptist church. We swing by Buzz's gas dock to refuel.
Amazingly, after all these years, Buzz is still working there—and grumpy
as ever. "Makin' me get up early on a Sunday morning, are ya?"

He sleeps in a hammock inside a small shed at the end of the
dock, and a bell signals when he has customers. He calls it his house-
boat. He comes waddling out in nothing but a pair of trousers held
up by suspenders. No shirt. His hula dancer tattoo is eight years bigger than before. She started out skinny, back when Buzz was young
and skinny himself. But since she's tattooed right on his stomach,
they grow bigger together every year.

Good old Buzz. I remember thinking as a kid that he was one of the most fascinating people I'd ever met, with his dancing hula tattoo. It's still nice to see him again—he's part of the original cast from the good old days.

❧

When we enter the sanctuary, Danny asks me where I'd like to sit. I'm kind of torn. My first inclination is to sit in the back corner so I don't make a spectacle of myself. But since Danny's preaching, I should probably sit closer to the front. I decide to compromise and sit halfway up in between. At least we get to sit together during worship. A little girl in my pew keeps looking over and smiling at me. Once Danny goes up front, I may just scoot over next to her and pretend to belong to her family.

Leaning over, I whisper in Danny's ear, "Are you nervous?"

"Mmm, not really. I'm preachin' on something you'll like," he whispers.

"What, men submitting to women?"

Danny stifles a laugh. "No. The stars."

❧

I have never seen Danny standing behind a pulpit before, but it is a sight to behold. He looks so tall and statuesque up there, a young Billy Graham in the making. Danny's wearing a dusty blue shirt with a tie, and beige corduroys. I'm sure I'm not the only one in here who's noticed how handsome he looks. But I'm the only one in here wearing his promise ring.

"O Lord, our Lord, how majestic is your name in all the earth! You have set your glory above the heavens." Danny is reading from the book of Psalms. "When I consider your heavens, the work of your fingers, the moon and stars, which you have set in place, what is man that you are mindful of him, the son of man that you care for him?"

Danny launches into a sermon on God's merciful mindfulness of us. He goes into the wonders of the stars and the planets, and how all of His creation speaks loudly of God, that man is without excuse when it comes to finding Him.

When the sermon ends, the worship leader has us open our hymnals and leads us in "How Great Thou Art."

People are getting up and walking toward the door.

What? That's it? You're done? Where's the liturgy? Where's Communion? What about the Nicene Creed? You can't leave—we're not finished here, people! … People … People …?

❧

Danny and I walk across the street to St. Peter's Parish to catch the second Mass. I had no idea that our two churches differed so much in their delivery. But then, I've never wandered into a Baptist church before. I'm going to have to keep a close eye on Danny—he has no idea what he's in for. Could be a bit of a shock.

The priest makes his entrance in formal vestments, followed by his ministers and the altar boys. We sing an opening hymn while the priest reverences the altar with incense.

"In the name of the Father, and of the Son, and of the Holy Spirit."

"Amen."

We move through the liturgy: the reading of the Holy Gospel, the homily, and our profession of faith, the Nicene Creed, which the entire church body stands and recites from memory. Danny's expression is one of amazement and curiosity rolled together.

The priest begins to prepare the Eucharist.

"Is this Communion?" Danny whispers.

I nod.

Danny waits in the pew while everyone goes forward.

After silent prayer on our knees, the priest gives us his blessing. "May Almighty God bless you, the Father, and the Son, and the Holy Spirit."

"Amen."

"The Mass is ended, go in peace to love and serve the Lord."

"Thanks be to God."

Walking to the car, I turn to Danny. "Well?"

"Well …" He rubs the back of his neck. "We have a lot to pray about."

* * *

Island Journal: Yikes! Okay, so, we do worship a bit different from one another. God—I'm counting on You here to somehow bring Rome and Oklahoma together to find common ground in You. You can do this … Right?

❦ 11 ❦
School Daze and Disco Knights

School, day one: My Environmental Science and Chemistry 101 classes clue me in real fast—*we are no longer in high school, Toto.* I'll feel accomplished at something today if I can just navigate myself through the Compton Union Building cafeteria, conveniently dubbed The CUB, without dumping my food tray on anyone. It's kind of a relief not knowing anyone here until I have an inkling of what I'm doing.

"A. J. Degulio—is that really you?"

I whip around. "Rodney Gizmode?" The guy who locked me inside of the confessional when I was ten years old. Of all the people I could go without running into for the rest of my life, Rodney would be my first pick.

"That's right! Only I go by Rod now. Hey, mind if I join you?"

"Uh …"

He sits down at my table before I can answer, and opens his brown-bag lunch.

Rod looks like Opie on *The Andy Griffith Show.* Unfortunately for him, it's not as cute to look like Opie at eighteen as it is when you're eight.

"What kind of degree are you shooting for?" he asks.

"A vet degree."

"No kidding? Wouldn't you just join the army for that?"

I see the guy hasn't changed. "Um, that would be vet as in veterinarian, not veteran."

"Ah, right. I'm in the parks and recreation program myself, hoping to follow in the old man's footsteps. Once your dad left for Italy, my old man landed the head ranger position at Indian Lake State Park."

"Do you really have to go to college for that job?"

"It never hurts to be the one most qualified for the position."

According to Daddy, all he needed to get that job was to be the right size for the Smokey Bear outfit. I think it might be an improvement over the snazzy polyester outfit and platform shoes that Rod is wearing. He looks like he's about to break into a disco routine any minute. Rod takes out a smashed peanut butter sandwich on white bread, and what appears to have once been a Twinkie.

"Looks like someone backed over your lunch there, Rod."

"Actually, my brother was mad that I took the last Twinkie and smashed my lunch bag with his anatomy book—he's a first-year med student."

"Hmm." *Better find out what kind of doctor he's planning to be so I never end up on his operating table.* I start into my own lunch, which is lukewarm now.

Rod expounds on his future plans to become a park ranger. Before long, I realize he's talked the entire lunch break away, and I'm about to be late for my next class. "Oh, hey, I'd better run, but what a surprise to see you again."

"Tell me about it! I'm so glad to know someone else here.

Hey—I'll look for you tomorrow, same time." With that, he shoves half the smashed Twinkie into his mouth and chokes out, "See you moomorrow!"

My last class of the day is a biology lab. As if my first day wasn't long enough, who but Rod walks through the door and makes a beeline for the chair next to mine. "Hey, A. J., I just signed us up to be lab partners."

This is going to be *a long* semester. I miss Danny.

❦

Lunch line, day two: Sliding my tray along the tray lane, I spot Rod hunting around as if he's in search of his next wall trophy. I dart behind the pie display case as long as I can until it's my turn to pay.

He catches sight of me somewhere between the banana and coconut cream pies and moves in for the chase. "Hey, there you are. I've been looking everywhere for you!" He follows me back to my seat. Today he is into the Western polyester theme. "I have something for you."

A large bouquet of flowers is thrust across my lunch tray. A mismatched bouquet of dried flowers and green grasses lands in my soup.

"Wow. Where did you get … all this?" I diligently pick the floating flower petals out of my cream of tomato soup.

"Pretty nice mix of flora and foliage, eh?"

"Mmm." *Maybe if I were a horse.*

"My sister-in-law owns a florist shop, so I have the privilege of arranging my own bouquets." He flicks his choppy bangs back.

"Rodney … er, Rod, this is really nice of you, but you didn't need to go to all this trouble."

"Oh, hey, I don't do this kind of thing for just anyone."

Lunch line, day three: Another bouquet shows up, this one even more eclectic than the first, with a sappy little love poem attached. I try to drop the hint that I have another love interest, while waving my promise ring in front of him. Rod has only one answer for that. "No harm in getting reacquainted with an old friend, right? I haven't told you this but I'm rather accomplished at disco dancing." He puffs out his little chest, exposing a large gold medallion necklace. "Not to brag, or anything, but I've given dancing a bit of a new twist over at Ratskeller's. I'm kind of known around there as the Disco Knight."

"Really?"

"Yeah, I dress up as a modern-day King Arthur in a silver stretch outfit with black platform boots. Got some pretty funky moves that really bring the babes out on the dance floor. The Alpha Chi Omega sorority girls really get into it. I've put a whole new spin on 'Shake Your Booty.' Hey, how about you and me hittin' the dance floor this weekend—drinking age is only nineteen in Idaho."

"I'm eighteen, I don't drink, and I don't dance disco."

"No problem. I can get some fake ID for you from one of the A-Chi-O ladies, and no one will know you're not drinking if you just ask for a Coke with a slice of lime—looks just like a rum and Coke. I'll teach you the disco moves."

"Um, I really hate to miss out, but … I have scads of homework."

"Great, we'll study together before we go. I can help you with math—it's my best subject."

"Actually, I'm studying for an animal anatomy exam—I have to be able to name every bone in the entire skeletal structure of a dog."

"Oh, well, guess I can't help you there."

❧

First lonesome weekend: Sailor and I are spending a quiet Saturday morning in front of old Western movies. A much-missed tradition from long ago. Indian Island and Westerns have always gone together. *Shirley Temple Theatre* was also a favorite I rarely missed. I had to keep the volume down on Shirley when Mama was in the cabin. I can still hear her yelling from the kitchen, "If I have to listen to that kid sing 'Animal Crackers in My Soup' one more time, I'm going to flip that channel and bring her little tap shoes to a screeching halt! For the love of Pete, who puts animal crackers in soup anyway?"

I've never heard anyone but Mama call Shirley on that one.

❧

On my own, week two: Life on the island all alone is dreadfully quiet. I'm getting a taste of what Danny's life has been like since his grandfather died. No wonder he offered me a hamster to stay. I even took Stormy to Big Daddy Burger last night just for some company. She's in a tough spot for a twelve-year-old. It was good for both of us to be together again.

School is going well as far as the academics. I've had plenty of uninterrupted time to study. My dog anatomy exam was today. The teacher had every single bone in the entire skeleton of a dog displayed in random order around the room. We had to identify each bone with the correct name and placement. I aced my first test. *So pin a rose on me!* as Mama would say.

And speaking of roses, my thrilling social life at The CUB cafeteria continues to bring new surprises daily. Today's bouquet came along with an invitation to join Rod's Disco-Mania Dance Club. "We're having a 'Get Down and Disco' kickoff this Friday. We're trying to get Ratskeller's to play more disco and lose some of the country-western. Wanna come?"

"I'm sorry, Rod, but I really can't."

"Let me guess. You're memorizing all the bones in the skeleton of the horse?"

"This week it's the cat."

❧

"Hey, Sailor—I'm home!" I have this need to feel that there is someone on the island waiting for me—even if it's only my dog. He's usually down on the dock long before my announcement. He picks up on my boat motor, apart from all the other boats, before I'm even in his sight. The minute I dock, he climbs into the boat to greet me. "Hey, boy, I got another poem from the Disco Knight. Wait till you get a load of this one!"

I've had about all I can stand. I'm even having Rod nightmares where I'm buried under a pile of flowers and love poems, screaming for Danny to come rescue me.

Missing Danny, day eleven: On my way to school, I'm contemplating the best way to confront the Disco Knight in shining polyester. Ironically, as I'm thinking about this, I notice Rod's pickup truck in front of a florist boutique—but the shop isn't even open this early. Slowing down, I catch a glimpse of someone behind the shop mulling through the Dumpster.

Dumpster flowers? No way ... Sure enough, Rod hops out of the bin after gallantly wrestling a bundle of wild foliage into a shopping sack. I think of the ever-growing jungle currently taking over my small cabin. I was trying to be gracious by not tossing them out, but now that I know where they're coming from, my plans have changed dramatically. I can't get rid of them fast enough, which is the first thing I plan to do the minute school is over. For now, I need to prepare a little speech for our inevitable CUB cafe encounter.

I take a seat in the environmental science lecture hall next to another blond girl who could almost pass as my twin. When we look at each other, we both laugh, aware that we both feel like we're looking in a mirror. "Oh my gosh—I've just met my double!" she says. "I'm Celiene."

"A. J. Degulio," I reply. "Nice to meet you." *Where were you when I was forced to live in Italy for eight years? We could have switched lives!*

"Do you live on campus?" she asks.

"No, I'm commuting from Indian Island. How about you?"

"I'm a Kappa Kappa Gamma—I live in the sorority house.

Sometimes I wish I could live on an island! It's nearly impossible to get any studying done here. I think a lot of these girls are just here to get their MRS degree."

"MRS degree—what's that?"

"MRS—as in *Mrs.* Smith. Some of these ladies think that the men come here to get their bachelor degrees, and the ladies just come to hook a bachelor. Know what I mean?"

"Um, yeah, right."

"So, A. J., what's your major?"

"Veterinary medicine."

"Wow. Doctor Degulio." She laughs. "That's impressive."

Yeah, I probably won't mention that I'm soon to be Doctor Morgan.

The lecture begins. All I can think about is why people tend to think that it's either-or when it comes to school and being married—rather than "and." Oh well, it's nice to meet someone besides the Disco Knight.

❧

My stomach fills with dread as he approaches my table. Today's bouquet is a special blend of bruised baby roses, a few wilted daisies, and some ferns tossed randomly into the mix. "Hey, pretty lady," he says, holding out the Dumpster bouquet.

Oh, gag. "Hey, Rod." As soon as he sits down, which is always too close for comfort, I scoot over and turn to look him straight in the eye. "Rod, listen, I appreciate the flowers and cards, but it really needs to stop. I am not interested in pursuing a relationship. I'm already involved with someone else."

He appears not the least bit fazed by this news. "Well, unless you're married to this guy, I still have a chance, right?"

"*No,* you really don't." *Ever.* "I am promised to Danny Morgan." I hold my ring up for emphasis.

"Well," he says, looking miffed. "I wish you had told me earlier. If you weren't giving me mixed messages, I would have asked one of the A-Chi-O ladies to be my dance partner."

"I'm sure they'll be glad to have me step down."

"Yeah, no doubt."

❦

The minute I get home, I toss the *last* batch of flowers on the table, next to the numerous other bouquets and poems. This place looks like a funeral parlor. My first plan of action is to go redump the flowers out back where I don't have to see them anymore. "C'mon, Sailor, let's go find something to load all of this 'flora and foliage' into and lay it to rest." I should probably just dump it all into the lake, but with my luck, I'd have to watch it wash in and out with the waves forever.

I head out to the old shed in search of the wheelbarrow. This way I can load everything up and be done with it in one big dump. Ashes to ashes. An old, rusty yard cart propped up against the shed looks like just the ticket to do the job.

Wheeling around to the front of the cabin, I notice the screen door standing open. I'm sure I'd closed it. Sailor doesn't act alarmed in the least—he wags his tail, runs up the stairs, and heads inside. The door suddenly swings wide open.

"Danny!" I run up the steps, "You're home *three days early!"*

I try to hug him, but he doesn't hug me back. Dropping my arms, I take a step back. "What's wrong?"

"What's *wrong?* Maybe a better question would be *who's Rod?"*

"Rod? Rod!" *Oh my gosh—the flowers!* I burst out laughing at the thought of what Danny just walked into. *Rod's Dumpster delights and his illusion of love.* "Danny, this is *not* what it seems!"

"Ya know, somehow I'm missing the humor in this. Is there something you want to tell me about the guy who's filled your living room with flowers and love letters?"

Oh, no, I feel my mother's laughing curse coming on. Just the thought of Danny feeling threatened by the Disco Knight sends me into hysterics. Bad timing. "Danny, it's not … it's not … if you could see …" It's no use. I can't stop laughing. I'm gone. Deep breath, exhale slowly … repeat. "Okay … I'm okay."

"Well, I'm glad *you* are. Let me know when you think you can explain this to me." He turns and walks away.

"Danny!"

He stops in his tracks.

"It's not what it looks like, *really."*

He turns around. "A. J., is anything *ever* what it looks like with you? Look, I've had a really long trip, I'm still on Kentucky time, and I'm going to bed." This time he turns and keeps walking.

I want to run after him, but it's obvious he's not in the mood to listen until I can pull myself together. Returning to Papoose, I see for the first time how all of this must have looked through his eyes.… Not good. Not good at all. I would have a hard time buying this story myself. But this is ridiculous! I'm going over there. If Danny can't trust me by now … *Okay, so I've done a few off-the-wall things lately, but he should at least trust my loyalty to him.*

One hour later, I arrive on Danny's doorstep determined to present my case as seriously as possible. It takes a while for him to answer the door. He's changed into his comfort clothes: worn-out Levi's and a flannel shirt. Judging from his scruffed-up hair, he must have fallen asleep. "Hey," he says, flatly. He's not investing a lot of emotion right now.

"May I come in?"

He steps aside. This feels far too familiar—the last time it had something to do with blackberries. I shuffle inside and sit on the far couch—the one designated for misunderstandings. Danny takes the couch across from me.

I can only imagine what must be going through his head, but here goes. "Danny, I know how bad this looks. I'm sorry for laughing—I would not be amused either if I were in your shoes. I can clear this all up in about two words."

"I'm listening."

"Rodney Gizmode."

"Who?"

"Summer of 1968—Big Island Bash, *remember?*"

"Gizmode? The strange little kid with the red cowboy boots?"

"Exactly! Only he's older and stranger now. He goes to WSU—and calls himself the Disco Knight. Instead of cowboy boots he's wearing platforms. Anyway, he got all the flowers from a *Dumpster.* I told him about you—he wouldn't take no for an answer. He wanted a disco partner. When you came home, I was just digging a hole to dump all of the flowers into. That's it. Really."

Danny leans his head against the back of the couch and recaps what I just said. "A guy at WSU named Rod, who wears platforms— gets flowers from a Dumpster, wants a disco partner, won't back off. You were digging a hole to dump the flowers in." He stares back at me. "Did I get that straight?"

"Y-eah. I think so."

He cocks his head to the side like a confused cocker spaniel. "What was that you were saying before I left for Kentucky? Something about 'What could possibly happen in two weeks?'"

"Okay, so it sounds a little crazy ..."

He raises his eyebrows. "A little?"

"What do you expect? This is *Rodney Gizmode,* for Pete's sake!"

Danny releases a heavy sigh. "Rodney Gizmode." He thinks about that for a minute. The weariness begins to drain from his face. "Rodney Gizmode, a disco knight in platform shoes ..." He shakes his head. "I don't know, A. J., you might want to reconsider. Maybe you two were meant for each other." He cracks a grin.

He *finally* gets it. I release a heavy sigh of my own.

Danny gives me a look that says he knows I'm eventually going to drive him insane.

"So why did you come home early?"

Danny hesitates, like he's weighing out his answer. "It's a long story ... that will have to wait."

"Oh, come on, you can't come back three days early and expect me to wait to find out why. I hate waiting."

Danny looks at me point-blank. "A. J., I have waited eight years for you to come back from Italy, then I waited while you decided if you were going to join a convent or not. And now, after waiting another ten days to see you, I've just come home to a bunch of flowers and love poems from a disco nut."

"Knight."

"Good night."

"Not night like good night. Knight like the Round Table. I was saying that Rod is a disco *knight,* not *nut.* But actually, he's kind of both...."

Now he's staring at me like I have driven him beyond insanity. "Come on, I'll walk you home. I have to get up early for work. I'll give you a ride to school in the morning."

❦ 12 ❦
Freshwater Pearls

The noise from Danny's skiff cuts into the stillness of the morning and rouses Sailor from his sound stupor. I grab my backpack full of books and head for the dock with Sailor on my heels. Sailor is beside himself when I climb aboard without him and howls pathetically as we pull away. "Poor guy. He's going to have to deal with being alone again since school started up."

"He's not the only one," Danny mutters.

Danny knows my days on the island are numbered. With the temperatures dropping I'm going to have to stay in town with Grandma Angelina soon. Big Chief is the only cabin insulated well enough to bear the winter months. The other two cabins were intended to be used only as summer cabins. Unless you have someone around to stoke the fire all day, too much heat is lost between the logs. Besides that, having to cross the water at the crack of dawn in freezing temperatures is something only Danny is willing to brave.

Besides having missed me, Danny has been wanting to see the veterinary medicine facilities where I'll be spending the majority of my life and offered to drive me all the way to school today.

Once we hit the main campus, I direct him over to the south hill—by the creamery, where they make the Cougar Gold cheese.

After a quick drive-by tour of the vet school buildings, I have him swing me back to the lecture hall for my first class. Danny pulls up to the curb, looks over at me, and sighs.

Whatever it is that's going on in that head of his, he's not sharing. He forces a smile. "Want me to carry your books for ya?"

That's cute. "Better not. I wouldn't want Rod to get jealous." Just trying to lighten the mood a little. Reaching in the backseat for my backpack, I spot Rod's pickup truck. "Danny—it's him."

Danny turns to look. We watch Rod hop out of his truck. He's wearing a one-piece, stretchy silver suit with four-inch black disco boots. This must be his King Arthur outfit. Lo and behold, he's carrying a bouquet of flowers.

"Those aren't for you again, are they?" Danny asks, incredulous.

"I'd venture to guess that those would be for a new disco damsel in distress."

Danny looks over at me with a subtle smile. "You know, I still think you two would have been good together."

"Yeah, thanks. I'll remember that if you ever leave me."

Danny leans over and wraps an arm around me. "Never gonna happen. Call me when you're out. I'll pick you up and take you to visit your grandma while I finish up on a few things at work. Maybe we can grab a burger at Big Daddy's when I'm off." He kisses me good-bye.

I watch his smile fade as he pulls away.

Over a warm bowl of clam chowder, I have the pleasure of watching Rod make his move for a new dance victim ... er, partner. Surprisingly, she's kinda cute. Even more surprising, she appears to be enjoying his attention. Between Rod's slick jumpsuit and her stretch black dress with loud geometric shapes, they look like a match made in heaven. I have to give the guy credit. His persistence is amazing.

✽

After school, Danny drops me off at Grandma's. She's sitting out on the back porch, enjoying the Indian summer afternoon. It only takes about five seconds from the time I sit down for Grandma to say, "Come on, A. J., out with it."

"Out with what?"

"Don't give me that. You have a new ring on your finger, and a pair of sorry eyes to go with it. What's the story?"

"You don't miss a thing, do you, Grandma?"

"That's what grandmas are for. Tell me whatsa matter."

I slump into the seat across from her and hold up my left hand. "It's a promise ring. It belonged to Danny's grandma Scarlett."

Grandma takes my hand in hers and admires my ring. "That's a beautiful ring. So why aren't you smiling?"

"I'm happy about the ring. It's just that ... ever since I've been back from Italy, it seems like everything keeps coming between Danny and me."

"Like what?"

"Well, besides nearly joining the convent, and Danny's camp conference in Kentucky, now I'm busy with all of my studying, and

I'll soon be moving back over here. Then I'll be in school for who knows how long, and Danny is just getting started with his summer camp and will be busy working out there all the time. It's like everything is good when we're together, but we're hardly able to be together."

Grandma gets up and returns a few minutes later with a small wooden jewelry box. She lifts the lid and sweet Italian music begins to play. "This was my wedding gift from your grandfather." She holds up a strand of blue pearls.

"Are those real pearls?"

"They're black freshwater pearls. Black pearls come in different shades, from black to silver to blue." She hands the strand to me.

I love how every pearl has a color and shape of its own. "The only pearls I've ever seen are white and perfectly round."

"The saltwater pearls are round. These freshwater pearls have their own uniqueness—that's what makes them special. When your grandpa gave this to me, he said, 'These pearls reminded me of you, because they're not like all the other pearls, and you are not like all the other girls.'" She smiles, remembering.

"Oh, Grandma—I wish Danny and I could just be together."

"So get married."

"What? Now?"

"Why not?"

"Well, because … because I'm just starting school … and Danny is trying to get a summer camp started up on the island."

"So get married *and* go to school while Danny starts his camp."

"Are you serious?"

"Angelina, I wouldn't say this about just anyone, but there aren't many Danny Morgans in the world these days. That young man knows what matters in life, and he'd be good for you." Grandma shakes her head. "I don't understand this new generation—everybody's waiting until they've done *this* and done *that,* got *this* career or *that* much money. Some wait too long and it's too late. Let me tell you something, Angelina, in the olda country, the family always comes first. What's more important in life than having a family? Remember what your grandpa says?"

"*La famiglia è tutto,*" I reply.

"That's right: The family is everything. That's why God gave us the holy family in heaven, and our earthly family here. We all do better with each other."

"Why did you only have one child, Grandma?"

"My mama always told me, 'Have your babies when you're still young enough to play with them.' So we did. And it's a good thing, because Sonny was the only baby we were blessed with. He was the joy of my life. I was young, and he was all I had. We had a lot of fun together."

"That's probably why Daddy's such a happy person. Good beginnings."

"I like to think so."

"Danny is a lot like Daddy in that way. And I know that Danny is the only one for me."

"Then if you know this is the man you want to spend your life with, what's to stop you from getting married now?"

"What's to stop me? Mama, for one! She'd say I'm way too young to get married, and I know she wouldn't want anything to get in the way of my studies right now."

"How old are you, Angelina?"

"Eighteen."

"You know how old your mama was when she married my Sonny?"

"Nineteen?"

"That's right. And how many years does it take to get your animal degree?

"Um … about eight."

"I don't know many men patient enough to wait that long to be married. You know, Angelina, when my Sonny asked your mama to marry him, your Grandma Juliana didn't think my son was good enough for her daughter. Your mama married my Sonny anyway. You're big now. You make up your own mind like your mama did. That's what your grandpa and I did too."

"What did you do?"

"We eloped."

"You and Grandpa *eloped?*"

She nods, smiling.

"Grandma, I'm surprised at you!" *The Degulio family secrets never cease to amaze me.*

I stare at the strand of pearls still in my hand. Grandma reaches over and closes my hand around them. "When you're ready, you wear those for your wedding. The bride is supposed to wear something old, something new, something borrowed, and something blue. These are for your *something blue.*"

I cannot believe my grandmother and grandfather eloped! I glance down at the strand of pearls in my hand. I even ponder the thought of eloping … until Mama's face pops into the picture. *Forget it.*

Danny and I have hardly seen each other all weekend. And I'm *still waiting* to hear what he's *still waiting* to tell me. Meanwhile, I've been moving some of my clothes from Papoose over to Grandma's. Between Indian-summer days and electric-blanket nights, I've just been biding my time out here on the island, but I know I can't stick it out much longer. In gathering up a few of my favorite things to take over on my next trip to town, the first thing on the list is Jomo, the big, plush monkey Danny brought me from Kentucky. I reluctantly add him to the pile, wishing we could both stay here on the island. Jomo is the one thing I have that reminds me of Danny when I miss him. Not because he looks like a monkey, but because Danny gave him to me. And he's big enough to hug.

My favorite Tony Bennett record album is playing on the old record player. I was the only kid who even knew who Tony Bennett was. Now I'm the only eighteen-year-old who knows who he is. When "Fly Me to the Moon" begins to play, I think back to the times I found Mama and Daddy dancing in the moonlight. It has always been reassuring for me to see Mama and Daddy in each other's arms, dancing.

Scooping up Jomo, I start twirling around the room to the music. Whirling past the doorway, I suddenly notice Danny standing in the doorframe watching me.

"Miss me?" he says, looking amused.

How embarrassing. "Um, maybe a little."

"How would you like the real thing?"

"… Okay."

He comes over and takes the place of his monkey, tossing it aside. We sway around the room in each other's arms. When the music stops, I play one more song, "Moon River." It always reminds me of when we were kids. I always thought of Danny as my huckleberry friend.

Danny notices the pile of clothes I've laid out. "Are you packin' up?"

"Yeah, just a few things to keep me warm on cold nights."

He looks at me. "Taking volunteers?"

I just sigh. "I wish."

He smiles back, takes the monkey, and hands it back to me. "Lucky monkey," he mumbles. "I feel like getting outside. How does a walk to the beach sound?"

We grab a blanket and matches and head down the Pitchy Pine Trail toward Juniper Beach. Maybe this is where he's planning to say what he hasn't been saying all week.

I tell Danny about Grandma's freshwater pearl necklace along the way. It's a beautiful, clear night with a fall chill in the air. While Danny's getting the fire started, I lay my blanket down in front of a big log to use for a backrest.

Once the fire's going, Danny comes over to join me.

"Twilight is my favorite color of night," I mention.

"Twilight is not a color," he informs me.

"It is so."

"It is not."

"Is *so*."

"Is *not*."

"So."

"Not."

"It's the blue shade between day and night," I enlighten him.

Danny turns to face me. "Twilight is the transformation of the atmosphere between evening and night; *twi* meaning *'tween,* as in between light and dark."

"You made that up. That's not even scientific."

"And yours is?"

"Yes, as a matter of fact, it is. *Twi* is the scientific abbreviation for twinkle. Twinkle plus light, equals twi-light."

Danny shakes his head. "You can't lose a debate, can you?"

"Not if I can convince someone that I know what I'm talking about even when I don't."

"I think you'd make a better lawyer than a vet."

"Think so?"

"Yeah. Know what else I think?"

"Hmm?"

He slips his arm around me. "I think I've missed you a lot lately."

"Think so?"

"Yeah."

"So what should we do about that?"

"Well, I'm seriously thinking about kissing you until your twilight turns from twinkle to midnight blue."

"Oh. Well ... okay."

"You sure you're okay with that?"

"Yeah, I'm pretty sure I'm okay with that."

When the sky is about halfway between twinkle and midnight blue, Danny stops kissing me. "Hey, A. J.?" he says.

"Hmm?"

"I can't do this anymore."

"Can't do what?"

He gets up, then stares out at the water. "I don't know." He turns away and walks toward the shore.

I'm sitting here wondering what it is that he doesn't know. I move closer to the fire to keep warm while Danny stands at the shoreline. The sky turns from midnight blue to pitch-black. So does my mood. He finally returns. Without a word he sits down beside me, looks at me, and sighs.

That's not very reassuring. Can I have another hint?

"I gave my notice at the church today," he says, staring into the fire.

"You *did?*" I look at him. "Why?"

"I had to make a decision. If I wanted to be a pastor, it would mean going away to seminary and devoting the next few years of my life to it. But if I'm ever going to realize this summer camp, I've got to be able to work on the island full-time in order to get it up and running by summer. I can still preach to kids at camp. But I can't help feeling more drawn to serving God in a camp setting than in a church setting. I think He made me for the great outdoors. "

"If that's what you really want to do, what's the problem?"

"The problem is … us."

"Us? What's wrong with *us?*"

He looks down at me. "What's wrong, A. J., is that I want to realize this dream *with you.* I don't want my dream to take me one direction and your dream to take you another. I want our dreams to be reached together. I want to be with you all the time, not just now and then. We've been apart more than we've been together since you've come back from Italy. I'm tired of saying good-bye and good night. I want you to stay with me. I want to fall asleep with you in my arms and wake up next to you every morning. But when I think of waiting who knows how many years … it makes me crazy just thinking about it—you make me crazy!"

What can I say to that?

He turns and looks into my eyes. "I want to be *married,* not *crazy.*" His eyes are searching. "I love you, A. J., but I don't know what to do about you."

He loves me—he said it—Danny Morgan said he loves me—out loud! But he also said I make him crazy. That part doesn't sound so good. So this is what's been bothering him so much—he's thinking about how long he'll have to wait for me. I think of everything my grandma said. I think about what Danny's saying, and I'm thinking about how I feel. I know Danny's expecting to hear me say I'm too young, that I want to get better established in school, or worse, that I plan to finish the whole eight years before marrying. But what he doesn't expect to hear is: "So why don't you just marry me?"

A large crease appears across his forehead. "What?"

I try a new angle. "Is there some reason you need to wait to get married?"

"Me?"

I nod.

"No. Of course not."

"Well then, what's to wait for?"

"But I thought … *you* … what about school?"

"Being married wouldn't stop me from going to school."

"Are you sayin' … what are you sayin'?"

"I'm *saying*, why don't you just *marry me*, Danny Morgan?"

"*Now?*" He blinks.

"Maybe not this very minute, but soon."

"Soon … as in, how soon is soon to you?"

"As in … as soon as I can work up the nerve to tell my parents they're invited to a Christmas wedding."

"*This* Christmas? Do you mean this *coming* Christmas?"

"That would be the one, yes."

"You *mean* that? You would do that?"

"Well, you might have to help me—Italian fathers kind of like the future son-in-law to ask their permission first."

"Right. Sonny. He'd probably like a son-in-law who's employed, too. He's gonna want to shoot me, isn't he?"

"No, I don't think so. It's my mama who will take the first shot, and Nonna will finish you off for being a Baptist. It could get pretty messy before it's over, but it will have to happen at some point anyway, right?"

"Right. I guess it won't matter when we're getting married—they'll resent me either way."

"They'll get over it. Italians have to react first, then they settle back down. It's just their way."

"Wow, I feel so reassured by that."

✺ 13 ✺
The Wedding Planner

"Okay, cowboy, you're up." I hand Danny the phone after dialing the number.

Danny looks at me like I'd better be worth whatever it is he's in for.

"Hello, Sonny?" Danny nods at me. "It's Daniel Morgan, from Indian Island."

"..."

"Yes, A. J.'s cowboy." He looks at me funny. He knows nothing about the cowboy concept between Daddy and me. "Is this a good time to talk?"

"..."

"Oh, is it that early?" Danny's sweating bullets. "Well, sir, I ... uh ... happen to be in love with your daughter, and I believe she loves me, too, and I would really like ... I'd like ... to ask your permission to marry her, sir."

"..."

"No, I haven't officially asked her to marry me yet—I wanted to ask you first."

"..."

"Yes, sir, I know you're already married. I'm not asking to marry you. I'm asking for your permission to marry A. J."

Oh, Daddy, don't make this harder on him.

"..."

"You mean, what if she says no?" Danny shoots me a strange look. "Well, sir, I'd ... I'd be devastated."

"..."

Danny smiles at me and whispers, "He said, 'Good answer.'" He shifts back to the conversation. "Uh, yes, sir ... I can ride a horse." He eyes me again, suspiciously, like it just clicked that I had asked him this same question before.

"..."

"Actually, no, we were thinking more like this Christmas, when y'all are thinkin' of comin' to visit."

"..."

"Uh-huh, this *coming* Christmas."

"..."

"Yes, sir." Danny hands me the phone. "He wants to talk to you."

"Hi, Daddy."

"A. J., is that you?"

"Yes, Daddy, it's me."

"You sure you want to marry this cowboy?"

"Yes, Daddy. I love him." I smile over at Danny. "I know you wanted me to wait until I had a few good years of school under my belt—but I think we'll be happier being together while I'm at school, and Danny's planning to turn the island into a summer camp—did he tell you that?"

"No, he didn't. A. J., are you sure this is what you really want? You're still so young...."

"I'm sure."

Daddy groans. "Let me talk to Danny again, then I'll have to deal with your mother—and her mother—but that's not your problem. Just remember, after I tell your plans to the women in this family, in case I don't live to tell you this, I love you and only hope the best for you."

"I love you, too, Daddy. Thank you!" I hand the phone back to Danny.

"Yes, sir … yes, sir … yes, sir … Okay, thank you, sir. Good-bye."

"What did he say?"

"He says I have his blessing, but if I ever do anything to hurt you in any way, shape, or form, he's coming after me. Then he reminded me that you come from a tight-knit family and there's also J. R., Dino, Benjamin, your mother, and her mother to deal with. Then he wished us the best."

The phone rings. Danny picks it up. "Hello? Yes, Mrs. Degulio, she's right here."

Danny hands me the phone. "Your mother."

"Mama?"

"Angelina Juliana Degulio, are you trying to put me in an early grave, pulling this on me right now?"

"No, Mama. I'm sorry it's so soon, but … remember what it was like when you wanted to marry Daddy and you were only nineteen?"

"That was entirely different."

"Why?"

"Because that was me, and this is you."

"But I was hoping you could help me plan a Christmas wedding."

"Plan the wedding? Oh … that's right. We'll need to plan the wedding—a *Christmas* wedding." Mama's entire tone changes. It's nice to know she has a weak spot I can take advantage of at a time like this. "Oh, wow, that doesn't leave us much time—let's see, not much left of September, October, November … You just leave this part up to me, kiddo—this is my department—you just leave the details to your mama—that's what the mother of the bride is all about. I'd better get scooting—lots to do before December. Now listen up, A. J., send me your measurements for the gown. I'm going to see if Adriana can scoop up one of those fancy designer wedding gowns that she models."

"Uh … okay, Mama, but nothing *real* fancy, keep it kind of simple …"

"Sure thing. Gotta run—gotta call Adriana before she leaves for work—I'll let you know what we find—*ciao,* kiddo!"

"*Ciao,* Mama—but I want the reception at Big Chief …" *Click.*

"Keep what simple?" Danny asks.

"My wedding gown. At least it got Mama behind the wedding—if there's one thing she loves, it's planning a party."

"You sure you want her planning the whole wedding for you—your gown and everything?"

"Honestly, Danny, don't you know my mama any better than that? Do you really think I have a choice, now that she's in on it? Let's just consider it a blessing that we have her behind us on this. All I really care about is marrying you, and with Mama making the plans, all I'll have to do is show up for the ceremony and everything else will be taken care of. Trust me." *I can only imagine what she'll come up with for a Southern-Baptist-Roman-Catholic-Italian wedding.*

Danny and I look at each other. "Well, I guess the only one left to ask now is you," Danny says.

"Oh, that's right. Yes!" I throw my arms around him. "I never thought you'd ask."

"... I didn't."

"Oh. Yeah, I guess you didn't." I drop my arms to my side. "But now it won't be a surprise. I always dreamed about it being a surprise. Can you wait and surprise me when I'm not expecting it? Let's wait until you buy the wedding ring since I always pictured being asked with a ring. But since I'm already wearing your grandma's ring for my engagement ring, you'll have to ask me with the real wedding ring—but only show me the little box that it comes in, because I don't want to see the real ring until the wedding. Okay?"

Danny shakes his head, then nods. "Y-eah, sure." He gives me a quick good-night kiss. "If I don't go insane first," he adds, then he gives me a big hug and heads for the door.

❧

Five a.m.: Ring-g-g—ring-g-g!

"Hello."

"A. J.?"

"Mm-hm."

"You up?"

Yawn. "Mama?"

"Hey, listen, I need phone numbers for Danny's mama and all of his aunts. I'm enlisting them to help cater this wedding reception.

Remember all that great Southern food they cooked up when we were all on the island?"

"Oh, Mama, you're not going to make them cook for my wedding, are you?"

"Listen, kiddo, that's the Southern way. Southern women live to cook. Trust me, I know these things—they'll be hurt if we don't ask."

"I'll get the numbers from Danny. I think he's telling them the news today, so maybe give them a week before you hit them up for the cooking."

"Okay. Next, I'm having the invitations made up here on special Italian paper. Then I'll mail them from here so everyone gets an Italian stamp on their invite. I'll need all the addresses on the Morgan side of the family. Then there's a few of our Italian and Greek relatives …"

"Greek relatives? You mean *besides* Uncle Nick's family?"

"Well, maybe just a few of them—after all, they are family, remember?"

"Yeah, I know … I mean, I'd really like them all to come … it's just … there are so *many* of them … and what about Nonna? It might give away the secret that Uncle Nick is really Greek. I'm not sure I want that to happen at my wedding. Are you sure she's well enough to make the trip?"

"She wouldn't miss it for the world—even if we wanted her to. So, listen, you take care of the church and the priest.…"

Priest?

"Then get those phone numbers to me, and a wedding date for the invites. I'm thinking December twentieth might be nice, right before

Christmas; that way we'll all come on the fifteenth, have five days to pull everything together, then stay through Christmas—maybe even New Year's. Then you and Danny can take your honeymoon after we all leave. Sound good?"

Oh, why not? What's the use in fighting any of this? I just want to be married.

"Uh, sure, Mama, whatever works."

"Okay, then, I'll just go ahead and get these invites printed up for December twentieth. And Adriana is trying to track down a designer dress for you. What's your size?"

"About a five."

"That's going to be a challenge to find something short enough in the modeling collection—the waist size is probably okay, but we may need to chop a foot or two off the bottom. Well, take your measurements and get me those phone numbers. We'll surprise you with the dress."

I can only imagine. "Okay, Mama. I'd better get ready for school now."

"Okay, kiddo. Go dissect some frogs for me!" She laughs.

"Sure will—I'll think of you the whole time."

"Ciao!"

Maybe we should just elope after all.

I break the news about Mama's two-week-long agenda to Danny on the way to the main shore.

"They're staying that long?" He's not smiling.

"If it gets to be too much, we can always take off for a honeymoon and leave them all here together."

"Probably not a bad idea," Danny replies. "Better keep that in mind for a backup plan. I can't imagine they'll expect us to stay with them the entire time they're here."

You obviously don't know my relatives.

Danny walks me to my car at the landing. "I'm curious how well a gathering of Greeks, Italians, and Southerners will all mix under one roof, aren't you?" he asks, opening the driver's door for me.

"Um, well, with Grandma Juliana coming, I'm not sure *curious* is the word I'm thinking of," I reply, climbing into Stewie. "Maybe closer to *terrified.*"

Same evening: ten p.m.: *Ring-g-g!*

"Hello?"

"It's Mama, A. J. Bad news."

"What?"

"Well, I wasn't planning to mention this to you just yet, but your father said I had to. I told my sister—your Aunt Genevieve—about the wedding, and she got so excited, she and Uncle Nick invited the entire Sophronia clan—including all of the courtesy cousins."

"You mean *all* of Uncle Nick's extended family, as in, half of Greece? How many are we talking about?"

"Well, there's about fifty—"

"*F-ifty* Greeks and Nonna in the same room? Mama, do you know what this could do to my wedding?"

"I doubt all of them will be able to make the trip."

"There's no way most of them can *afford* to make it. Right?"

"Well, if any of them can't make it, money won't be the reason."

"Why not?"

"You know how generous your Uncle Nick is."

"What's that got to do with it?"

"He offered to help anyone who couldn't afford it."

"Fifty Greeks—at my Southern-Italian wedding?"

"I don't think you'll have to worry about more than half of them actually making the trip. Are you saying you don't want them to come?"

"Of course I *want* them to come—I would love having them all here. The problem is worrying about what Nonna is capable of doing to my wedding day when she discovers the family secret."

"Don't worry, kiddo, they won't be staying on the island. We'll book them into the Squawkomish Cozy Inn and keep them away from Nonna as much as possible."

"Yeah, good luck."

"Angelina, you listen to me. This is your mother speaking. It's all going to work out fine. I'm in charge. Just remember that. No one rains on my parade and I'm planning the parade. Now, do you have those phone numbers for me?"

❧ 14 ❧
Second Thoughts

Thank goodness it's Friday. Nothing has been normal since we broke the news about the wedding. I'm still waiting for Danny to officially propose to me. At this point, I wouldn't be surprised if he comes up with a way to tell me that this whole wedding is *not* going to happen after all. Especially when he hears about the new guest list and the increased odds of Nonna discovering the big Degulio hush-up of the century. For the moment, I have to focus my attention on playing "dodge Rod" in the cafeteria. *Fortunately,* he has his new little disco doll by his side. Unfortunately, he seems bent on making sure I see them together. When I'm just about finished with my sandwich, he weaves his way to my corner table, pulling his gal behind him.

"Hey there, A. J., I have someone I'd like to introduce you to. This is Laura."

"Hi, Laura." I try to sound friendly behind my sympathetic smile.

"Nice to meet you." Her bright orange dress and gold coin belt are a perfect complement to Rod's black disco outfit with a bolo necktie. It's hard to take the cowboy completely out of the kid. They look like they're ready to go trick-or-treating.

"Hey, how about if you two ladies get to know each other while

I grab some lunch for us." He leans toward Laura. "Do you have five bucks?"

Laura forks over the cash, looking mortified that he's leaving us alone together. As soon as Rod walks away, she suddenly gets the jitters. Turning to me, she stammers, "I h-hope there are no hard f-feelings between us."

"Hard feelings? Why would there be?" *I am indebted to you for life.*

"Well, Rod told me how he broke up with you because of me and how upset you were…. I know it must have been quite a blow to you. I hope we can all be friends."

That screwball. "Well, Laura, I appreciate your concern. I'm doing my best to get over it."

"You know, Rod has a few brothers—one is even planning to be a doctor." She rambles on and on about the similarities between Rod and his big brother—as though settling for second best isn't all that bad. "Maybe we could double-date sometime, the four of us…."

"No!" *That came out a little loud.* "What I mean is, I'm already engaged, so no hard feelings, okay?"

A plastic lunch tray comes skidding across the table in front of us. "Did I hear you mention you're engaged?"

"I am."

Rod looks at me with pity, then at Laura. "Rebound," he mutters to her. She nods. "So, when's the big day?" Rod asks.

"Around Christmas." *And no, you won't be invited.*

"*Christmas?*" He tightens his bolo. "Sounds like a shotgun wedding, eh?"

I'm very close to reaching over and pulling his bolo so tight he can't utter another absurdity....

"Hey, good-lookin'."

"Danny!" My true knight to the rescue.

He leans down and gives me a kiss. Danny's six-foot-four frame towers over Rod, even in his platforms.

"Danny, I'd like you to meet Laura, and I'm sure you remember Rod."

Danny nods at Laura and extends his hand to Rod.

Rod shoots his hand out in a put-it-there fashion—which gets swallowed up by Danny's huge grip.

"Hey, buddy, mind if I steal my girl away?"

"Uh … guess not." Rod acts as though he actually has a say in this.

"Thanks. I appreciate that." He grabs my hand and whisks me off.

There are moments in life when things go so completely right, it feels like poetry. This is one of those moments. This is haiku.

❧

I have invited my fiancé over for a cozy night of popcorn and a TV movie by the fire—with hopes of finding the right moment to disclose the tiny family factoid that could blow our entire wedding to pieces. *Ah, the joy of family.* I told Danny I'd be studying until showtime and would call him when it's time to come over.

In the middle of my research project, I hear the sound of Danny's little motorized "get-around" darting back and forth outside, then suddenly, a loud crash. Bolting out the door, I find a pile of building supplies dumped outside Papoose. "What's all this?"

"Insulation. You're not moving off the island if I can help it!" He has rolls of fiberglass stacked under the lean-to and a pile of tools beside it. "I'm going to need to do this work eventually anyway, and it definitely has to be done before your relatives come for the wedding. Besides," he smiles up at me on the porch, "I hate the thought of being left out here in the cold all winter without you."

I return his smile. I didn't like that thought either.

He starts to work. "I may or may not get around to insulating Pocahontas in time, but I'll at least get Papoose done before you freeze to death."

"Why, thank you, sir."

"My pleasure. Let me know when it's showtime."

❧

To Kill a Mockingbird is scheduled for tonight's TV movie of the week. If anyone can help bring on a good mood, it's Scout Finch. I even bought sparkling grape juice to toast to our happy future. I sent Danny home to shower off before showtime.

To help set the illusion that all is well on the little island, I've graced the front room with dainty jelly jars filled with something wild I found growing in the woods. They look similar to sweet peas: bright fuchsia with a spicy-sweet fragrance. Someone needs to come up with a word for that combo. I'm torn between *speet* or *swicy*.

I throw on a sundress with a light cardigan, and a straw hat to add to the all-is-well theme.

Knocking a jelly jar off of the coffee table with his tail, Sailor clues me in that our guest has arrived. I greet Danny at the door with a chipper "Howdy" and bright smile, fully aware that by the end of the evening this could all go up in smoke and I will be single for the rest of my life.

"Hey, it's Rebecca of Sunnybrook Farm," he says, planting a kiss on my cheek on his way through the door. "Somethin' smells good, what is it?"

"Popcorn."

"… Oh. Well, can't beat that, can ya?"

"Nope, can't beat that." *Not with my cooking anyway.* We head to the Victorian couch in front of the fire.

"I have never seen you in a hat before, or cooking without a motive, so what's the occasion?"

"Us. Just us. I thought we could drink a toast to our future and just … be together."

Danny looks at me out of the corner of his eye. "I don't know about you. It's more than that, isn't it? You're settin' me up for something … let's hear it."

"Why would you even think that?" *The guy can read me like a book.*

"Well, so far you've gone after my beach, my island, and Papoose. You set me up with the Mafia kingpin to ask for your hand in marriage." He glares down at Sailor lying faithfully at my feet. "You took your dog back and got him to ignore the fact that I fed him for eight years—the traitor. I can't imagine what's next. Do I have anything left to offer?"

"Nope, just going for your soul this time."

"Yeah, that is all that's left, isn't it?" He laughs. "What's the movie?"

"Guess. It's my favorite movie. You, me, and J. R. all watched it together the summer of '68."

"Hot Rods to Hell?"

"Nope. That was J. R.'s favorite. I'll give you a clue. We pretended we were the characters all the way through the movie."

"Planet of the Apes?"

"Nope. This one was in the South...."

"To Kill a Mockingbird."

"Bingo. Remember how spooked we all got over Boo Radley?"

"Oh, Scout, how could I forget?"

"You remember!" I was Scout, J. R. was Jem, and Danny was Dill, the kid visiting for the summer. "You made a perfect Dill, with your Southern accent and all. Remember I called you Dill for days after—until you started to call me by Scout's real name, Jean Louise?" That shut me up pretty quick. Scout hated her real name as much as I did mine.

"Did you say you had some popcorn around here somewhere?"

"Popcorn? Right. Be right back." I retreat to the kitchen where I dump half a cube of melted butter into the popcorn bowl, add a little salt, toss it around.

Danny comes through the kitchen door. "Are we drinking that toast now?"

"Um, let's save that for ... later."

"You mean *later* after you tell me why I'm really here?"

"Daniel Morgan," I snap, with my sassy Southern accent, "I cannot believe you'd question my character like that." I hand him the popcorn and grab a couple Cokes from the fridge.

"Sorry, just getting used to being surprised by you."

Yikes. I turn to face him. "Well, okay, there is one small glitch."

Danny stops chewing his popcorn. "Yeah?"

"Mama called again. Remember my Uncle Nick and Aunt Genevieve?"

He nods slowly.

"Well, it sounds like they may be planning to bring a few relatives with them to the wedding."

"A few?"

"Uh-huh …"

Ring-g-g!

Saved by the bell … maybe. "Hello?"

"Morning, sunshine!"

"Hi, Mama. It's not morning here."

"Right. Well, anyway, I need to know if you're planning to have the ceremony at St. Peter's Parish or Our Lady of the Lake?"

"Um … undecided."

"What do you mean *undecided?*"

"Tell you what, Mama, you work out all of the reception details and I will deal with all the church details—and we'll both just show up and be surprised by each other. Know what I mean?"

"Well … just remember, we're all Catholic."

"We will let you know which church we're marrying in when we know ourselves."

"Oh, Angelina … for the sake of our family honor, can you marry in the Catholic Church just this once?"

"*Mama …*"

"Okay, fine, but just run the idea of a Catholic ceremony by

Danny. You can convert after the wedding if you really have to. The Baptists are much more understanding about this kind of thing than the Catholics are. *Ciao.*"

I look over at Danny, then pull a kitchen towel over my head. "It's going to be *The Alamo* all over again at our wedding!"

"The Alamo?"

"Yes, the Alamo!" I jerk the towel from my head and toss it aside. "You know, that old movie with the Duke as Davy Crockett—where they fought to the death to save a Catholic mission?"

"So now it's the Catholics against the Baptists when it comes to which church we're gettin' married in?"

"Mama's bad enough, but it's Nonna we'll have to worry about most. When she gets wind of something she doesn't like, she's starts out like a soft breeze and gathers wind as she goes. If we marry in the Baptist church, things could begin to fly. Then, when the Greek dancing starts up at the reception and she discovers the family secret, she'll turn from a tornado into a full-blown monsoon and leave everything and everyone lying in ruins...."

The look on Danny's face tells me I've probably said enough. "Geez, A. J, could you add a little drama to the picture? How do you come up with this stuff? Never mind. I probably don't need to know." Danny sets the popcorn bowl on the table and squints his eyes like he's almost afraid to ask. "What family secret are we talkin' about now, anyway?"

"The Sophronia family secret. That's what I was trying to tell you earlier. Mama called and informed me that a number of Uncle Nick's Greek relatives are planning to come to the wedding. As soon as Nonna realizes, after all these years, that her other daughter married into a bunch of Greeks instead of Italians … the feta is going to hit the fan! Can't we just *elope?* How about we get married in your little prayer chapel? Let's just call your pastor—we'll squeeze him inside with us. We could have tiny sweetheart roses and little candles everywhere—they wouldn't take up much room. And we'd have sweet, peaceful memories of our teeny-tiny wedding—just you and me.…"

"Only until your not-so-teeny-tiny family shows up and hunts me down."

"True."

Danny runs his hand through his hair with a heavy sigh, then gets up and holds his hand out to me. "C'mon, let's go watch a movie." He leads me out of the kitchen, flips on the TV, and steers me to the couch, propping pillows all around us. "You know, we don't really need to talk about the wedding right now. It's all gonna work out. One way or another, we're gettin' married. I'm sure it will get a whole lot worse before it gets better, but at some point it's all gonna be over, everyone will go home, and you and I will be married. Okay?"

"Okay." I look down at Sailor, who only cares about the next kernel of popcorn that falls to the ground.

Ring-g-g!

"No! It can't be!" I bury my head in the pillows. "I can't take anymore.…"

"I'll get it." Danny grabs the receiver. "Hello?"

"Jason! Hey, good to hear your voice … Yep, if I'm not at Big Chief, I'm usually here … Well, thank you. So Mama told you the news, huh?… Sometime around Christmas … So how are things with you and Cindy?… No way. Seriously?"

I'm trying to catch the gist of the conversation, but Danny's mostly listening with an occasional "I'm sorry to hear that." After about three of those, he says, "You're welcome to come stay out here if you need to get away for a while ... A. J.? She's invited me over for a movie and popcorn." He looks over at me and smiles. "She's crazy 'bout me—begged me to marry her ... I'm a little crazy 'bout her, too." He raises his eyebrows over Jason's next comment. "Adriana? She's a fashion model living in Milan. Out of your league, buddy." Danny laughs. "Okay, well, I hope you and Cindy work things out, let me know how it goes. Thanks for the call—we'll see you in December, if not before."

Danny hangs up, then comes around and plops back down on the couch next to me. "Apparently, Miss Amway is causing Jason a bit of grief lately. Seems she's been attending a few too many Amway conventions away from home, and Jason suspects there may be more than just pep rallies goin' on."

"Yikes. Well, it's like I said, if you can't trust someone to be nice to baby ducks ... I hate to say it, but I still think the poor guy would be better off raising ducks than marrying this gal."

"Yeah, you may be right. Strange how the tides have turned. Jason was used to bein' the heartbreaker until Cindy came along."

"Is he going to come visit?"

"It sounds like he wants to wait and see how things play out for now. He did have some good news, though."

"Really? What?"

"It looks like the baby ducks are gonna make it. One of the banty hens took them under her wing and is raisin' them as her own. It's kinda scary that his chicken is more compassionate than his fiancée."

"I would have raised those babies!"

"I know. That's why I'm marrying you. I hope to have a dozen of 'em someday."

"Kids or ducks?"

"Not tellin'. You'll just have to take your chances."

A dozen ... "Um, weren't we about to watch that movie?"

"Right." Danny turns up the volume and finishes the rest of the popcorn before the first commercial.

"I'll make another quick batch." I scurry back to the kitchen, cross the room, and lean my back against the far wall, hyperventilating. A dozen kids? "Take your chances"? *What am I thinking? What am I doing? Am I really ready to get married ... and possibly have a dozen children? What about school? What about my career? What about my sanity?* Maybe I'd better make sure he's talking about ducks.

I return a few minutes later with a huge bowl of popcorn. "This should last you awhile."

Danny is fast asleep. Must have worn himself out from all that pounding. I lay a blanket softly over him and sit down beside him. It's one of the few times I can just stare at him for as long as I want. My Danny ... the big, gentle giant ... not to mention cute and adorable. Yep ... he's a hunk. How could I *not* marry this guy? I'm so in love with him I could die. *I'm almost sure he was talking about ducks.*

Danny's still asleep during the scene where Scout's walking through the woods in the ham costume. As soon as the creepy music starts up, I shake him awake.

"Hmm—*what?*"

"Wake up, Scout's in the woods!"

Danny jolts awake, sits up, and looks around. "You woke me up to watch the ham—"

"Shhh!" I'm sitting on the edge of the couch. I accidentally whack him with the back of my hand when Scout gets knocked to the ground in her ham costume. "Sorry!"

"Geez, you're dangerous to watch movies with."

"Shhh—"

Danny yawns, closes his eyes, and falls back to sleep. He doesn't wake up again until the closing credits start to roll. "Did I miss Boo Radley?" he mumbles.

"You missed the entire movie."

"Oh." He yawns. "Hey, there's something I need to talk to you about, A. J., but it's gonna have to wait until tomorrow."

"Are you dumping me for hitting you during the ham scene?"

He laughs. "It'll take a little more than that to get rid of me. I have a meeting in town tomorrow. Can I meet you back here tomorrow, late afternoon?"

"S-sure." This kind of suspense kills me. "What's the topic? I mean, can you give me a hint?"

Danny stands up, pulling me up by the hand. "Um, no." Then he gives me a quick kiss, says he'll see me tomorrow, and walks out the door. Just like that.

This man can be so infuriating at times. He'd better not make a habit of this.

15
Apache Falls

I hate suspense when it involves me being the one left in suspense. I
phone Big Chief right after Danny leaves, then wait for him to pick
it up the minute he walks in his door.

"Hi, A. J."

"At least give me a hint what to expect."

"I will—tomorrow afternoon."

"Ah, c'mon, how am I supposed to sleep without even a clue?"
Silence. "Okay, fine, I'll settle for a topic. Can you give me that
much?"

"Our future. It's about our future," he tells me. "Sweet dreams,"
he says, then laughs. Click.

Great. I worry all night, wondering if this means we won't have
a future together. Maybe he's backing out. Maybe he's had enough
of Mama, and my family … or me. Maybe he's going to tell me I'd
make a good nun after all.

❦

By the time Danny finally shows up on my doorstep, I'm a nervous
wreck. I've set out a large supply of chips. Mama always told me

when you have some serious planning or decisions to make, be sure and do it over a bowl of chips. The crunchier the better. She said the crunching sound helps to keep your brain alert and makes you think more clearly. As a little kid, I remember thinking that heavy people must have a lot on their minds, because I always saw them eating chips.

I take a seat across from Danny and pop a chip in my mouth. "Tell me you're not here to call the whole thing off." *Chomp.* "Because if you are, I'd rather you just get it out, right now, none of that letting-me-down-gently rot—just be a man and say it like it is. No, wait … if that's the way it really is, let me down gently."

Danny looks over at me with a straight face.

"Danny?… *Danny?* You still want to marry me … *right?*"

"How does this afternoon sound to you?"

A wave of relief washes over me.

I can tell by his grin that he knows he had me going. "I'd elope in a minute, but your father would come after me loaded for bear."

I shovel a handful of chips in my mouth. "Okay, I'm listening. Let's hear it."

He reaches for the chips and slides the bowl to his side of the table.

I reach for the bowl and slide the chips back to my side of the table. Looks like it's going to be a real chip-chompin' conversation.

"We need to talk about religion."

Chomp-chomp. I get a pang every time this comes up.

"There is just no middle ground when it comes to merging Roman Catholicism with the Southern Baptist church. We are definitely different. I know how important Catholicism is to your family, but I'd really like to know how you feel. I mean, do you realize how different these two churches are?"

"Well, other than the liturgy ... *chomp,* and the sacraments ... *chomp,* and Mary ... *chomp,* and the traditions of the church ..." I try to smile, and reach for another chip. "I'd say we're pretty close as far as Jesus goes."

"That doesn't sound real convincing."

"Well, I've been wondering, what would you think if I went to both churches ... for a while, anyway? I could go to the early service with you at the Baptist church, and the late mass at Our Lady."

Danny looks at me intently. *Chomp, chomp, chomp.* "How about if we go for a long country drive and air out? I could use a break."

"From me?"

"No." He smiles. "From everything but you."

❧

The two of us are driving through downtown Squawkomish, singing along to Mungo Jerry's *In the Summertime,* feeling carefree for the first time in ages. You can't sing that song and not feel carefree, at least until the song is over. I wish I could hit replay about ten times in a row right now.

Once we've passed through our two-stoplight town, Danny heads south. Just before we hit the outskirts of Moscow, he makes another turn and heads east. The drive to Apache Falls takes us past long, barren stretches of hay fields. Seems there's only one house about every fifty acres. I always wonder what it would be like to grow up out here. *Bye, Mama, goin' to the neighbors'—see ya in a week.*

Before long, road signs start to point to the falls. At the foot of the mountains, there are twin waterfalls that dump into the Apache River.

"This place look familiar?"

"It does. Didn't we come here as kids?"

"Yep, this is it. Freeze Your Fanny Off Falls. Didn't your mama name it that?"

I roll my eyes. "Who *but* my mother would name it that?"

Climbing out of the Jeep, we head toward the trail that takes us to the falls. A quarter of a mile in, deep in the Fry Your Fanny Off Forest, I feel like I'm walking back in time. I remember this part well. Just when I'd feel like I couldn't take the heat of the day any longer, there she was in all her glory: the Great Old Swimming Hole where the falls make their final splashdown. This was *the* place to go when the thermometer hit scorching temperatures. The pool felt so refreshing on hot days.

Standing here, I begin to play back the memories like it was yesterday; kids splashing and diving from huge rocks, sunbathing on warm, smooth slate … I blink and they're gone. Where did everyone go? There used to be kids everywhere. Has everyone grown up and moved away? Our long, hot summers usually held on until the end of September. If we were lucky, an Indian summer would take us through October.

Thank goodness, today is one of those Indian summer days. I kick off my tennis shoes and dive into the icy pools in my cutoffs and T-shirt.

Danny is quick to follow. My bloodcurdling scream shatters the calm, and I shoot out of the water as fast as I went in. Again,

Danny is quick to follow. We find a big, warm river rock to help zap the chill from our bones. "Wow—colder than I remember!" Danny exclaims.

"No *kidding!* My body's in shock."

"Maybe we had tougher skin as kids," Danny says.

"Maybe we just didn't care."

Danny reaches over and holds my hand as we defrost on the warm slate. It feels so good just to lie here again and remember.

❧

"You awake?" Danny asks.

My eyes flutter open ... *where am I?* Trees ... waterfalls ... oh yeah. "I am now." I must have been pretty tired to fall asleep on a rock. We meander back through the trees in search of the Jeep. Its forest green paint blends in a little too well with the surroundings, but we finally hunt it down.

❧

Cruising through the small town of Apache Falls, I notice it hasn't changed much over the last decade. Same old brick shops, same small white plaster church with the gold onion dome steeple. After living in Italy among my Greek relatives, it's easy to recognize what kind of church it is. But it's so small it looks like a miniature of the big churches in the Old Country. Danny slows down and pulls right up in front of Saint Nectarios.

"Why are you stopping at the Orthodox church?"

"How did you know this was Orthodox?"

"Half my family is Greek Orthodox."

Danny cocks his head to one side like he'd never considered this before. "Oh, right. Do they have Orthodox churches in Italy?"

I look at Danny. "Of course they have Orthodox churches in Italy. All churches were Orthodox for the first thousand years."

"Did you ever attend one in Italy?"

"Yeah, of course I did."

"Really?" He looks at me funny.

"Are you kidding? Between all of the weddings, baptisms, and feasts that our relatives have celebrated together, I am well acquainted with the Orthodox Church. I'm just trying to figure out how one ended up in Apache Falls."

"Greek immigrants from 1920," he replies matter-of-factly.

I stare at Danny. "How did you know that?"

He sits back with a sigh and says, "A. J., there's something I've been wanting to tell you."

"Is this *the talk?*"

"This is it."

"Okay …"

"Well," he rearranges himself to face me, "after attending Mass with you, I realized how little I knew about your church—and church history in general. So when I went to the camp conference in Kentucky, I spent some time in the church library and began reading about the early church and the apostolic fathers. I didn't know that the Orthodox Church was the church of the apostles from the time of Pentecost. They keep the same liturgy and traditions of the early church. They are the *One Holy Catholic and Apostolic Church* of the Nicene Creed. Anyway, it all struck me as really interesting. When I came home from Kentucky, I looked for an Orthodox church in the area, and this was it. I've been meeting here with Father Demetrios ever since I've been back."

The meetings. "You've been coming *here?*"

He nods. "Like you said, all Christian churches were Orthodox in the beginning. Turns out all the things you said you'd miss about your church—the liturgy, sacraments, traditions—all came from Orthodoxy. It was pretty surprising to find this church out here in the middle of nowhere. Is this where your Uncle Nick attended when his family lived around here?"

"No, Uncle Nick attended a big Orthodox church in Spokane. We used to go along for some of their family events when I was little."

"I've never even read about the apostolic church until now, but it amazes me to find that it's still the same church today as it was almost two thousand years ago. Hey, did you know that Orthodox priests can marry?"

"Oh, *really?* Are you considering becoming an Orthodox priest now?"

"At this point, I'm just interested in learning about Orthodoxy, period." Danny looks over at me. "I'm thinking of attending a service here Sunday. Interested in coming along?"

"Um … sure, why not?" *What's a little more confusion added to my life right now, anyway?*

Trying to balance my time between studying for exams, dodging Rod, investigating churches, and planning a wedding—or, more accurately, watching Mama plan a wedding—has me a little bit on edge. I am ready for a good dose of group therapy. I slap together a tuna sandwich on Wonder Bread, grab a bag of Fritos and some Oreo cookies, stuff them into a beach bag, and I'm out the door. "C'mon, Sailor, time for our therapy session." I toss my lunch in the dinghy, untie the bowline, load the oarlocks, and away we go. Drifting … again.

As soon as we hit a good tailwind, the oars go on the floorboards, and I resume my position in drift mode. Sailor is always in drift mode. He finally outgrew the life jacket. On my back, face to the sun, my mind can wander off to my happy world. Daydreaming about the Cartwrights from *Bonanza* was always my best therapy. Little Joe Cartwright and me out on the Ponderosa. But now that I'm a soon-to-be-married woman, Little Joe has to go.

Today's daydream is just Danny, Sailor, and me, sailing around the world. We're out in the San Juan Islands, sailing away from Friday Harbor, for our year-at-sea honeymoon. A new novel begins to take shape:

The wind was little more than a hush … but no one was in a rush…. Worst-case scenario, it would take two years at this pace. The newlyweds had just said their wedding vows at the Catholic/Baptist/Orthodox (pick one) church. It was a beautiful ceremony. The bride's mother graciously orchestrated the entire wedding according to her daughter's every wish and desire. The cake was a towering steeple of two parts frosting, one part cake—as all cakes should be.

A radiant summer sun shone down on the tranquil couple sharing a watermelon on the bow. "Moon River" played as the two set sail on their life's journey together. Their goal: to enjoy life. Their motto: to stop and smell the seaweed along the way.

Little did the couple know of the storms that awaited them out on the dark and treacherous sea....

Would they reach their goal? Would they ever return home? Perhaps they'd be shipwrecked on a small, deserted white sand island in the middle of turquoise waters, where they would eat nothing but fresh bananas and pineapples, and never have to cook. They would sleep in hammocks and never have to make a bed or hear the roar of a vacuum cleaner.

She would write stories and never have to deal with annoying people or make complicated decisions. And he would build little rafts to ship their manuscripts to publishers, and receive royalties back in a bottle....

Drifting and dreaming. Therapy.

✤ 16 ✤
Far Above Rubies

Entering Saint Nectarios is like stepping into another realm. Flickering candlelight beckons me into the dark sanctuary. The glow of the candles reflects off of tiny gold tiles in the mosaics along the walls. A quiet reverence emanates from the faces of worshippers. Standing among them, facing the altar, I'm overwhelmed by the mystery of heaven intersecting with earth. God reaching down to man. There is still a place in this world to find the sacred. In His church.

Danny is transfixed by the mosaic of Jesus filling the dome overhead. He was told by Father Demetrios that the thousands of tiles that make up the mosaics were numbered, shipped from Greece, and reassembled here one tile at a time. Mosaics of Mary with baby Jesus and many of the saints who were martyred for Him surround us like a cloud of witnesses. A gentle peace falls over me. *A hospital for the soul.* That's how my Aunt Genevieve once described the Orthodox Church. My soul could sure use a rest in the ICU about now.

Father Demetrios, in colorful vestments, stands before the altar, praying the Divine Liturgy. "For holy art thou, our God, and unto thee we ascribe glory: to the Father, and to the Son, and to the Holy Spirit: now and forever, and unto the ages of ages." I close my eyes, listening to the small choir sing the liturgical hymns. The liturgy is

meant to reflect the worship going on in heaven. By participating in
the liturgy, we're participating in the worship of heaven along with
the angels and saints. "Holy God, Holy Mighty, Holy Immortal,
have mercy on us." My mind wanders back to the days of the apostles. Back to when they walked with Jesus—and then, to the cross,
where they watched him die. And mysteriously, He has kept the
hope of heaven alive in hearts of men for nearly two thousand years.

Danny and I slip into the foyer during Communion. "Well?" I
whisper.

"Different," he says. "Really different … but definitely awe
inspiring. What do you think?"

"… I think it's about as close to heaven as I can get from here."

"What would you think about getting married here?"

"Hmmm …" My eyes take in the reflection of flickering candlelight, as my heart takes in the peace and stillness. "It would be a
marriage made in heaven."

❧

At the end of our catechism class, Father Demetrios invites us to stay
for a meal. He's a kind old man with warm eyes and a long gray beard
that makes him look really wise. His small parsonage is just behind
the church. Over lamb and potatoes, he tells us all about his journey
to America as a young boy. When his family settled in Apache Falls
in 1921, his father helped to build St. Nectarios. He was the priest
for nearly twenty-five years before he passed away. Father Demetrios
grew up in the church and continued his father's legacy. He's now a
widower with three grown daughters.

Danny brings up the topic of marriage within the Orthodox Church. "There are only certain times of the year that weddings are performed—excluding December during the Nativity and again in spring during Pascha—or Easter, as you call it."

Danny looks concerned.

"Is there a problem?" Father Demetrios asks.

"Well, we were kind of hoping to be married in December."

"That is a problem," the Father replies. "That's right in the middle of the forty-day fast."

"The *forty-day* fast?" I exclaim. "You mean, no one eats for *forty* days *straight?*"

He smiles. "Oh, we eat. We just fast from certain foods and try to keep our focus more on the Nativity than on the *activity* of the season."

I look at Danny.

"We'll work around it," he says, matter-of-fact.

"We can't work around *that!*" I blurt out, rather loudly, the second Danny hops into the Jeep to leave. I'd nearly bit a hole through my lip during the meal while Danny and Father Demetrios calmly disassembled my entire Christmas wedding.

Danny stares at me. "Look, A. J., God is in control of this, not us. I know you were hoping to have a Christmas wedding with your family here and all...."

"What do you mean *were?* I still *am!* I don't care what you say about it, I'm having a Christmas wedding, *with* or *without you!*"

Danny's staring back at me, probably wondering how long it will take for me to realize what I just said.

... *Okay, so that won't work.* Why do I feel like my mother right now? Probably because that was a perfect example of something she would say.

We head down the highway in silence. Halfway home, Danny glances over at me.

I glance back.

He smiles.

I don't.

"You know, A. J., I wouldn't mind getting married next month."

I look at Danny bug-eyed. *I'm surprised you're still interested after that little display of insanity. Maybe you're talking about marrying some-one else.*

"Could your family come in November instead?"

❧

"Mama? Hi, it's A. J."

"How's my little Christmas bride-to-be?"

"Um, Mama? What would you think of pushing the wedding up a little—to maybe, November fifth?"

"That's real funny, kiddo. Your father told you to say that for kicks, didn't he? I'm not falling for it this time. Hey, I just ordered the most gorgeous Christmas ornaments so we can decorate a giant Christmas tree for the reception at Big Chief."

"Mama, I'm not joking about the date. It's the only time we can get the priest to perform the ceremony."

"Angelina Juliana Degulio, if you are pulling my leg, you will be so sorry, and if you're not, you'll be better off dead than alive."

"I'm not pulling your leg."

Silence. Three … two … one … "You must be *out of your mind!*" I'm holding the phone a foot away from my ear and can still hear her.

"I have just printed all of the invitations—with the date—on special Italian paper, *and* ordered Christmas ornaments from here to Timbuktu! This is already October … do you really think I can pull this all together in a month?"

"I know you can pull off anything you put your mind to, Mama."

"That's right, and I have put my mind to a Christmas wedding, and that, by George, is what we're having! Give me the number of the priest; I'll have a little chat with him. Either that or we'll find a new one."

"No, Mama. This is the priest Danny and I both want."

"Well, it will be a cold day in Phoenix before I trade in my Christmas angel ornaments for turkeys and pumpkins. Unless you and Danny are planning to stand at the altar dressed up like pilgrims, I suggest you find a way to make this Christmas wedding work!" *Click.*

"So what'd she say?" Danny asks.

"Oh, good grief, she's already bought up every Christmas ornament in the North Pole for the reception. She's probably hired a team of elves to help her decorate too."

"I'm sorry, A. J., I didn't mean to make things harder for you."

I slump onto the couch. "I'm so confused I can't even think straight." Am I Catholic, Baptist, or Orthodox? Cathobapdox. Am

I having a wedding or a funeral? According to Mama, a funeral. You would think this is her wedding, not mine! I can't even elope if I want to without dying from guilt.

Ring-ring …

"If it's my mother, I'm not here!"

Danny braces himself and picks up the receiver. "Hello?"

"… What's that? … Wow. That is a *great* idea. Wish I'd thought of it. I'm sure she'll be fine with it."

"I'll be fine with *what?*" I hiss, giving him *the glare* for speaking for me about matters involving the rest of my life.

"I'll let her know. And thank you—you've just saved my life."

As Danny hangs up the phone, a wave of relief washes over his face.

"What?" I demand.

"Your mother says we're on for November fifth."

"Oh, *really?* What about her Christmas wedding?"

"We're having Christmas in November. We are going to have *our* Christmas wedding after all."

"We are? We're having a Christmas wedding in *November?* Will anyone besides me think this is weird?"

❧

Ding-ding-ding-ding! I'm jolted from a deep sleep. Sailor's running back and forth between me and the door, barking his head off. The bell on the mainland is ringing wildly. My eyes shift to the clock: 1:13 a.m. I'm acutely aware of how Danny felt when I ran away from Peaceful Pines and rang the same bell in the middle of the night.

Certain that Danny must have heard it too, I hop out of bed, throw on some warm clothes, slip my feet into cold boots, grab my parka, and run out the door. Sailor and I charge down the Pitchy Pine Trail toward Big Chief, hoping to catch Danny before he leaves for shore without us. The thought that there's no school tomorrow helps to ease my mind about running around in the wee hours of the morning.

"Danny, wait for us!" Sailor and I race down the bank to the dock where Danny is untying the tug. The engine is already running. The tug is the only boat he can use at night since it has navigation lights.

"Ahoy, mates!" he calls back. "At least I know it's not you ringing the bell this time."

Danny grabs my hand and pulls me aboard. Sailor's already on the bow wagging his tail over the excitement of a new adventure. "Expecting anyone early for the wedding?" he asks.

"Not this early. It's a month away." I take my place in the first mate's chair, and we head across the cold, dark lake. From out on the water we can see the silhouette of someone standing on the landing dock. At least we know it's not a couple of pranksters trying to wake up the whole town, like J. R. used to do for kicks. Nearing the shoreline Danny squints his eyes. "It's my brother."

"Jason? How can you tell? It's pitch-dark out."

"I know his stature. That's him."

"Looks like a six-foot blob to me."

Pulling up to the dock, Danny hops down from the bow. "Jason!" He extends one hand and hugs him with the other. "What in the world brought you here?"

"Long story," he answers. "Mind if I stay awhile—like until the wedding?"

"Don't mind at all." Danny grabs his bags and tosses them onto the tug. "You okay?"

"Nope, as a matter of fact, I'm not."

"Well, hop aboard," Danny says. "Let's get you to the island and you can fill me in."

Jason climbs on board and notices me standing by the cabin door. "A. J.?" he says in amazement.

"That's me." I smile and hold out my hand to him.

"Wow." He looks at Danny, "Wow, brother." He ignores my hand and gives me a hug. "I'm glad to see one of the Morgan men has done well for himself."

Jason looks identical to Danny, only with darker hair. He's equally as burly and handsome.

We all duck into the cabin, where I surrender my first mate's chair to Jason. Sailor and I take the bench seat along the wall. Sailor must know family members by scent—or just has a really good memory. He doesn't seem the least bit concerned about the new guest.

The tug pulls away from the dock. Everything turns dark again as we head out on the water. "She dumped me," Jason says.

❧

On the front porch of Big Chief, I turn to go. "I'll let you catch up with your brother," I tell Danny.

"You don't need to go, A. J.," Jason says over his shoulder. "Come in long enough to give me hope that there are still nice women left in the world."

"I'm probably not the one to do that, but I'll stay for a few minutes anyway."

"Good."

I start for the kitchen to put some hot water on. "Anyone for hot tea or coffee?"

"Coffee sounds good," Jason replies. "Doubt I'll be able to sleep tonight anyway."

"Tea, please," Danny adds.

I take down three mugs and a tin of very crispy chocolate chip cookies—my latest attempt at baking for Danny. A tad overdone, but still edible. While Danny stokes the fire, Jason plops down on the couch and puts his feet up on the coffee table, cowboy boots and all. "Sorry about the short notice," he says.

"Short notice? Try no notice," Danny laughs. "But we're glad you're here."

"Yeah, well, I couldn't get here fast enough—hardly had time to even think about what I was doing—I just knew this is where I needed to be."

I set the steaming mugs and cookies down by Jason's feet.

"Thanks, A. J." Jason reaches for his coffee. "You want the long or short version?"

"Up to you," Danny says.

"Okay … for the full impact, picture this: I'm out on the tractor checking on some damaged fence lines, when Cindy's car pulls up to the guesthouse. That's where she was planning to stay until our wedding. I'm thinking maybe she came home early from work to have lunch with me or somethin'. So I start driving toward the guesthouse. Next thing I know, she's throwing suitcases into the trunk of her car. Seeing me comin', she leans against the car to wait for me.

"I ask her what's goin' on.

"She stands there in her business suit and high heels and tells me that she realizes she isn't cut out to marry a farm boy and she's done playing *Little House on the Prairie*.

"So I ask if this has anything to do with the Amway guy who keeps hauling her off to conventions.

"She went on about never reaching anything beyond ruby status in the company, and that *Clark* is already at diamond status, and how much he motivates her to be more than what she is."

"She's leaving you for a guy named Clark?" Danny asks.

"Apparently so." Jason heaves a loud sigh and looks over at me.

"It sounds like you just lost yourself a true Proverbs 31 woman," I say.

Jason and Danny look at me like I must be crazy.

"Well, thanks to Clark, with his diamond status, Cindy's worth will soon be 'far above rubies,' just like the Proverbs 31 woman."

Jason looks at Danny. "She's cute," he says. A subtle smile crosses his face. "Little does Miss Ruby realize, but that *Little House on the Prairie* is worth a lot more than anything she'll ever get out of Amway, or Clark."

"This all just happened?" Danny asks.

"Yep. Told my ranch hands I was headin' out, and to hold down the fort. I was packed and on the road that afternoon and just kept driving. Took me three days and a few hotels, but here I am. All I could think of was the island. I had to get to the island. I felt like I was headin' home. Know what I mean?"

"Yeah, this place has a way of drawing people back," I tell him. "Speaking of home, I think I'll head to my cabin for the night."

"You mean what's left of the night," Danny says. "C'mon, I'll walk you back."

❧

Very early a.m.: Ring-ring!

"Hello?"

"A. J., is that you?"

"Yes, Mama, it's me." Yawn.

"Hey, little missy … we have found *the gown of all gowns!*"

Oh no.

"But listen, there is absolutely *no way* we will know if this will fit you unless you try it on. We'll need time to have it altered if it needs adjustments."

"You want me to fly back to Italy to try it on?"

"No, smarty-pants. I'm sending Adriana to deliver it to you next week. She needs a break after her assignment in the jungle."

"What did you just say?"

"I said, she just went to the Amazon.…"

"No, not that. Did you say Adriana is coming here next week? The wedding is still a month away!"

"Your sister could use a month at the island. She's just had a run-in with a hoity-toity cover girl, and I think the island will do her some good. So Adriana will be arriving next week with *the gown.* I'm also enlisting her to pick up a few things for the cabin—guest towels, dishes, kitchen things. The two of you can fix things up a little for the wedding guests."

"Why—who's staying at Papoose?"

"We are. And don't forget to keep that fire burning or you'll freeze your little fannies off."

"Good news: Danny's nearly finished insulating Papoose."

"Atta boy, Danny!"

"But I'm not going to be real good company for Adriana with school going on."

"Adriana's a big girl, she'll keep herself occupied—just let her spice the place up while you're off performing those triple bypasses on hamsters. Well, I've gotta run and get the plane tickets for your sister pushed up. You are going to *flip* when you see this dress!"

That's what I'm afraid of.

When Mama hangs up, one word comes to mind. *Jason.*

❦

"Danny, meet me at my cemetery *right now—alone!*" I hang up the phone and dash out the door with Sailor. The sun is just rising over Juniper Beach. I continue on down the trail, beyond the chapel to my Haven of Rest critter cemetery. "Mornin', Saint Francis," I say, on my way through the guarded entrance.

"Good morning," an eerie voice answers back.

Euwww. I about faint.

Danny steps out from behind the rose arbor. "Mornin', Scout."

"Oh, it's *you.* I didn't think Saint Francis would really sound that creepy."

"So what's the urgency?"

"You'll understand when I tell you." I notice Danny's half-mast eyes. "You look tired, did I wake you up?"

"No." He yawns. "I haven't gone to sleep yet. Jason kept me up all night rehashing memories of the Little Barbie Doll on the Prairie."

"Well, now she's the Little Barbie Doll off the Prairie." And it's a good thing for both Jason and the ducks.

Danny smiles. "What's this secret meeting about?"

"I didn't want to risk Jason hearing this. Adriana's flying in next week."

"Here?"

"Yep, right here on this very island."

"I guess she's gonna stay, then? Till the wedding, I mean."

"Uh-huh. The *whole* month. Mama's sending *the gown of all gowns* with her to make sure it fits right. And as far as Jason and Adriana … it will be interesting…."

"Kind of ironic that Jason just got a taste of the way he treated your sister."

"I know. Do we tell them, or let them find out on their own that they're not alone out here?"

"They managed to find each other the first time. Might as well let nature take its course. Hard to say how they'll react to seeing each other again."

"They'll see each other at the wedding anyway. What difference could a month together on a small island make to a couple of old sweethearts?"

We look at each other and laugh.

✵ 17 ✵
A Walk in the Woods

"I am *dying* for a Big Daddy burger, fries, and shake!" Adriana announces, while tossing her suitcase and large hanging bag on my bed. "For once I can eat whatever I want!"

"Great—let's go eat! Danny left the skiff here in case we wanted to go to town."

"Good. But first, we have got to try this gown on you!" She whisks the hanging bag back up from the bed and holds it out in front of me. "A. J., you are going to die when you see this."

Very possible.

Adriana yanks the zipper down and whips out a billowing white cloud of lace and fluff. "Ta-da!"

Oh boy ... I'm pretty sure this gown belonged to Catherine the Great of Russia. Now all I need is one of those hoops that make the skirt stick out five feet in every direction.... Here comes the bride ... big, fat, and wide.... I'll need to wear a "wide load" sign just to get down the aisle....

"... A. J.?"

"Huh?"

"I asked if you like it?'"

"Like what?"

"The *gown*."

"Oh. Um ... it's really ... *something*. Wow."

"Mama just went wild over it when I showed it to her."

Let her wear it. "What if it doesn't fit? Can I get a different one?"

"We'll make it fit. C'mon, let's try it on!"

Within minutes, I'm standing in front of the full-length mirror staring at myself. Lord have mercy. I am Catherine the Great. Hear me roar.

❧

Approaching the public docks, we can see a giant rotating burger, the town's prize trademark, spinning awkwardly on a crooked axle over the Squawkomish skyline. Big Daddy Burger is still the place to go for burgers—the *only* place to go for burgers, actually. It's also Mama's old stomping grounds for playing her Sophia Loren game. She looked so much like the real Sophia and loved fooling tourists into thinking she was the famous actress. My mother the imposter: She used to trick the entire town into asking for her autograph. Her autographed photo is still hanging on the wall above our table. Thank heavens she learned her lesson in Rome a couple years ago when she caused a mob scene and needed a police escort to get her out of the mess. She's kept a low profile ever since.

Adriana orders a Double Daddy burger, large fries, and a chocolate shake. I guess she means it when she says she's going to eat anything she wants. She takes the burger and sinks her teeth right into it. "Mmm-mmm," she moans, devouring it in a very unladylike manner.

I'm content with my routine Coney Island dog and Coke. It's

been a long time since I've seen my sister with ketchup and mustard smeared across her face. "I wish I could get a picture of you to send to *Mademoiselle* magazine."

Adriana laughs while plunging her straw into her shake. "Me too. I'd love to send a copy to the models of Milan. They'd be so jealous. You have no idea how restricted our diets are when we're working. One bonbon too many and we're out of a job."

"So what's the latest on the modeling scene?" I figure that's a better approach than *Mama says you had a run-in at work.*

"Don't ruin my appetite. I'm enjoying this too much to think about it."

"Sorry. Okay, tell me about the family."

"I've been so busy working I've hardly had time to see the family. At least I'll have time to see everyone while I'm here. I'm not planning to go back to work until after the wedding. The last photo shoot did it for me."

A good journalist will always find a roundabout way to get the story. "Really? Where was the shoot?"

"The Amazon," she replies.

"The Amazon *jungle?*" So Mama was serious after all.

"Yep. The jungle."

"Oh." I nod. "Why?"

Adriana sets down her shake. "Some big shoe company was launching a new line of snakeskin shoes and purses. They wanted photos of beautiful women with real snakes crawling over the tops of their snakeskin shoes."

Euwww. "So they sent you to the real jungle? Why couldn't they just go to the zoo and shoot it at the snake exhibit?"

"They wanted the real thing. They also requested our agency's top two models. My agency sent me ... and Zahara."

"Zahara? What kind of name is Zahara?"

"Swahili. Anyway, we shared a tree house together for five days."

"A tree house?"

"Yeah, they're supposed to keep you from being devoured by wild beasts at night. In retrospect, I would have been better off rooming with a jaguar. A quick death would have been less painful. The entire experience can be summed up in two words: *jungle torture.*"

Adriana launches into a blow-by-blow account of her jungle trip with Zahara:

"The jungle was swarming with mosquitoes the size of hummingbirds. I came fully equipped with a big can of bug spray. The first night I went to look for it, it was gone. So I lay there all night getting eaten alive. I tried to wake up Zahara to see if she had some repellent. She mumbled something about how Swahili blood doesn't attract insects. The next morning I was covered with welts. Zahara didn't have a single bite.

"That afternoon, I climbed back up to the tree house during a break to take a nap. When I entered the hut, there was Zahara spraying away—with my bug repellent!

"'What are you doing with my bug spray?' I asked.

"'Oh, I just found it under your cot—it must have rolled under there,' so she said.

"I would have been happy to have shared it with her—had she *asked.* Things like that kept happening all week long. I had missing clothes, shampoo, makeup.... By the end of the week, I looked a mess. "

"Did you ever find out why she did it?"

"The story finally broke that Zahara was aiming for 'Top Model of the Year.' Apparently, she thought I was a threat and she was trying her best to sabotage my appearance so I'd look lousy in my photos."

"Did your agency hear about any of this?"

"Did they ever. Not just from me, but the whole crew was ready to leave Zahara in the jungle. The agency gave me a paid month off to recover and Zahara is no longer with us. She'll be lucky if she can get into Bonne Bell's charm school with her new reputation."

"So how did the photos turn out?"

"Not as bad as I thought they would. They were able to airbrush my welts out of the pictures." As Adriana glances around Big Daddy's, her eyes suddenly stop. "Oh my gosh. Do you remember Mindy Osmund?"

I whip my head around. Sure enough, there she is, bigger than life. "It's her!" The girl who told everyone she was Donny Osmond's cousin, even though their names were spelled differently.

"Remember we always had to play the Osmond Family whenever she came over?"

"Yeah, well, at least you got to be Marie Osmond. I always had to be Donny, so she could play his girlfriend." While I'm staring over at her, I suddenly notice two guys outside walking past the window toward the front door. *Yikes!* Danny and Jason. This does not feel like the right time for a reunion at all. "Adriana, come on, let's sneak out the back before Mindy notices we're here." I get up and turn toward the back door.

"A. J., what's the big deal if she sees you?"

"I never gave her troll doll back. Come on!"

"Oh, brother," she moans, and slowly climbs out of the booth.

I whisk Adriana toward the back door just as Danny and Jason are coming in the front. Danny's eyes suddenly spot me. He looks as mortified as I do. He quickly moves in front of Jason as I pull my sister out the door.

I look for the tugboat, but see Danny's Jeep instead. Must have driven down from the mainland. Danny and Jason are sitting in a window booth. Danny's looking straight at me. I give him a quick wave and hop into the skiff.

It's only a matter of time before Romeo and Juliet meet again.

❧

I poke my head in Adriana's room before leaving for school. She's dead asleep, still on Italian time. I decide to leave a note rather than wake her up:

Mornin' Sunshine!

Won't be back from school until late—spending the afternoon in study hall. You might want to explore the island for Danny's new additions since you were last here. I'll send you on a scavenger hunt. Here's what you need to look for:

*Danny's prayer chapel

*The new garden surrounding my critter cemetery (do not step on burial plots marked with little wooden crosses)

*The tree fort and lookout tower for the future summer camp

*Major fire pit on Juniper Beach
Good luck and don't get lost!
XOXO

Your ever-lovin' little

sis

Evidently, some things never change between siblings. I still find great pleasure in annoying her.

When I return home via my tug escort, I find a note in place of the one I left.

Dear Beaver Teeth,

I decided to be a good sport and take you up on your stupid scavenger hunt. If I'm not here when you get home, I am likely to be at Juniper Beach or wandering in the woods. If I haven't returned by dark, call the ranger to come find me, provided it's not Ranger Rod.

Your favorite sister

P.S. A little person named Stormy called for you—wants you to call her back.

On my way to raid the snack cupboard, the phone rings. I grab the receiver and continue in the direction of the cookies, stretching the cord to its limit. "Hello?"

"It's me," Danny says.

"Hi, you. What's new? Haven't seen you for at least five minutes."

"I just noticed that Jason's not around and was curious if he might have popped in over there?"

"Not here. But Adriana's not here either...."

"Really?"

"Well, hey, I'd better run. Lots of homework today."

"Homework, my foot. You're going out there to spy on them, aren't you?"

"Who, me? What would ever possess you to think such a thing? That is such an immature thing to say."

"A. J., I know you...."

"Hey, gotta go! Tons of homework." *Click.* Some people are so immature, I can't believe it. I do the Snoopy dance on my way out the door. "Nope, not this time, Sailor. You botch it up for me every time." I close him inside and brace myself for his cries of rejection. Three ... two ... one ...

"Ouuuooo-oo-oo-o."

Let's see, where on the scavenger hunt would they have run into each other? I don't hear a peep in the woods, so I work my way toward Juniper Beach. When I reach the trailhead to the beach, I suddenly spot them. Jason and Adriana. Sitting on a log. If I can work my way along the overgrown trail that parallels the beach, I might be able to catch some of their conversation.

Creeping through the tall beach grass, I follow the path until I'm directly behind them, then dart behind a tree trunk for cover.

"Sounds to me like you're probably better off without her," Adriana says.

"Yeah, I know, you're probably right. I just hate the thought of being dumped for a guy named Clark in Amway."

"Yeah, that is pretty pathetic," Adriana says and bursts out laughing.

"Hey, you're not helping much," Jason replies.

"Sorry. I guess what goes around comes around."

Ouch! I can't believe she said that, obviously referring to the way Jason treated her. I lean a little closer, trying to catch Jason's response to that zinger.

"Yeah ..."

I'm suddenly grabbed from behind!

"Aaaagghh!" I scream at the top of my lungs. Whipping around, I find Danny doubled over with laughter. It's straight from the ham scene in *To Kill a Mockingbird*.

"How immature of me to think you'd be out here spying on your sister!" Danny mocks me.

"I was just catching the best part ... now look what you've done."

Jason and Adriana are on their way over. "Oh, look, it's my little sister. Haven't we done this before?"

"I think we did," Jason replies. "She caught us kissing in her critter cemetery once. She screamed even louder back then."

Thanks for reminding me.

"Well, now that we've all found each other, anyone up for a trip to the big city?" Danny asks.

"Downtown Squawkomish?" Jason asks.

"The one and only."

Jason and Adriana look at each other. Adriana shrugs. "Why not? I'm sure it has as much to offer as Rome."

After changing from casual island wear to casual dinner wear, we all pile into the tug and head to *the big city* for a night on the town. For me that means changing from my dirty overalls to clean ones. Adriana changes into a two-piece silk number that makes her look like a million bucks. Actually, she'd look like a million bucks wearing a potato sack. It's not every day that one of Milan's top models makes an appearance in downtown Squawkomish. I've often wondered what it would feel like to turn heads everywhere you go. Actually, I know exactly what it feels like, due to tripping over things.

We hop off the boat at the marina—if you can call a dock that moors a half-dozen boats a marina. Not exactly a hoppin' place—but it's all the excitement I need. Our dining options are somewhat limited, but it makes life less complicated. When it comes right down to it, I am probably the most boring individual I know. My idea of a dynamite night is a good book, a couch, and a fire with a sleeping dog in front of it.

"Okay," Danny announces, "we can eat at Pop's Pizza, Flip's Fish-n-Chips, Big Daddy Burger, or the Spaghetti House."

Being that we've already been to Big Daddy's and Flip's recently, I cast my vote for the Spaghetti House. Everyone seems to be in agreement. It's probably the nicest of the four and has some seriously good Italian food.

Strolling down the boardwalk, Adriana points out the playhouse where we saw *Annie Get Your Gun*. "Hey, A. J., isn't that where you got your arm caught in the candy machine trying to steal a candy bar?"

"No, that was Benji. I got in trouble for telling him to do it.

I had to pick up every candy wrapper in the state park for that."
Daddy always had a flair for poetic justice.

"You deserved it." Adriana looks over at Jason and Danny. "Poor
Benji. That kid did everything we told him to."

"Yep, poor Benji was always an accident waiting to happen," I
add. "Then he fell off the roof of the villa." Adriana looks back at me
and the moment turns somber. That was a turning point in all of our
lives. That's when we stopped taking family for granted.

As we enter the Spaghetti House, I'm hit with a blast of garlic
from the kitchen. "*Buongiorno,*" our Italian hostess greets us, and
leads us to a quiet, dark corner facing the lake. The classic candle in
the Chianti bottle beckons us to our table.

While Adriana's busy glancing at the menu, the gentlemen at the
table across from us are busy glancing at Adriana. She doesn't seem
to take notice, but Jason does, and shoots a glare in their direction.
One point in my corner. I'm tempted to start wagering some bets on
Romeo and Juliet.

"Too many choices," Adriana says. "Order for me, A. J.—I'm
too tired to figure out what I want. I'm still on Italian time."

"What do y'all say we order a big bowl of spaghetti, family-
style?" Danny suggests.

"Sounds good," we all agree.

The waitress drops off a basket of crunchy bread sticks. Adriana
looks down. "Where's the *antipasto?*"

"Welcome to America," I tell her.

"Don't worry," Danny says. "I've never left this place hungry."

"So," Jason says, crunching on a breadstick, "Danny mentioned something about Adriana's wild jungle adventure. That must have been a pretty interesting trip."

"Only if you call working with snakes and backstabbing women *interesting,*" I comment.

Jason looks surprised. "Oh, I guess we hadn't gotten to that part." He turns to Adriana. "Sounds like the modeling world and Amway have a lot in common. It's nice to know there's a place to go when it all goes wrong out there." He holds up his glass. "To the island."

We all raise our glasses. "To the island."

❧ 18 ❧
The Wedding Diary

October 10, 1976

I've decided to journal the events leading up to my
wedding day. Of course it won't hurt to secretly chart the
progress of Jason and Adriana. I don't want to lose my
bet with Danny. I'm convinced Adriana has been in love
with Jason all this time—which, I'm equally convinced, is
why she has not had a boyfriend since she left the island.
The whole breakup happened because of me exposing
Jason's two-timin' secret. Adriana holds Jason responsible
for my childhood boating accident—so I'd like to help free
them both from their past heartaches.

Because we live in such close quarters these secret
diary pages are being hidden between the covers of my
rose-petal scrapbook, entitled "My Wedding Diary," for
safekeeping.

October 15, 1976

To date, I'm losing my bet with Danny over Jason
and Adriana. I predicted that one or the other would be
showing some obvious signs of romantic interest by our

wedding. So far, other than the basic courtesies, nothing. Nada. Not even a blush or a twinkle in the eye. Dang. I do not like losing—especially when it comes to love. I'm still hopeful. I'm also hoping for Jason and Adriana to pull through for my new novel so I can say it's based on a true story.

Working title: "Mending Sails"

Character Sketch

Adriana Degulio: burned-out fashion model from Milan, returns to the summer cabin of her youth where she unexpectedly finds herself sharing the same island with her first true love, Jason, the schmuck who broke her heart.

Jason Morgan: tall, dark, and dashing Oklahoma farm boy, gets dumped by gorgeous gold digger who runs off with an Amway salesman. Jason returns to Indian Island in hopes of restoring his shattered heart and life.

Synopsis: The two meet again

Jason, the former no-good two-timer, has finally been hit with a good dose of his own medicine. He suddenly senses deep, deep, gut-wrenching remorse for what he'd put Adriana through years ago as a young, trusting girl. Yes, beautiful women can be a pain, but

Adriana is different—she comes from a family who
believes in love and being true. Jason decides he will
do whatever it takes to prove that he can be the man
Adriana deserves.

Adriana, tired of the backbiting, backstabbing fashion
world, is strangely drawn, heart and soul, to the idea of
relaxing on a nine-hundred-acre hay farm. She daydreams
of raising baby ducks and collecting fresh farm eggs in the
morning to fry up for her hungry hunk-a-hunk farm boy.
No longer consumed with worry over having to fit into a size
two runway gown with toe-pinching high heels, she relishes
the thought of going barefoot in a one-size-fits-all muumuu,
while fixin' up some fried chicken-n-biscuits with gravy every
night for dinner.

Can they do it? Can they forgive, forget, build a bridge,
and move on? Or are they stuck in the past, destined to
live separate, miserable lives, next door to each other on
a lonely island for the rest of their lives? Will they sit
on a porch swing together when they are old and gray,
and reminisce of the day they got over it and came back
together? Or will they rock alone, whining until the day they
die about the things that happened sixty years ago? Things
they barely even remember? Only time will tell.

They have all afternoon to restore my hope. They're on the island
alone all day today. I'm headed to Grandma's.

While Grandma and I are having a nice chat in the front room, a delivery truck backs into the driveway. A big guy hops out and begins unloading boxes. Must be the beginning of Mama's shipments. She mentioned she'd ordered a few decorations for the wedding reception and was having everything shipped here. I've been wondering how much stuff she actually ordered.

The hand truck should be the first clue. Box after box comes wheeling past us and is stacked by the front door. By the time the truck pulls away, there are six large boxes blocking the entrance to the house. We can barely open the front door to see what he's left here. "What in the world is all of this?" Grandma wants to know. "Why don't you open one and find out?"

"Good idea." I've got to get over the idea that this is Mama's wedding instead of mine. There is nothing wrong with opening boxes for my own wedding. On the other hand, do I really want to know? What if I don't like what I see? There's not much I could do about it at this point, with only two weeks to go. Might as well get it over with and see what I'm in for.

Grandma returns from the kitchen with a butcher knife.

I'm hoping this doesn't turn into an oh-happy-dagger scene from *Romeo and Juliet* once I see how bad it is.

"You do the honors," she says, handing me the knife.

I raise the handle and plunge the blade into the top of the first box.

"You don't have to kill it, Angelina, it's not alive. Just slide the blade along the tape under the flaps."

"Oh, right." *Freudian slip of the wrist, I guess.* With a bit more caution, I slit the tape along the opening and pull up the flaps. *Angels.*

We are looking at angels. A ton of gold and silver angel ornaments holding every musical instrument imaginable to mankind. "Looks like the theme is angels," I say to Grandma.

"It would appear so," she replies. Grandma lifts an angel from the box and dangles it over her head. "Well, they'll go nicely with both Christmas and your name, won't they?"

It could be worse, I guess. Like pilgrim ornaments. I open the next box, then the next, until all six boxes lie open. Angels, angels, angels! I believe this must be all nine choirs of angels in heaven, including the seraphim and the cherubim, not to mention the archangels Gabriel and Michael, complete with weapons. I can't recall the names of the others, but I'm sure they're here.

We not only have angel decorations for the Christmas tree, we have angel plates, angel napkins, an angel cake stand—with angels holding up the cake platter, an angel punch bowl with angels etched in crystal—with matching angel glasses. I have a sudden vision of Mama strapping a pair of angel wings on my back and launching me from the rafters to make my grand entrance. I'm still trying to come to terms with the gown of all gowns.

While we're standing here surrounded by angels, the mailman pulls up. He steps out and hands me a square envelope with Italian postage. With the knife still handy, I slit it open. A wedding invitation—to *my* wedding! Fancy black lettering printed on Italian watermarked paper. Then, there's an angel sticker flying across the middle of my invitation, blowing a trumpet, right between the time and the date. Out of curiosity I peel the sticker off and quickly realize why it's there: Mama had December twentieth crossed out and used the sticker to cover it up.

Sonny and Sophia Degulio
along with Jack and Stella Morgan
request the honor of your presence at the
marriage of their daughter,
Angelina Juliana Degulio, to Daniel Jackson Morgan
One o'clock in the afternoon
xxxxxxxxx xxxx November fifth
Nineteen-hundred-seventy-six

St. Nectarios • 303 Main Street • Apache Falls, Idaho
Reception following at Big Chief on Indian Island

October 20, 1976

    I have gone out of my way to get Jason and Adriana
thinking about each other. I even made brownie sundaes tonight
to create a little get-together. After Jason and Danny arrived, I
made Danny go for a walk with me so Jason and Adriana would
be alone. Danny thinks it's a hopeless cause. I made him a
new bet—if they show interest by the end of our wedding day,
Danny owes me a pirate ship.

    When Danny and I returned to the cabin, the two of them
seemed to be pleasantly engaged in conversation. After Jason
and Danny left, I asked Adriana what she thought of Jason.

Quote: "Jason is a very nice, extremely handsome hunk who
nearly caused my sister to drown eight years ago."
Not real encouraging.

October 25, 1976
The four of us went to dinner at Big Daddy Burger tonight.
I begged Danny to help me find out what Jason thinks about
Adriana now. When Adriana went to the ladies' room, Danny
said, "Adriana is sure looking well these days, don't you think,
Jason?" Jason's reply: "Buddy, 'looking well' doesn't even begin
to cover it."
That was encouraging. So I said, "You know, Adriana would
probably really like a break from modeling. I think she's always
had a secret desire to have a little farm of her own, with some
cute baby ducks."
Jason's reply: "You know, A. J., there's something about
beautiful women and hay farmers that just don't mix." I shot
Danny my say-something stare.
Danny: "Well, Adriana's actually very down-to-earth."
Jason: "Don't even start, little brother. If you'll recall, the
last beautiful, down-to-earth woman in my life just stomped all
over my heart in her high heels."
At that very moment Adriana strolled out of the ladies'
room in her black satin pantsuit and stiletto heels. Bad timing.

October 30, 1976
I was feeling desperate today for these two to get over
the past and give each other a chance. Once the family arrives,

there won't be a lot of opportunities for them to be alone again. For my last-ditch effort, I had Danny build a fire at Big Chief, and told Adriana that we were invited over for a card game.

"I hate cards," she said.

I called Danny. "Tell me everything that's on TV tonight."

He read me the TV Guide, show by show. When he got to the reruns, I began to lose hope, then he read the words Mod Squad.

I practically screamed, "Mod Squad? That's it! Adriana absolutely loved Mod Squad! It came out just following the summer she and Jason were together. It's sure to spark some old feelings."

It sparked old feelings, all right. Adriana remembered it as the show that coincided with her blue period—the most miserable period of her life. She had been so blissfully happy—until, thanks to me, she found out she wasn't the only girl Jason was going steady with. He had another girl back home at the same time. Strike three.

❧

Monday morning, I wander into my environmental science lecture hall half asleep. If I have any intentions of passing this course, I have got to get back to my former life as a serious college student—the second my family goes home. I am beginning to understand why people wait to get married. It's not being married that's the problem. It's all of the relatives and distractions leading up to the marriage that is throwing me off course. I'm already planning to take Friday and

Monday off to give us a four-day wedding weekend. But the scary thing is, *the Family* hasn't even arrived yet and I'm already falling behind.

"A. J.!" A hand is waving me over from the far side of the lecture hall. After arriving at row D, I have to squeeze my way past a half dozen occupied desks, with my book bag bumping the heads of students in the row in front of me. I finally take a seat next to Celiene.

"Morning. What's *that?*" I whisper. I am viewing a slide show of cows standing knee-deep in mire.

"Feedlots."

"Feedlots?"

Celiene nods. "Feedlots—the most disgusting form of raising beef and most damaging to the environment, all for the sake of saving space and money."

The projector clicks from one slide to another, more cows, more manure. I'm just thankful we don't get to experience the stench to go with it.

"I signed up for the field trip," Celiene whispers. "Want to go with me? It's next Wednesday."

"A field trip to feedlots?"

"Hey, it beats cramming in reading about it for the exam, don't you think? Besides that, I signed myself up for the five-day feedlot tour, by bus, over winter break." Celiene is actually beaming over this news.

"*Why?*"

"Because *he's* going." She tweaks her head to the side, trying to be discreet, pointing someone out to me. "One row behind us, third from the end."

I jerk my head around, dying to know who on earth would be worth a five-day bus tour to feedlots.

It's Abe the Babe, as she calls him. Dark hair, olive skin, big brown eyes. "He's planning to be an *environmentally conscientious* cattle rancher."

"Really? Are you sure this guy is worth spending your break with five hundred cows in manure?"

"It would be worth spending my life married to a cow farmer if I could wake up to *that* every morning." She glances back at Abe while stifling a laugh. "Hey, think how good I'd look to him next to all those cows."

I look at the current cow clip on the screen, then back at Celiene. "You may have a point there." So much for not merging the bachelor and MRS degrees.

❦

November 1, 1976

It looks like I will be going from wearing white on Saturday to trudging through manure on Wednesday. A real '70s kind of gal! Talk about identity clash. I still cannot believe Celiene is willing to take the five-day cow tour just for the sake of a cute guy. Of course, she questions me leaving behind the romance of Rome and Tuscan vineyards just for Danny. Oh, the things a girl will do in the name of love.

❧ 19 ❧
When the Saints Come Rollin' In

Standing on the bow of the tug, I can see a mob of hands waving at us from the main shore landing. Behind them, a big bus pulls away and parks beside Danny's Jeep. Mama had mentioned something about leasing a bus for the week to ensure that everyone gets to the island, rehearsal, and wedding all together and on time. Is there anything this woman has not thought of?

My cousin Nicky Jr. hops out of the bus—obvious choice for the designated driver, being that he spends a good deal of his time at the Italian raceway test-driving fast Italian cars. I'm not sure how reassuring that is—he was the one driving the boat when I was taken for a joyride on an inner tube and nearly lost my life.

Chugging our way to the landing, faces slowly come into view.... "My family! They're here!" I suddenly realize how much I've missed them. *Mia famiglia. All* of them. Nothing can beat our family gatherings. And from here out, there won't be a moment of quiet until they all go home.

Mama is leading the pack. She has everyone throwing confetti and singing "Arrivederci Roma." Then there's Daddy, right at Mama's side, always willing to give her center stage—and knowing that if he doesn't, she'll take it anyway. Beside my three brothers, I spot Nonna, my Grandma Juliana, waving like mad, not at us, but at some strangers on a passing boat. That's my Nonna, all right!

As the tugboat merges with the dock at the landing, the crowd storms the deck of the tug. We are quickly engulfed in hugs and kisses, passed from one relative to another: Mama first, followed by Daddy, Benji, Dino, J. R., Nonna, Uncle Nick, Aunt Genevieve, Nicky Jr., Stacie, a dozen cousins, aunts and uncles, more courtesy cousins, and one unexpected guest: Angelo, dear old Angelo—our favorite toothless neighbor from Tuscany. The hugs continue on. Even Jason is embraced as family. While all of the hoopla is going on, Danny slips away from the crowd back to the helm and heads us all back to Indian Island.

I don't know why I'm surprised that nobody waited until the wedding reception to dance. Who needs music when you have Greeks? *Opa!* The *kalamatianos* is in full swing on the deck of the tug. When we hit the dock, everyone rolls off the boat and continues dancing up the ramp to Big Chief, where Danny's relatives are ready and waiting with piles of Southern fried food for the welcome party.

"Stella!" Mama yells, as she shoots across the room and throws her arms around Danny's mama. They haven't seen each other for eight years. "You look fabulous!" Mama gushes, then gives a two-finger whistle to get everyone's attention. Attempting to cover all bases, she gives her best Italian greeting in a Southern accent. *"Buongiorno, buongiorno!* I'd like to officially welcome y'all here, from our family to yours. Welcome, welcome!"

Okay, Mama, news flash: This is their island, not ours—you're the guest....

Mama begins introducing Stella and Jack—and all of the Morgan clan, to our *entire* family, one person at a time. Our family tends to be a bit overwhelming at times.

"I sure hope y'all are ready for the big cook-off tomorrow," Mama announces to the aunts, continuing in her Southern drawl.

They all smile. "We are more than ready," Stella replies.

"Wonderful! I am looking forward to your down-home cookin' and sweet tea. Not to mention your fabulous Jell-O molds—no one does Jell-O like y'all."

I pull Danny aside. "I'm sure your mama is just thrilled to be given such an honor by my mother," I whisper to Danny.

Danny smiles. "Actually, the Jell-O thing is a big deal back home. Mama and my aunts won a blue ribbon at the Oklahoma state fair this year for their armadillo mold."

I look Danny in eye. "They did not."

He laughs. "Yeah, they really did."

I look over at Mama, who is still going on about the Fourth of July flag mold that the Morgan women made on the island in 1968. "The American flag is one thing, but finding an angel mold was tough. I finally located one through a mail-order catalog from Texas. It should be here soon. You're going to love it."

I turn back to Danny. "So they don't think it's weird that my mama has asked them to cook for our reception?"

"Not at all. They consider it an honor to be asked."

I nod in disbelief. Does this mean I'll have to learn to make Jell-O since I'm marrying a Southerner?

In the midst of my Jell-O dilemma, Mama swooshes over to me. "Hey, kiddo, what do you have to say about that fancy wedding gown of yours?"

"It's fancy, all right."

"You'll need to let me see it on you as soon as things settle down. We need to make sure it fits right. Besides that, I'm dying to see it on you! Where is it, anyway?"

"I have it lying out on the bed at Papoose. Adriana said you had a few adornments to add to it."

"She's right, I do."

I look around the room for Sailor. "Mama, have you seen Sailor since we got off the boat?"

"Oh, I had Benji run him back to the cabin. I didn't want him hounding the guests all night."

"Oh, poor guy. He hates to miss a party. I think I'll go feed him."

"Yeah, well, leave him over there. We had our little reunion already."

I let Danny know I'm sneaking out.

"Wait, I'll come with you."

Neither one of us are used to so much commotion on the island. It's time for a quick breather for both of us. On our way out the back door, Nonna spots me. "Angelina Juliana, is it really you?" My grandma's looking a bit more feeble than when I left Italy. The trip has probably worn her out.

"Nonna!" I give her a big hug—it's the first chance I've had to talk to her alone since the family arrived.

She casts a leery glance at me. "How did you get here? I thought you'd died."

"Died? Why would you think I died?"

"Because you were gone. I knew my Angelina Juliana would never leave me if she were still alive, so I figured you must have died. Is this heaven? Wait—this can't be heaven—your father's here."

"I'm fine, Nonna. I just came back to the island to go to school, remember?"

"School? You left me and all of the saints so you could go to school? Do you have any idea how upset they will be to hear that?"

"They? They who?"

"Saint Francis, Saint Augustine, Saint Christopher …"

"Why would they be upset that I'm going to school?"

"Because you didn't say good-bye. They talk about you all the time, but we all thought you were dead."

How sad that she forgot. "But didn't Mama and Daddy tell you where I was?"

"Of course they did. I figured it was a bunch of nonsense. Your father's always feeding me baloney. Anyway, I'm glad to see you're not dead."

"Me too." I give her a gentle kiss on the cheek. "I'm so happy you've come for the wedding."

"Wedding? Who's getting married?"

Angelo comes over and takes Grandma's arm. "*Angelina Juliana si sta per sposare.*" Angelina Juliana is getting married.

"Oh my stars!" As she's looking at me, a strange sense of clarity appears in her eyes. "I hope it's to that nice Morgan fellow. I always liked that boy." She smiles at Angelo. "*Ci si può sedere?*" Can we sit down?

They hobble off, side by side, toward the porch swing.

Sailor is nowhere in sight when I enter Papoose. I thought he'd be sitting right inside the front door pulling his howling number. I wander down the hall to my room. "Danny! Come quick!"

Danny darts down the hall. We both freeze in place, speechless. Sprawled in the middle of my bed, on top of the once-pure white satin wedding dress, my big, hairy, wet dog is chewing away on a piece of driftwood that he obviously dragged in from the lake on his trip back to Papoose. The lace veil is tangled around the driftwood, looking like a mesh fishing net. "My *gown of all gowns ...*" I whisper. "Mama ... my poor Mama!"

"A. J., are you in here?"

"It's Mama," I gasp. "What do I do?"

"A. J.?" She sees us standing at the bedroom door. "There you are." Both of my grandmothers are following on Mama's heels. "Nonna wants to take a little rest.... Daniel Morgan, you are not supposed to see that gown until your wedding day, young man."

We look at each other, then back at Mama.

"What? What's going on here?" Mama peers in the bedroom.

I watch the blood drain from her face like a thermometer on a cold day. Her eyes zero in on Sailor, who cowers under Mama's glare. "You ... mister ... you just earned a trip back to the dog pound. And if they don't put you down, I will!"

"*Mama!*"

"Don't you Mama me, Angelina, in defense of that sorry mutt. You have no idea what we have gone through to get you the perfect gown—*no idea!* Now look at it! Do you see that—do you see that filthy mess?"

"Yes, Mama, I see it...." I also see the huge snag down the front of the gown, where the driftwood caught on the satin.

Grandma Angelina steps forward. "Listen to me, Angelina, I have an idea."

We look at her. Mama has her *I'm listening* eyebrows raised, accompanied by an obvious air of skepticism.

Grandma turns to me. "Do you remember me telling you about your grandfather and me eloping?"

I nod.

"Your grandfather still wanted my wedding to be special. He bought me a beautiful gown to wear for the ceremony."

At this point, Mama's looking even more skeptical.

"I still have the dress, and it's in perfect condition. I used to dream that one of my granddaughters might wear it for her own wedding. But then Adriana shot up like a bean stalk and I knew she was out of the running. I was going to mention the dress to you, but it seemed you already had your heart set on … that one." She glances over at the tangled heap of satin and lace on the bed. "Would you like to see my dress?"

I notice she's asking me, not Mama. "I would," I answer, without waiting for Mama's approval.

Mama takes a deep breath. "Danny, would you be so good as to escort my daughter and Grandma Angelina over to the mainland to take a look at the dress—but, mind you, you are not allowed to see it until the wedding."

Danny looks at me with a slight smile. "I'd be happy to."

With that, Mama turns and walks out the door.

❧

When we enter the house, Grandma goes to her closet and brings out a plastic hanging bag. She carefully lifts the plastic to reveal a simple ivory-tinted gown: a sleek, formfitting bodice, with delicate organdy sleeves, and a subtle organdy ruffle along the bottom. No poofs or billowing fluff. Just simple and sweet. "Oh, Grandma … I love it," I whisper.

"Try it on," Grandma insists.

I reappear from the dressing room and stand before my grandmother, who is sitting on the bed waiting for me. "Oh … *bella, bella signorina* …" Tears fill her eyes. She goes to her vanity. From a floral hatbox, Grandma lifts a long, gorgeous lace veil with a pleated organdy-and-pearl crown. Our eyes meet. We pause. She knows her dream has come true. "Something old," she says softly, and places it on my head. We both sense the sacredness of this moment. Through tears and sighs, my grandmother's heart is revealed: *Through this granddaughter, my legacy lives. La famiglia è tutto.*

❧

Leaving Grandma's house, it occurs to me that this is the second time Sailor has saved me. With all due respect for Mama's efforts and feelings, alas, I will now be wearing the wedding gown of my dreams.

❧

Returning to the party, I weave my way through the crowd, trying to find Mama. She has Daddy and Mr. Morgan cornered, enlisting them to hunt down the perfect Christmas tree on the island and chop it down first thing in the morning. "It will be the main attraction at the reception, next to the bride, of course. I'd like it to stand tall enough and full enough to hold a few hundred angels. Once you get it hauled in here, I'd like it to go right over—*Angelina!* You're back!" Her eyebrows shoot up, asking the silent question.

"I *love* it. It's over at Papoose if you'd like to see—"

Before I finish, she is heading for the door.

"Just don't let Sailor inside!" I yell after her.

She glances back at me with her *well, obviously* look and bolts out the door.

I rejoin the festivities, now in full swing. With the gown tragedy behind me, I feel like I can finally relax and enjoy the party. I look around at my family and relatives, all together under one roof. Uncle Nick's voice booms out over the crowd, as one might expect from a loud, lovable Greek. I remember a time when I thought him obnoxious and annoying … until he saved Benji's life. I look over at Benji. He's becoming quite the young gentleman. He looks just like Daddy.

The younger cousins are running all over, laughing and giggling with one another. Nonna has Grandma Angelina cornered. She's explaining to her that the first grandbaby will be named after her this time. "If itsa girl, she'll be Juliana Angelina; if itsa boy, he'll be Julio Angelo." Then she tells Grandma Angelina that the coin toss was rigged when they went to flip for my name, and it's not going to happen again. She also tells Grandma Angelina that Saint Francis told her that Danny and I will be having a dozen children.

Beautiful accents, Italian, Greek, and Southern, fill the air, blending together like a symphony. I spot Danny across the room. He glances over at me with that adoring smile—which I will soon be the lucky recipient of for the rest of my life. This is a moment frozen in time. I am one happy bride-to-be.

❦ 20 ❦
Christmas in November

"A little more to the right, Sonny ... oops, too far ... whoa, whoa, whoa. Jack, watch the top, you're scraping the ceiling."

Wandering into Big Chief, I find Mama playing the wedding director. She was up at the crack of dawn dragging Daddy out to the Pitchy Pine Forest in pursuit of the perfect tree. Daddy and Mr. Morgan chopped it down and hauled it to Big Chief at sunrise.

"Okay, Sonny, that's perfect—let's set it up right there."

"Want some help with the ornaments, Mama?" She has her legions of angels strewn around, all ready to descend upon the branches at her command.

"No, thanks, kiddo. This is all for you to enjoy on your special day. You just go paint your toenails red or something and leave the decorating to me."

"Okay. So what are the plans for the rehearsal?"

"We need to leave the island by three, be at the church at four, then we'll all be going to the country club afterward for dinner."

"How many of us will be going?"

"Between us and the Morgans, there will be close to seventy."

"S-eventy? They're *all* in my wedding party?"

"When it comes to our family, nobody wants to feel left out, so yes, they are all in the wedding party."

Only my immediate family and the Morgans are lodging on the island in the three cabins. Uncle Nick and his brood, including all of the Greek relatives and courtesy cousins, are lodging at the Cozy Inn in town. I'm sure there will be stories circulating around Squawkomish for weeks to come.

Mama stands at the base of the tree looking up. "Okay, gentlemen, it's a wrap! Thank you for your sweat and hard work. I'm sure the Morgan women have a nice hearty breakfast waiting for you over at Pocahontas by now."

"Does that mean you want us to leave?" Daddy says.

"It does, indeed. Time for the flight of the angels—now scoot, before one bumps you in the head."

"C'mon, Jack, let's grab the big farm-boy special over at Pocahontas. I hear Southern housewives actually cook for their men, is that true?"

Jack laughs and wisely heads for the door.

Mama saunters over to Daddy and gives him a big, sweet smile. "I'd be happy to cook for you, darlin', so long as you don't mind bein' married to a woman the size of a barn." Mama's faux Southern accent puts mine to shame.

"Stella and her sisters are nowhere near the size of a barn," Daddy replies, smiling back.

"Of course they're not, *sweetheart*. They burn it all off scootin' around their big farm kitchens and runnin' through hay fields to round up their men for chow three times a day. Now, if you'd like to drive a combine on a nine-hundred-acre hay farm in the blisterin'

summer sun, rather than sittin' on your behind on the balcony of
your Tuscan villa, I'd be most happy to scramble you up some eggs.
I'm sure Jack wouldn't mind tradin' places with you."

Daddy gives Mama a big grin and a kiss on the cheek. "Never
mind," he says, and heads out the door after Jack.

❧

"A. J.," Mama says, "speakin' of roundin' people up, would you go
round up your sister for me? Tell her I need her to find some nice
boughs and pinecones in the woods. She can help me make a few
evergreen swags. Oh—and grab one of the boys to go along with her
to do the cutting."

"Yes, ma'am," I answer with my own Southern twang for old
times' sake, and march out the door.

I toddle my way over to Pocahontas, where I know I will find
a bunch of strong, healthy males feasting on the finest homemade
Southern cooking ever to grace these parts. Sure enough, the second
I step foot on the porch, the smell of warm maple syrup and bacon
comes swirling out the door to greet me. Half a dozen strapping big
boys and men are sitting around the big kitchen table laughing and
gorging themselves silly on flapjacks drenched in syrup.

"Excuse me, Jason, my mama wanted me to ask for some help
with cutting tree boughs for her decorations. Would you mind helping when you finish eating?"

Jason looks up while shoveling a forkful of hotcakes into his
mouth. He gulps down half a glass of milk, then says, "Love to."

"Great. I'll be rounding up one of the ladies to show you what to cut. How about if I have you both meet up at Danny's chapel in, say, fifteen minutes?"

"I'll be there with my handsaw."

"Perfect. Thanks."

I whistle my way back over to Papoose. "Oh, Adriana, where are you?"

Adriana steps out of the bathroom with a green mud mask covering her entire face. "Okay, green is not a good color for you, glamour girl."

"Need something?" she asks, barely able to move her lips.

"I do. Rather Mama does. She wants you to pick out some nice evergreen boughs from the Pitchy Pines, then help her make up some swags for the reception hall. One of the guys will meet you by the chapel in about ten minutes to cut them for you."

"Ten minutes?" she mutters. "But this is supposed to stay on for thirty minutes. Maybe I'll just go like this and rinse it off afterwards."

"Um, you know, I wouldn't. I mean, being out there in the woods and all, you might end up with all kinds of dirt and pine needles sticking to it. I've heard those masks can be very drying to the skin if left on too long."

She rolls her eyes at me. "You'd better be worth all this," she says, and goes to wash it off.

Whew!

Five minutes later, Adriana is on her way out the door, glowing complexion and all. I know better than to try and follow her this time. Some things are just better left up to fate. Of course, I may have to pass that way shortly to discuss a few wedding details with

Danny. By the way, where is Danny? I haven't seen him all morning. He wasn't at breakfast with the rest of the guys.

𝒩₊

"Mama, have you seen Danny anywhere?"

Mama's hanging her second legion of angels from a ladder near the top of the tree. Four more boxes to go.

"Come to think of it, I have not seen Danny since last night. Maybe he changed his mind."

Real funny. "Thanks." His own mama will know where he is. I head into the kitchen where the great wedding cook-off is in full swing. Danny's Aunt Charlotte and Aunt Rebecca are cutting and chopping away. "Anyone here seen Danny?"

"Not lately," Aunt Charlotte says. "Try his mama, she's still workin' on breakfast cleanup back at her cabin. You must be gettin' pretty excited 'bout now, I'd imagine."

I imagine I would be if I knew I still had someone to marry. On my way to Pocahontas, I detect Adriana's voice in the forest.

"No wonder she left you," she laughs, "you can't even use a handsaw without hurting yourself. Come on, I'll fix you up back at Papoose."

Jason walks into view holding his hand up with Adriana's scarf wrapped around it. "Hey," I yell over, "you okay?"

"He's okay," Adriana answers for him. "He used the handsaw a bit too literally, but I think he'll live."

"Has anyone seen Danny?" I ask.

"Nope. Not out here, anyway," Jason says.

Adriana takes hold of Jason's arm, trying to keep it elevated while they walk toward the cabin. She glances back at me. "Danny probably realized this was his last chance to escape."

I love my family.

Approaching the cabin, I hear the delightful sound of little Southern girls playing in the woods. "It's the bride, it's the bride!" one of the girls squeals, and they all run behind a tree to spy on me.

"Have any of you seen the groom?" I yell to them.

"Nope, haven't seen him *anywhere!*" one of them yells back.

Danny's mama is shaking out a rug on the front porch when she spots me coming through the woods. "Mrs. Morgan, have you seen Danny anywhere?"

"No, come to think of it, I haven't seen him since last night. Maybe he and J. R. got up early this morning to do some fishin'."

That's it. That's got to be it. I feel somewhat relieved and run down to Juniper beach to look for the skiff. I finally spot J. R. with his fishing pole a good way out. He's alone. Peering out at the lake, I spot the tugboat heading out for an afternoon voyage to Squawkomish. I know Danny's not on it this time. His Uncle Tracy and my Uncle Nick have really hit it off together since they met each other. Mama talked them both into taking a bunch of the little guys to town to keep them out of the women's hair while they cook and set up for the reception. I can only imagine what those two uncles will come up with for kicks.

❦

A few hours later, the tug returns and pulls up to the dock at Papoose, obeying Mama's orders to keep all young males on this side of the island. The second the boat docks, a herd of rowdy boys hop off and come charging up the ramp past me. "How was town?" I ask as they fly by.

"Oh, A. J.," Adonis announces, "Uncle Tracy is crazy!" He skids to a halt long enough to fill me in. "They took us all to Big Daddy Burger for lunch. Uncle Nick stayed with all of the kids and sent Uncle Tracy and me up to the counter to order for everyone. For Uncle Nick, he ordered the Big Daddy double cheeseburger special. But then he said, 'Hold the mayo, hold the onions, hold the cheese, hold the meat, hold the fries. I'd like a side of ketchup—in a little paper cup, please. Oh, and I'd like a Coke with that.' Then he gave them Uncle Nick's last name to announce in the intercom when it was ready, and he pronounced Sophronia *Sefferonio*. So when they called his name over the speaker, Uncle Nick went to get his order and came back with only pickles on a bun, a side of ketchup, and a Coke. And he ate it! It was the funniest thing I've ever seen! We were laughing so hard we had everyone in the whole place looking at us!"

Oh boy, Uncle Nick has just met his match.

Tromping up the front steps of Papoose, I hear hysterical laughter inside. *Adriana and Jason. My plan must be working.* I push open the screen door to find the two of them sitting on the couch doubled over in laughter. Jason's hand is all bandaged up, and he's obviously free from pain. Adriana looks up at me and laughs even harder. After repeated attempts to catch her breath, she finally blurts out, "You know, A. J., I have this sudden urge to give up my modeling career so

I can run around a big farm kitchen in a muumuu and fry up some chicken-n-biscuits!" They both burst into sidesplitting laughter.

My eyes fall on my wedding diary lying open on the coffee table in front of them. "Adriana, you should know better than anyone that it's not nice to read other people's journals."

"I learned that from you, little sis. And don't even try to tell me that you didn't read every word of my Indian Island diaries."

"That was different—we were kids."

"Well, if you're going to write a novel about me, I'd at least like to know how it ends."

"Hey, I didn't write anything that wasn't in your best interest. I think the farm life might do you some good. Think about it, Adriana—you've spent the majority of your adult life in the Milan rat race, putting up with rodents like Zahara."

Adriana looks at Jason. "She has a point there. What do you say, buddy, think we should give it a go?"

Jason looks back and smiles. "I'm game if you are."

Adriana is obviously joking, but something in Jason eyes leaves room for question. I'm not giving up this easily.

The phone rings—a nice diversion from the embarrassment of having my personal journal exposed. Maybe it's Danny, calling from Mexico to explain why he can't go through with this. "Hello?"

"A. J.?" A small voice on the other end barely comes through. "Yes?"

"It's me, Stormy. My dad …" She sobs. "… He died."

I sink onto the couch. "Oh, Stormy. When?"

"Last week. I called you, but …"

"Oh, I'm *so sorry*—I've been so busy, and …"

"It's only me and my mom now. Nobody else. We're all alone."

"Where are you?"

"At my neighbor's house. The neighbor lady's watching me while my mom's at work."

"Listen, Stormy. How would you like to be in my wedding tomorrow?"

"Your wedding? To Danny?"

"That's the one." *I hope, anyway.*

"For real?"

"For real. I'll call your mom and make sure it's okay." She gives me her mom's work number and the number at her neighbor's. "Okay, I'll call you right back." What's one more bridesmaid added to Mama's lineup of *bellas?*

After a sad chat with Stormy's mom, I ring Stormy back. "Okay, kiddo, I'm coming to get you!"

❧

"What do you mean we're adding another bridesmaid?" Mama bellows. "I already have a dozen of them and only a dozen dresses."

"Mama, this little girl just lost her father, she has no brothers or sisters, no friends, nobody."

"I don't care if she's the president's daughter, A. J., there is no way we can add her this late in the game! I have nothing for her to wear!"

"Mama, I don't care if she has to wear the matching tablecloth, I want her in my wedding. Show me one of the dresses and I'll take her shopping for something similar."

"Oh, Angelina, you are bound and determined to give me heart failure before this is over, aren't you?"

Wait until you find out that my groom ran away and the whole thing is off.

"Just go get the kid and bring her back here. I'll have to figure out what to do with her." Mama has that look of resolve in her eyes. She'll find a way to make it work.

"If Danny shows up while I'm gone, tell him to stick around until I return, will you?"

✵

An hour later Stormy and I return to the island. I introduce Stormy to everyone we run into, but the young girls her age are nowhere in sight. "Where are all of my little bridesmaids?" I ask Adriana.

"Mama's holding them hostage over at Big Chief. She's orchestrating the dress rehearsal to make sure all of their dresses fit."

"Great, we're just in time."

Stormy and I arrive at Big Chief to find twelve girls, ranging from three to five feet tall, standing in a perfect line in perfect height formation. We have four Southern belles, three Italian *bellas,* and five Greek goddesses, all donned in gold satin gowns matching the angels on the Christmas tree. We will soon be adding one freckle-faced redhead to the lineup. We also have two tiny cherubs—Zara and Olympia, my little Greek flower girls. Cousin Stacie, Adriana, and I are all exempt from having to wear our dresses for the rehearsal. Mama already cleared us for our fittings.

"You must be Stormy," Mama says, whisking her off and placing her right smack in the middle of the others. "Don't you worry, angel, we'll get you all wrapped up in gold in no time. Grandma Angelina will be right over to measure you for your new dress."

I pull Mama aside. "What are you making it out of?"

"Well, your comment about wearing the tablecloth …"

"You didn't …"

"I did. Just so happens I have one spare gold tablecloth and a seamstress for a mother-in-law."

I've wondered all my life if there will ever come a time when my mother is stumped over anything. *Anything!*

"Well then, I guess I'm leaving Stormy in your hands for now. Has anyone seen Danny?" I address the crowd, expecting that someone may have seen him.

Silence.

"Okay then, I'm off for now."

"Don't go far, we're leaving for the rehearsal in about an hour."

Great. I hope I'm not going alone. Come to think of it, he never did officially ask me to marry him, did he?

🦌

Wandering out of Big Chief, I hear some loud banging inside of the boat shed. Flying down to the dock as fast as my legs can carry me, I call out for my hopefully-husband-to-be. "Danny! *Danny Morgan,* are you in there?"

After a slight rustle, Danny comes strolling out as though this were just any ordinary day in history. "Hey there, cute stuff. How's my bride?"

"Don't you *cute stuff* me, Danny Jackson Morgan. *Your bride* has been looking for you all day."

"Huh?" Danny looks completely miffed. "I've just been workin' in here."

Oh. I guess to a guy that would be a normal thing to do up until the minute he has to show up at the church. *I can get over this. Deep breath, count to three.* "Um, never mind. Just thought I'd let you know it's probably about time to get ready to go to the rehearsal."

Danny comes over, eyes me funny, and wraps his arms around me. "You're ticked, aren't you?"

"No," I reply, avoiding his eyes at all costs.

He smiles and zeros in on me, forcing me to look at him. "Yeah, I think you are."

I grit my teeth. "Am *not.*"

"Are too." Now he's laughing.

"Okay, fine. You were nowhere to be found all day, so I just assumed that maybe you'd changed your mind and hopped a train to Mexico."

"You and your wild imagination. How can you live with yourself when it's in overdrive like that?"

"I can't," I confess. "It's pretty miserable sometimes."

"I guess." He looks back toward the boat shed. "Let me put a few things away, then I'll get cleaned up and be ready to go."

"Okay. Promise you're coming?"

"Promise." He gives me a smile and a sweet kiss to go on.

21
Paper-Doll Bride

Approaching the cabin, I suddenly realize I haven't even thought about what to wear for the rehearsal. Adriana greets me at the screen door and pulls me into Papoose. Inside, thirteen little bridesmaids, each holding a roll of toilet paper, have been instructed to turn me into a paper-doll bride. Their goal is to make my entire gown and veil out of nothing but TP.

I am turned, twisted, twirled, wound, and bound in a mile of white tissue. Then they put the finishing touches of toilet-paper bows all over my "gown." After the gown, they go to work on the veil. Streamer after streamer of tissue is added and tucked into my paper halo.

When the final embellishments are added, I'm paraded in front of the full-length mirror, where I'm pleasantly surprised at the reflection of such an exquisite piece of work. I am seriously impressed with how I look in thirteen rolls of toilet paper; billows of ribbons, streamers, and bows. My train alone probably took up three rolls; it cascades clear down the hall, where it culminates in another room. I think once they tucked the opened end of the rolls into my paper waistband, the rolls were set free and will continue to unwind wherever I go. I guess this takes care of the what-to-wear issue. There will probably be a trail of toilet paper from here to the church, to the restaurant, and back to the island by the end of the night.

We're all water-taxied to the mainland on the tug to meet up with the rest of the so-called wedding party. After talking to a few of the kids, I'm convinced of one thing: This town is sure to never forget Uncle Nick and Uncle Tracy. Nonna has announced she will make this trip to the church only once and has opted to come to the wedding rather than the rehearsal, lessening the chances for a family crisis tonight, anyway. Angelo agreed to keep her company on the island. They're planning to watch one of Grandma's favorite movies together: *Arsenic and Old Lace*. She said something about getting some new ideas for dealing with Daddy.

We are a sight to behold, all piling onto the big bus together. Between the bridesmaids in golden gowns and the guys wearing black tuxes with white shirts, we look like a busload of angels and penguins. I was not expecting to do a complete dress rehearsal tonight, but with Mama in charge, this is just the way it is.

"Hey, A. J.," Mama shouts, as we pull up to the church, "what's the deal with the funny steeple—isn't this what you kids used to call the Ice Cream Cone Church? I never realized it was a Catholic church before."

"That's no Catholic church, Sophia," Uncle Nick roars. "That's as Orthodox as any Orthodox church I've ever laid eyes on."

Here we go.

"Nick, what in the name of Pete are you talking about? This happens to be Apache Falls, America, not Constantinople. It was enough of a fluke that you ever found an Orthodox church in Spokane when you lived here, but you're nuts if you think there's one out here in the middle of nowhere."

A little voice from the back of the bus pipes up. "Cousin A. J. said it's a little mission church to America that a Greek priest started when his family migrated years ago, Auntie Sophia."

Mama's eyes dart to my eight-year-old cousin, Adonis, then back to me.

"It's true, Mama. This is a Greek Orthodox church. It's a long story, but for the sake of time, I think we'd better go in, don't you?"

Mama struggles to collect her wits about her. "All right, troops, everybody off the bus and into the ... sanctuary." She shoots me a stern look. "That *is* what it's called, isn't it?"

"Yes, it's a sanctuary. A *quiet, holy* sanctuary." *Hint, hint.*

Mama walks past me mumbling something about how her mother is not going to take all of this very well tomorrow.

"She probably won't notice the difference between this and the Catholic church, Mama, if you don't point it out to her."

"My mother, not notice? She knows every Catholic saint, song, and tradition. You won't fool her for long."

Hopefully, between her hearing loss and poor eyesight, we can get through the ceremony without incident.

Mama raises her chin with an air of resolve and leads the pack into the sanctuary. Just entering the doors brings a degree of calm to my spirit ... until Mama enters. She pushes through the double doors, yelling, "Okay, places, everyone!" like we're shooting a movie on a Hollywood set. Everyone scatters and falls into their pre-assigned line, in order of height.

"Excuse me," Mama says, "but where are the pews?"

Uncle Nick bursts out laughing. "Did you hear Sophia? She wants to know where the pews are."

The Greek relatives have another good roar at Mama's expense. Mama is not amused. Uncle Nick puts his arm around her. "We're just having some fun, Sophie. Actually, we're honored that these two are marrying in the Orthodox Church. But not all churches have pews, Sophie. We usually stand in our churches."

"Well, welcome to America—now, where are the chairs?"

"The chairs will be delivered in the morning, Mama."

"Good. Glad to hear it," she states. Without missing a beat, she removes Uncle Nick's arm from her shoulder and continues to direct the show.

I shoot a glance over at Danny, who wipes his brow in relief. I nod in agreement.

Mama snaps into action. "Dino, go find the priest, will you, and let him know we're here. A. J., wait in the back, bridesmaids up front, flower girls in the back, best man and groom over here, everyone else sit down. Or stand up. Whatever the case may be."

I'm watching Stormy mentally mark her spot in the front of the sanctuary, and can't help smiling. She is all sparkle and shine in her shimmery gold tablecloth, and couldn't look happier. I can't imagine being an only child. She probably won't be able to either, after spending a weekend with us. The other girls are all crazy about Stormy's long, wild red hair and have taken her in as one of our own.

"All right, I need my bride and father of the bride. Let's have you two scoot down the aisle together."

"What aisle, Sophie?" Uncle Nick's at it again.

"The aisle that's going to be here when my chairs show up!"

Daddy takes my arm and walks me down the *imaginary* aisle toward Danny, who is waiting at the front of the sanctuary for me. He looks so handsome standing there. As I walk toward him, his eyes reassure me that we are going through all of this for a good cause. Each other. By tomorrow night we'll *hopefully* be able to look back and know that it was worth all of the chaos.

Father Demetrios appears in the entrance of the sanctuary, looks around, and goes over to Mama. He whispers something that drains the color out of her face.

"All right, everyone, cut! Father Demetrios is going to explain how this ceremony will go." Mama steps aside, clearly ruffled about handing over the reins, yet trying to contain herself.

"May I have the bride and groom up front, please?" Father Demetrios says calmly.

Everyone else wanders over to the benches along the walls to take a seat—except for Mama, who stands right by Father Demetrios, watching him with an eagle eye. He leads us to a table in the front of the sanctuary. There are two crowns and two candles placed in the middle. Father Demetrios explains the order of the ceremony ahead: the betrothal with the rings, the lighting of the candles, the joining of right hands, the crowning, the common cup, the walk, and the blessing. Then he walks us through each of these traditions, all very different from the "I do's" of Western wedding vows.

I can tell Mama's busting at the seams to add a few of her own touches, but fortunately, she has the courtesy to just sit tight and watch. Or maybe I should say, *stand tight* and watch. It's tough to buck two thousand years of tradition. With a loud sigh, she finally sits down on a bench and crosses her arms over her chest. She looks relieved when Father Demetrios says, "That's all, as far as the ceremony goes."

"What about the 'you may now kiss your bride' part?" Danny asks.

"I'll let you follow up with that tomorrow at the wedding, but for now, if you'll please excuse me, I need to attend to another appointment."

As soon as the Father walks out, Danny pulls me over. "I think we need to rehearse this part," he says, and attempts a trial run of the wedding kiss.

"Cut!" Mama calls from the sidelines, reassuming her director role. "Hold up there, mister. It's bad luck for the bride and groom to kiss the night before the wedding."

Danny reluctantly drops his hands to his sides. I get the feeling I'm not the only one that the *wedding coordinator* is beginning to get to lately. It's hard to feel like you're in charge of anything with Mama around. Danny's not used to having someone else call the shots for him.

❧

Down the hall in the ladies' room, Mama's busy changing her legion of angels in gowns back into little girls in jeans while I'm busy trying to unravel a dozen rolls of toilet tissue from my body.

"Ah-ah-acht, Angelina, you keep that on for the rehearsal dinner so everyone knows who the bride is."

I am *this close* to just ripping it all to shreds right here in front

of Mama and running off to elope on some deserted island in the
South Seas.

❧

Mimicking my mother under my breath, I march my way back down
the hall. Suddenly, out of nowhere, a hand reaches out and grabs me,
yanking me into a dark closet! On the verge of screaming, I realize it's
Danny. "S-h-h-h!" He slams the door behind me. In the pitch-dark,
a small velvet box is pressed into my hand. "A. J. Degulio," he says in
his deep Southern voice, "I am hopelessly and crazy in love with you
and will be till the day I die. Will you marry me?"

I am so surprised I can't believe it! He did it—he really did it!
I thought maybe he was holding out on me until the rehearsal dinner—and was gonna ask me in front of everyone. This is so much
more romantic! I close my hand around the tiny box and start to cry.
It's so perfect … I'm speechless.

"A. J.?"

"… Yes," I sob.

"Um … is that a yes as in yes, you will marry me?"

"*Yes,* as in yes, I will marry you, Danny Jackson Morgan!"

Sigh of relief. "With all due respect for your mama, I'm not a
superstitious man and don't believe in bad luck." He takes me in his
arms and kisses me for the last time as A. J. Degulio.

❧ 22 ❧
Thanks for the memories

The Squawkomish Golf and Country Club is the one and only place in town large enough to accommodate our wedding party. Mama reserved the grand banquet room that overlooks the water fountain and golf course. Being that this is November and freezing out, we had no problem getting the place reserved on short notice. It's not a real hoppin' place this time of the year. It's not a real hoppin' place in the summer either, but more so than during the winter.

Oohs and *ahhs* ring out as we enter the banquet room. The whole place is lit up in tiny white twinkle lights. "It's the least they could do," Mama says, "after they refused to put up a Christmas tree and deck the halls, as I'd *requested.*" She was also annoyed that they couldn't put us all at one table, as we're accustomed to in our Italian villa, with our mile-long table. They said tables don't come that size in these parts.

Instead, we're split up among six big round tables that seat up to a dozen apiece. I've decided I'll be the roaming toilet-paper bride and make my way from table to table throughout the night—kind of like a progressive dinner—one course at each table. That way I'll get a chance to visit with everyone here—after all, they did come all this way just to celebrate with us. I'm thinking I'd really like to start at the kids' table.

Just as I'm about to sit down, Mama starts flagging us down from her table by the front window. "Angelina, you and Danny are sitting over here!" Danny pulls me back from the kids' table and reroutes us to Mama's table marked *Reserved*. Looks like we'll be joining my folks, Danny's folks, my Grandma Angelina, Danny's Grandma Morgan, and his ninety-four-year-old Great-Aunt Beulah.

Once we're all seated, Mama clangs her wine glass to get everyone's attention. "Welcome, family! We are so honored to have you all here to celebrate with us for this very special occasion—and from all three corners of the globe! Our entrée for tonight is plank salmon with risotto, which will be served shortly. Please join us in giving thanks." She nudges Daddy, who takes her cue and asks a blessing over the dinner, the evening ahead, and our wedding.

Halfway through my salad, Mama starts telling stories about when I was little. "A. J. was the silliest little kid." She turns to me. "Tell everyone about that time your goldfish died on Easter."

"That's okay, Mama, it wasn't really that interesting."

"So, anyway," Mama plows right into it, "A. J. leaves her gold-fish floating belly up while we go to Mass on Easter Sunday, and she writes on the little donation envelope, "Dear God, since Jesus rose on Easter, would You please let Goldie rise from the dead too?" She breaks out laughing. "When we got home that fish was still deader than a doornail, but A. J. wanted to wait until midnight before she'd flush him down the toilet … just in case.…"

I roll my eyes. *Great story, Mama—right when everyone's about to eat fish.* By the third "little A. J. story," I give Danny an SOS nudge. Save our sanity.

He picks up the hint. "Excuse us, please; we'd like a chance to visit with some of the other guests, if y'all wouldn't mind."

"Oh, sure, you go on." Mama turns back to her audience. "… so, I look in her room, and darned if A. J. doesn't have every pet from the entire neighborhood in her bedroom." She turns around as we're walking away. "Don't let A. J. sign up for any of those save-the-animals foundations, Danny. They sent me so many solicitations for funds, it took drastic measures to get off of their mailing lists."

"What'd you do?" Danny asks.

Here it comes.…

"*Well,* every time one of those little collection envelopes showed up with *return postage paid* stamped on the front, I just took a big box, filled it full of bricks, taped that postage-paid envelope on the front of the box, and shipped it back to them. They took me off their lists real fast."

I take hold of Danny's hand and pull him away before she can go any further. Little does Mama know, I just joined a trust that supports an elephant orphanage in Africa that rescues orphaned baby elephants. They have matriarch mama elephants to help care for the babies. The babies are called *ellies.* How can anyone say no to that?

Danny and I begin making our rounds. We have the Greek section with Uncle Nick, his three brothers, two sisters, and their spouses. We also have a table with the extended Greek relatives and courtesy cousins. We have the Southern section with Danny's four aunts and their husbands. And then there's the kids' section. This is where Jason and Adriana ended up, and I *will* be watching—closely.

While we're visiting with Cousin Stacie, rumblings of the Greek anthem start up at Uncle Nick's table. Following their lead, Dino and

Benji launch into *Il Canto degli Italiani,* the Song of the Italians. Not to be outdone by a few Greeks and Italians, Danny's nieces and nephews, along with Stormy, join Uncle Tracy in "The Star-Spangled Banner."

It sounds like an international music competition. As voices grow louder, it quickly becomes the International Music Wars. It's hard to tell who's winning, until Uncle Nick and Uncle Tracy go head-to-head. After a painful couple of stanzas sung in two different languages simultaneously, Uncle Nick finally clinches it for the Greek section with his booming Hercules tenor.

Danny and I work our way around to the little kids' table in time for dessert. Baked Alaska. My favorite.

"Speaking of baked Alaska, the fountain down on the patio is frozen." Dino grins. "You up for a little ice skating, brother Benji?"

Within minutes, all of the kids are sliding around the frozen fountain. One of them finds the master switch and flips on the power. All of the fountain lights burst into color. Due to the cold, the pump doesn't work—until one of the kids breaks through the ice. Fortunately, the water is only a foot deep. The new game is to break all of the ice so the pump can work. I'm enjoying watching all of this from our window above the fountain, over a cup of hot coffee. Luckily for them, Mama has her back to the window and is too engaged telling embarrassing stories to notice the chaos developing outside.

Uncle Nick, Nicky Jr., and J. R. suddenly get up and head outside. It's probably not a bad idea to have a little adult supervision out on the patio.

"Woo-hoo!" Cheers ring out from the kids below. The fountain has sprung to life amid the colorful lights, with great pillars of water shooting straight up in the air. Then Uncle Nick, Benji, Nicky Jr., and J. R. dart out onto the patio driving golf carts and start racing each other around the fountain. We have the winter ice follies going on below, and all Mama can say is, "You know, one winter, A. J. had the whole neighborhood climbing up on the roof of our house for a snowball fight...."

Danny asks if I'd mind if he spends some time with his grandma and great-aunt.

"Not at all, I'll be fine."

Aunt Beulah is very hard of hearing, so this could take awhile. I suddenly have an urge to go play in the fountain and race golf carts. I whisk off down the staircase and out to the patio in my paper dress with toilet-paper streamers flowing behind me. "J. R.! Take me for a spin!" I yell after him. He turns his cart around and comes screeching to a halt in front of me. "Your carriage awaits you." I hop in, and away we fly—five laps around the fountain, laughing hysterically.

Dino and Benji are up for the next race, so I climb in with Dino. Suddenly a light flashes on Benji's cart and a security guard is in full pursuit. Both golf carts shoot off toward the fairway in a big hurry. When we hit the greens, Benji hops out and takes off running. Dino hops out too, but realizing that the security guard is right behind us, he points toward Benji and yells, "Hey, that kid tried to steal my father's golf cart!" Never mind that he and Benji look identical and are dressed identically. We watch Benji hightail it over the greens and disappear somewhere beyond the eighteenth hole. "Maybe you can help us get that cart back to the clubhouse, sir," Dino suggests.

"Sure thing," the guard answers, and hops into Benji's cart.

While we were gone, Uncle Nick snuck his cart back to its parking slot. Once the other two carts are parked safely back where they belong, the security guard departs, along with the keys to all of the carts. It's another fifteen minutes before Benji is sighted sneaking back down the fairway.

Once the twins are reunited, I round them up for a Kodak moment. "Now that the race cars have been impounded, why don't you two climb to the top of the fountain and pose as statues? I'd like a snapshot for my wedding album. It would go nicely with my photos of the golf cart races."

Dino and Benji agree to be fountain statues as long as we turn the fountain off. After flipping the switch off, they scale to the top of the fountain and strike a pose as Apollo and Hercules, facing opposite directions. Right as I'm snapping my photo, someone flips on the master switch and Dino and Benji light up in full color with water shooting out from under them. That finally got Mama to stop with the A. J. Story Hour.

"Dino and Benji!" Mama comes storming out on the balcony. "You two get your soggy behinds down off of that fountain this instant! For the love of Pete, the last thing we need right now is another trip to the emergency room!" Mama looks at me and notices the camera in my hand. "What on earth are you thinking by encouraging your brothers to do something so idiotic?"

I try to explain that I just wanted a photo of my rehearsal dinner for my wedding album.

"Well, why don't you just point that camera over here and take a picture of me having a heart attack while you're at it?"

I get the feeling that seeing Benji up on the fountain triggered some bad memories for Mama. Benji's fall from the villa was enough to last her for a lifetime. Now it looks like she's ready to call it a night. She's starting to herd all of the kids out toward the bus—probably telling them stories about when I was their age.

🪶

Sailor runs to greet me the instant I step foot back on the dock at Indian Island. I'm in dire need of a long, cool walk on Juniper Beach with my dog.

"A. J.," Mama says, "come on up to the cabin—I need to try that wedding gown on you one more time. Oh, we also need to come up with something old, something new, something borrowed, and something blue...."

"*No!*" I yell.

Mama's head jerks around. "*Excuse me?*"

I plant my feet firmly on the dock. Right in front of everyone unloading from the tug, I rip my toilet-paper dress to pieces, tossing the shreds into the lake as I go. "I said, no! No, I do *not* need to try on my gown *again,* it's fine the way it is. No, I don't care about something old, blue, borrowed, or stolen! I just want to get *married* and that is *all I want!* That is, of course, if Danny still wants to *marry* me, after hearing all about what a *weird* kid I was, *thank you very much!*" I storm off of the dock, with Sailor at my heels, and head for Juniper Beach.

🪶

After a good, long cry on my beach, one question comes to mind: *What have you just done, you idiot?*

It has not escaped me that Danny hasn't come looking for me. Our wedding eve was probably not the best time to allow my emotions to get the better of me. Maybe Danny's decided he doesn't like the real me, which is too bad, because I don't particularly like myself much right now either.

Sifting sand between my toes, I begin to wonder, *Am I really mature enough to be getting married? Will I act this way with Danny when he gets on my nerves?* Amid the rustle in the trees, I hear the sound of footsteps. Expecting to see Danny, I'm surprised when Daddy emerges instead.

Just looking at him starts me crying all over again. He sits down and pulls me to his side.

"Hey, little fig, it's going to be okay," he says in his soothing way.

"I'm an idiot," I tell him. "But I'm so mad at Mama. Why is she acting like this? Why is she making me so crazy?"

Daddy just holds me.

"I don't understand what her problem is. Besides telling everyone embarrassing stories about me, she has been so bossy ever since she got here. Has she gone nuts or what? She's not the same, Daddy. Did something happen to her that I don't know about?"

Daddy sighs. "Before you're too hard on your mother, A. J., you have to remember there are two sides to the picture here. There is more for her to deal with right now than you could possibly understand."

"Like what?" I wipe my face with my sleeve and sit up.

"Well, to begin with, it wasn't easy for your mother to say good-bye when you left Italy. She's had to say good-bye to both of her girls—Adriana is traveling all over, you're in a different country. That is hard enough on a mother. As soon as she was adjusting to all of that, she learned that her baby girl is getting married. Granted, to a very nice young man, but *married*, A. J., at age eighteen. That's more than just moving away from home. That's good-bye. You know how much your mother loves you, don't you?"

"Yeah."

"Don't you think she wants to make this the most wonderful celebration she's ever thrown for anyone?"

"Yeah, I guess."

"You have no idea what it takes to pull off a wedding in one month. Picture what that was like for her when you pushed the wedding date up—after she had already printed the invitations. Your mother wants everything perfect for you. That's pretty hard to do in such a short period of time. From *Italy*, no less. Not to mention Sailor ruining the wedding gown. And of course there's her mother, your Nonna, to deal with—need I say more?"

I shake my head.

"As far as the childhood stories … maybe that's her way of reminiscing about the child she feels she's losing.…"

My tears start to fall again, but this time they're for my mama instead of for myself. I feel horrible. "I must have made her feel awful."

"She understands, A. J. She knows when one of her kids has hit the wall. I'm sure she feels bad for you, too."

"What about … Danny? Do you think he'll still want to marry me after all of that?"

Daddy smiles. "I'm pretty sure he still wants to marry you."

"How do you know that? He didn't even try to find me when he knew I was going to Juniper Beach."

"That's because we were having a nice talk ourselves. He knows I'm with you."

"What were you talking to him about?"

"Oh, just a little bit of everything. I tried to help him understand where his new mother-in-law is coming from so he wouldn't feel put off by her. And I didn't need to explain where you're coming from—he already knows."

"He does?"

"Danny knows you pretty well. I have to admit, you two are a lot alike. He struggles the same way you do when surrounded by all of the company and chaos. I'd say you're both loners at heart. I told him I thought his plans for the two of you to get away for a few days after the wedding is a good idea."

"He told you? Do you think Mama will understand?"

"She'll be fine. We'll all have plenty of company while you're away. You just need to go have some fun and unwind together."

"Should I go talk to Mama?"

Daddy gives me a gentle hug. "How about if I let her know you're okay, and you can both get a good night's rest. Besides, I think there's a young man who's anxious to see you. I told him to head down here after I talked to you—figured you might like to see him before your wedding day."

"I love you, Daddy." I give him a big hug.

"I love you too, *ficcucia*."

※

A short while after Daddy leaves, I see Danny's silhouette coming down the beach. He throws a stick for Sailor, then sits down beside me. Without a word, he just holds me. We spend our wedding eve stargazing in peaceful silence. Two loners, together. The sky turns from twilight to midnight blue, then all the way to pitch-black. "Still want to marry me?" I whisper.

He tightens his arms around me. "Yeah," he whispers back. "I do."

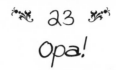

23
Opa!

I have never seen a more beautiful chapel for a wedding: the soft glow of candlelight through red glass vases, a sense of awe and mystery throughout the sanctuary. Simple and cozy, yet sacred and holy. I'm surrounded by the love of my entire family here and the Heavenly Family above, and it's everything I have ever dreamed of for my wedding.

"In the name of the Father, and the Son, and the Holy Spirit." Father Demetrios begins by blessing our rings. He makes the sign of the cross over our heads. "The servant of God is betrothed to the maid of God...."

"Christos Anesti!" A loud cry suddenly cuts into our sacred ceremony. *"Christos Anesti!"*

Nonna?

All eyes turn to Grandma. *"Christos Anesti! Christos Anesti!"* she yells again.

"What is she saying?" Mama asks.

"Christ is risen!" the Greeks all reply. And with that, my wedding ceremony comes to a screeching halt.

Grandma stands up and lifts her hands toward heaven. "My mother," she says, with tears streaming down her face. "My mother brought me to the Greek church for *Pascha*...."

"*Pascha,* that's Easter," Uncle Nick announces.

"I was very small. My mother carried me to the Greek church for *Pascha.* My father wouldn't go. His family was Italian. They didn't like Mama. They didn't like that she was ... Greek...."

"*Greek?*" My mama stands up. "Are you saying you're *half* Greek? Dear Lord, that means *I'm* Greek!"

"Well, if you're part Greek, Mama, then so am I!" I'm in shock. I am a blond Greek-Italian.

"Oh my gosh!" Adriana yells. "That means all of us are part Greek!"

Daddy looks at us as though he just found out he has a new family.

"That means my children are *more* than half Greek!" Aunt Genevieve yells. "Why didn't you tell us this before, Mother? I've had to keep Nick's Greek heritage a secret all this time."

"Oh, I knew Nick was Greek all along." Nonna flicks her hand at Genevieve. "I didn't want your grandfather to know because I never told him I was Greek. I didn't know if he would marry me if he knew. We lived in Italy, so I told everyone I was Italian. But being here in this church," Grandma looks around in awe, "I remember. I remember Mama...." With that, Grandma starts to sing the entire Pascha hymn: "*Christos Anesti ...*" And all of the Greeks—who already knew that they were Greek—join in.

"Excuse me," Danny says, looking somewhat concerned, "but are we still getting married?"

"Does it matter to you that I'm part Greek?" I ask him.

"Greek is good, not a problem. I can go with Greek." Danny looks over at the priest. "Um, Father, can we move forward here?"

Father Demetrios looks to my mama.

"Mama?" I say. "Can we ... get married now?"

"Oh. Right. The wedding. Well, I guess if no one has any further surprises or objections about this Greek-Italian bride and her Southern groom ...?"

"*Opa!*" Nonna yells.

Everyone cheers back, "*Opa!*" As the echo subsides, Mama looks at Father Demetrios and nods.

*

"The servant of God is betrothed to the maid of God in the name of the Father, of the Son, and of the Holy Spirit." We exchange our rings. Danny's wearing his grandfather's gold ring and had a matching band made for me. It's perfect.

After lighting our candles, Father Demetrios joins our right hands together to unite us as one. He places a floral crown on each of our heads, which means that we are the king and queen of our home, serving God together. I breathe a silent prayer of thanks that God is letting us serve Him *together.* I ask Him to help us to pass along the legacy of our Christian faith to those coming after us.

We each take a sip of wine from the common cup to remember Jesus turning the water to wine at the wedding in Cana. Father Demetrios says that, from this moment on, we will share everything in life; our joys will be doubled and our sorrows halved because they'll be shared. I like that math.

Danny and I are led in a circle around the table—taking our first steps as husband and wife. We're married.

I can hear all the women in my family crying, which, of course, brings on my own tears. Family trait. We have to either laugh or cry at every event.

Father Demetrios gives each of us a blessing. And now, Danny stands before me as my husband. Gazing at me with those blue, blue eyes, he kisses me tenderly. I close my eyes and remember the first time I ever heard him say my name. My heart has longed for him ever since.

Emerging from the church as husband and wife we are greeted with shouts, cheers ... and rice. Trying to make our way down the front steps to the bus is like trying to navigate our way through a whiteout. When we've finally moved through the rice storm, we're engulfed by hugs and kisses from every side. I emerge a disheveled bride with a crooked crown, feeling like an angel who missed her landing.

The bus has so many angels and balloons attached to it I'm surprised it's not floating above the ground.

The moment I climb on board, I'm aware that the party has already begun. Danny and I are given the seat of honor—the big bench seat in the back of the bus—so everyone can turn around and see our happy faces all the way back to the island. With Nonna on board, she has all of the Greeks singing *Christos Anesti*. We're a little out of season, but as long as we're celebrating Christmas at Thanksgiving, why not add Easter as well? "Don't worry, A. J., you'll learn the words to this one soon enough," Uncle Nick informs me.

"I'm sure I will." Probably by the time I reach the island.

❧ 24 ❧
Setting Sail

As a true Italian mother of the bride, Mama greets each of the guests as they arrive at Big Chief with *"Eat! Eat!"*

Danny's aunts have really gone all out to prepare an authentic Southern feast. Forget about ice sculptures—we have Jell-O sculptures. I have never seen such a display of Jell-O art: a pink flamingo made from strawberry Jell-O with fluffy whipped-cream feathers, a Jell-O tower that resembles the Leaning Tower of Pisa, even cantaloupe with Jell-O molded into the centers. Each slice has a perfect sliver of Jell-O wedged inside. It's called *stained-glass melon*. Add to the Jell-O display: fried chicken, barbecue pork ribs, shrimp gumbo, three varieties of potato salad … it just goes on and on.

When it's apparent that all of the guests have arrived, Mama makes an announcement: "All right, everyone, it's time for the father-daughter dance."

"Hold on right there!" My Aunt Genevieve is the only person brave enough to override Mama … and live. She's still the big sister in the family. "First, it's time for the *nyfiatiko!*"

The next thing I know I'm being abducted by Uncle Nick's sisters and all of the Greek women in the room. "Now that you are officially married *and* Greek, it's time to learn the Greek bride's dance."

Oh boy, here we go!

"This is how we do it ... this is how we do it," I hear over and over. Not only do I get to learn this in front of everyone, I get to *lead* it, kicking and dipping my way through Big Chief. All of the Greek women and girls join in, coaching me along as we go. By the time I finally have a few of the steps mastered, it's over.

Once we've had a chance to catch our breath, Mama announces, "Okay, now it's time for the father-daughter dance!" She signals to Daddy and hits the music. "Fly Me to the Moon" begins to play.

Nonna and Angelo join us out on the dance floor. Grandma is smiling and has a little glimmer in her eyes that I haven't seen for years. Then to my delight, I see Jason make his way over to Adriana, and darned if they don't end up joining us too. "What's going on?" I whisper to Adriana as I whirl past her.

"Just friends," she whispers back, the second time around.

At the start of "I Left My Heart in San Francisco," Danny cuts in and takes me away from Daddy. My heart fills with mixed emotions. Love for Danny, bittersweet sorrow for Daddy. This can't be easy on him.

Jack and Stella join us, bringing back childhood memories of the power of God's grace in restoring their broken hearts and family.

I whirl by Adriana again. "Still just friends?" I whisper.

"Get lost," she whispers back. We both laugh.

The music takes a sudden turn and some very lively Greek music comes blaring through the speakers. Uncle Nick takes center stage. "In honor of the Degulios' long-lost yet newly found Greek heritage, we dedicate this dance to you."

And we're off! My first time dancing the *kalamatianos* as a true Greek. This time with my entire family. *Opa!*

Everyone in the room is kicking up their heels in one big circle. Nonna must have learned this as a child. She hasn't missed a step yet. What's really a hoot is watching all of the Southern folk get in on it. Adriana is doubled over with laughter trying to help Jason get the basic steps down. *I smell victory.*

Mama dances herself into a frenzy, then bows out, collapsing in a big La-Z-Boy by the fireplace. I excuse myself from the circle to join her.

"Mama?"

She looks up at me and smiles. I can tell she's exhausted. How could she not be? I kneel down beside her chair in my gown. "Hey, Mama."

She turns and looks into my eyes. "Hey, kiddo." She reaches over and holds my face between her hands. "How's my little bride?"

"Happy," I tell her.

"That's all I need to know." She looks over at Danny. "I knew you'd find your prince," she says, still smiling. She searches the room until her eyes land on Daddy. "A good prince is hard to find." She looks back at Danny. "I'd say your chances look pretty good from here. I'm betting on that one."

"Mama, thank you for my wedding ... I'm so sorry...."

"*S-h-h-h.*" Mama gets a little glint in her eye. "Angelina Juliana Morgan, don't you know that love means never having to say you're sorry?"

"Isn't that a line from a movie?"

She starts to snicker. "*Love Story*. Isn't that just the dumbest thing you've ever heard in your entire life?"

"It is!" I snicker back.

"Who would say such an idiotic thing?" she bellows. "That guy was the biggest jerk to his poor sick wife! She deserved a whole lot more than … 'I'm sorry'!" Mama is roaring now. "What a moron!" She's about to fall off of her chair.

I can't get any lower, I'm already on the floor laughing. "That's like saying, 'Oh, by the way, I've ruined your life … sorry.'"

"Sorry *my foot!*" Mama howls. "Try 'good riddance … you … *bonehead!*'" That did it. She's on the floor with me, kicking her feet, gasping for air. When we look at each other, it only gets worse. The tears start to roll. I'm suddenly aware that we are not alone. The entire room is now focused on us. I attempt to crawl away in my wedding gown, in search of an isolated room. Mama starts to follow me. "Get your own room!" I gasp. It's my only hope for survival.

Emerging moments later, I avoid all eye contact—especially with Mama. Danny's watching me from across the room, like he's not sure if it's safe to approach me just yet. I take a deep breath and saunter over to him as though nothing unusual has happened. "When are we cutting the cake?" I ask nonchalantly.

"Anytime you like. This is your party, princess."

"Well, then, how about now?"

"Done."

Our cake is one beautiful creation. A tower of white frosted perfection with a fine plastic replica of Danny and me perched at the top. Except if you look too close, the bride looks cross-eyed. We had the option of about ten different cake and frosting variations. The choice was simple: white on white, with white dots and white roses, on a big white doily. That has always been my idea of a good piece of cake.

While Danny and I are preparing to do the cake ceremony, the guests are preparing for a toast. Champagne, *ouzo,* and sparkling cider all around. Daddy comes and stands by me. "Don't worry, fig, I'll go easy on you."

"Thanks." I just used up my embarrassment quota for the day with Mama.

"Attention, please! I'd like to propose a toast to the bride and groom." Daddy looks at me with a reassuring smile as the guests all gather round. Now that Nonna's big secret is out, she has decided to toast us with a shot of *ouzo.*

Daddy takes the floor. "What I have to say isn't going to be easy for me." He has to look down for a minute. He looks at me and smiles. "Those of you who know A. J. well know that my daughter tends to wear her heart on the outside. This has always made me feel a little overprotective of her. I have prayed her entire life that the man she would choose to marry would appreciate this about A. J., and cherish and protect her accordingly. I prayed for a man who, before all things, would love God the way A. J. loves God. I knew if he did, he could love my daughter the way she deserves to be loved.

"As a child, A. J. was the most tenderhearted kid there ever was. She loved animals and people—in that order—and she loved life. She was a *hopeful romantic,* as we called her, and I knew it would take a special man to make that heart of hers beat the way it should." He looks right at Danny and lifts his glass. "And today, I thank God that she found you. I believe that you, Daniel Morgan, are the one man worthy of marrying my daughter."

Everyone raises their glasses, while Daddy and I exchange glances. I'm acutely aware that something in my heart is trying to make the adjustment from Daddy to a new man in my life, and Daddy and I both know it.

Dino raises his glass. "Geez, that sounded more like A. J.'s dying than getting married."

"To a father, it can feel like both," Daddy says. Then he excuses himself and slips outside.

Uncle Nick covers for Daddy. *"Na mas zisuon!"* he yells, raising his glass to Danny and me. "Live a long and happy life!"

Cheers ring out in three different languages. Danny and I toast each other, then Danny signals me with his eyes to go after Daddy.

I find him down on the dock, staring at the lake. He turns when he hears me approaching. "Hey there, fig."

I walk into his waiting embrace. "I'm sorry if I'm making you feel sad, Daddy."

He lets out a gentle laugh. "Hey, I'm happier for you than I am sad for myself." He looks down at me with a warm smile. "I guess this is all a little harder than either your mother or I expected. It's all just happening so fast—your leaving home—so far away, and the next thing we know, you're all grown up and married. But it's all part of the good life, the way God meant it to be." He pulls me to his side and turns us back toward Big Chief. "C'mon, let's go eat some cake with that cowboy of yours."

I take my place beside Danny and together we cut the cake. My groom is much kinder than I am when it comes to feeding each other wedding cake. I'm not sure what's gotten into me, but I give him a little more than he can handle in one bite. He makes up for it by giving me a big kiss with frosting all over his face.

After enjoying my very vanilla cake, I slip into the bathroom to wash off my white-frosted face.

By the time I emerge, my groom is nowhere to be found. Then I spot my two grandmothers sitting together at a table with Angelo. I have to get in on this rare moment; they've hardly spoken to one another since I was born. They're looking at me and whispering to each other. *"S-h-h-h!"* Nonna hisses as I come closer.

"Okay, what are you two up to?"

Nonna looks up, guilty as all get-out.

"Okay, Grandma, out with it. What are you smirking about?"

"Angelina Juliana! Just the girl we were talking about." She looks over at Grandma Angelina and winks. "It's a *great big* secret."

"It's big, all right," Grandma Angelina adds, and they both start to giggle like schoolgirls.

"How about a teeny-tiny hint?"

"Oh, all right. I was just sharing what I'm giving you for a wedding gift."

I'm sure I'm in for a treat. Glancing over at the gift table, I have an inkling it's the three-foot-tall package wrapped in newspaper and duct tape—with the feet sticking out of the bottom. Looks like Saint Francis will soon have a companion to help him guard the cemetery. "It's nice to see you two enjoying each other."

Nonna smiles proudly. "I have called a truce on our eighteen-year-old argument."

"Really? And how did you manage to make up?"

Nonna looks over at Grandma Angelina. "We've decided on a plan that will solve the old family feud."

"You mean the feud over my name?"

"That's the one!" Nonna says. "Saint Francis told me your first two babies would be twins, a girl and a boy, so we've agreed to name them both after me. Juliana and Julio."

"Is that right? Well, what happens if I just raise baby elephants instead?"

Nonna sits back in her chair and stares at me. "In that case, name them after Grandma Angelina."

"What do you mean by that?" Grandma Angelina remarks.

"I mean, if she's raising elephants, they should be named after the grandmother they resemble most." Nonna begins to snicker just like my Mama.

"*Nonna!*"

Nonna is still snickering when I reach for the bottle of *ouzo* sitting in front of her. "Hey, where're you going with that?"

"No more *ouzo* for you, Nonna. You're not saying kind things."

"It has nothing to do with the *ouzo*. I'm Greek—now hand it over." She gets that look of challenge in her eyes and I brace myself for the worst.

Angelo reaches over and places his hand gently on Nonna's arm. *"Ti va di ballare?"* Would you like to dance?

Nonna's eyes soften, a sweet smile appears. She gives him a shy nod and shuffles out on the dance floor without looking back.

I take a seat next to Grandma Angelina. "I hope you didn't take Nonna's comment too personally."

"Oh, heavens, no. I've known your Grandma Juliana long enough not to take anything she says too seriously." She reaches across the table for Nonna's purse, opens it, dumps her entire piece of wedding cake inside, snaps it shut, and sets it back. "She'll be happy to know that the elephant is starting her diet today."

🐿️

After watching Nonna and Angelo dance together, I start looking around for Danny again. I cannot, for the life of me, find my husband. Amidst all of the mingling and chatter, a sudden hush falls over the room. Glancing around, I notice all eyes are turned toward the front window. I follow their glances out toward the lake. *Oh ... my ... gosh!*

"It's my pirate ship!" I lift my wedding gown to my knees and run out the front slider, charging full speed for the dock. "Danny Morgan, wait for me!"

Standing on the bow of a thirty-foot pirate ship is my very own pirate in a dashing white swashbuckler's shirt, tight black pants with a belt and sword, and black boots. He even has the patch over the eye. The words *Two Drifters* are painted across the bow, and "Moon River" is playing softly from deck speakers. "C'mon, wench, let's hit the high seas!"

I run up the plank and throw myself into his arms. The entire wedding party gathers on the dock below. Mama is flashing pictures of the bride and the pirate. Adriana tosses up a suitcase that she's packed for me, then returns to Jason's side. *Hold on—Adriana and Jason.* I break from my own romantic embrace long enough to yell, "Hey, I have a bet on you two over this boat, and a book at stake! You sure you don't want to try out the farm life, Adriana?"

"Sorry, sis, my heart's in Milan. But I hate to think of *Mending Sails* never hitting the bookstores—just write the book—that's why they call it fiction!"

Danny raises the mainsail and prepares to cast off.

"So, Cap'n Dan, where did you ever find this boat?"

"Find it? I *built* it. I restored an old schooner and turned it into a pirate ship. Why do you think I've been spending so much time in my boat shed?"

"*This* is 'the project' you were always working on?"

"This is it. I thought maybe you'd discovered my secret when you made that bet with me for the pirate ship."

"I had no idea!" I look out at the lake. "Won't it be kinda cold out there at night? I mean, this is November."

"It has a heated cabin. I thought we'd sail away for a few days now, and plan a longer trip next summer."

This is just too good.

Our ship sets sail in a gentle breeze on the waters of Indian Lake. Standing on deck, with my wedding dress billowing in the wind, I wave good-bye to the cheering crowd on the dock.

What a great scene for my next novel … *Setting Sail …*

Their ship set sail in a gentle breeze on the waters of the Indian Ocean. The pirate and his bride are off to see the world.

Two young drifters, brought together by fate ... held together
over the years by a dog ...

Speaking of dog ... "Where's Sailor?"

"I think the kids fed him too much wedding cake—he's passed out on the bow."

Sure enough, Sailor's sacked out beside the anchor. Crossing the deck, I join my handsome rogue pirate and slip my arm around his waist. "Now I have almost everything I've ever dreamed of."

"What do you mean *almost?* You've got your dog, your boat, and me. What else is there?"

"You still owe me a hamster, you know."

Danny grins. "No, I don't."

"Yes, you do—you promised me a hamster."

"He's on board."

I look around. "Oh yeah, where?"

"In the captain's quarters." Danny scoops me up in my bridal gown and carries me over the threshold of the cabin. "C'mon, I'll introduce you."

... a little more ...

When a delightful concert comes to an end,

the orchestra might offer an encore.

When a fine meal comes to an end,

it's always nice to savor a bit of dessert.

When a great story comes to an end,

we think you may want to linger.

And so, we offer ...

AfterWords—just a little something more after you

have finished a David C. Cook novel.

We invite you to stay awhile in the story.

Thanks for reading!

Turn the page for ...

more Stories Behind the Stories

Do you ever wonder if the people who write romance stories really experience true love themselves, or do they just make it all up? Perhaps these writers are just a bunch of really lonely people with good imaginations and enough time on their hands to dream this stuff up. On the other hand, perhaps some writers really are hopeless romantics like A. J., and really do believe in true love … like, perhaps even … *this* writer …

**A word from the author on true
love and real-life princes …**

I first laid eyes on him when I was twenty-one: a big, hairy brute from Alaska, my best friend's brother. He was home from working on the fishing boats in Cordova for the summer. Six-foot-four inches of muscle and … I wasn't sure what … I couldn't really tell what he looked like beneath his bearded face and long hair. We'll call him Bear (which happens to be what I really do call him). Anyway, Bear had just worked his way through college and was now finished with school and fishing in Alaska.

A few months later I was walking through the shopping mall when I saw this clean-cut guy with the bluest eyes I'd ever seen. He looked right at me and I actually gasped—*gasped out loud*—then looked around to make sure no one heard me. I noticed he was with Dave, who happened to be an acquaintance of mine. I suddenly had a dire need to speak with Dave. I knew Dave worked on the fishing boats in Alaska too, so for the sake of keeping the conversation going (so I could stare at his friend's blue eyes some more), I asked if he ever saw Bear now that fishing was over.

The guy with the blue eyes looked at Dave, then at me, and said, "I am Bear."

"Oh. You look … different." Amazing what a cut and shave can do for a guy. Even more amazing was what he looked like beneath all of that hair.

My first thought was: *I wonder if he has a girlfriend.* My next thought was: *Even if destiny were to bring us together, there could be no future for the two of us anyway.* I was a respectable, churchgoing Catholic girl, and Bear, he was … well … I'd heard stories about those wild Alaskan fishermen. On a spiritual level alone, we're talking the Great Divide.

Never underestimate the power of prayer (more likely his grandmother's than mine). A few months later, I heard a new rumor: Bear had started going to church and was no longer wild.

That's when providence (and a bit of scheming) set in: I called Bear's sister to find out what Bible study he was going to. I didn't mention why.

"You know, you should really call my brother—he says it's a really good one."

"Oh really? *What's his number?*"

So I called. And I was scared—just like A. J. when she called Danny that first day back from Italy. My saving grace was that I couldn't see the hunk on the other end of the line while trying to pull this off, and I knew he'd have no clue that this was anything more than a Bible study inquiry. No, I did not yell "Howdy on ya!" in a

Southern accent when he answered. But I did say, "Hi, I'm a friend of your sister—she suggested I call you...."

Did I ever mention I once took acting classes?

※

When the big night rolled around, I spent an exorbitant amount of time preparing for this Bible study. Not in my Bible, mind you—in the *mirror.* Driving to the Bible study, I suddenly realized I'd forgotten something ... my Bible. I whipped my little VW Bug into a friend's driveway, ran to the door, and asked to borrow her Bible for the night!

Minutes later I gracefully walked into a room full of people with my Bible tucked under my arm, looking like Mother Teresa herself (with a cute little outfit and a smidge of makeup).

Bear looked up with *those eyes.* "Oh, hi," he said. "I remember you."

You do? Funny, I remember you too.

Bear even suggested that we pass around a sheet of paper so everyone could write his or her phone number down in case we wanted to get hold of anyone during the week. This was going well. The Bear was walking right into my trap. Then something went terribly wrong. Some guy (we'll call him Rodney Gizmode) with inch-thick glasses cornered me and wouldn't stop talking to me. "Do you want to be part of my vision ministry?"

Heck no, I don't even wear glasses!

Rodney sat next to me—very attentive—through the entire Bible study. When it was over, I watched as Bear made his way over to sit by me, then patiently waited for Rodney to stop talking. And waited … and waited … but Rodney never stopped!

I couldn't take it anymore—the most gorgeous guy on God's green earth was just sitting there while I was held captive by Rodney Gizmode. I had to make my escape before Blue Eyes took off, dashing my only hope of true love. I politely excused myself from Rodney, saying I needed to use the restroom (I turned toward Bear and almost gave him the silent canine command for *stay*).

"I'll show you where the restroom is," Rodney offered.

Uuuuggghhh!

He even went inside and turned the light on for me, then waited outside the door for me. I knew he was out there. I prayed for mercy. The minute I opened the door, I made a beeline for Bear!

꙰

As fate would have it, he did call me—Bear, not Rodney—and he invited me to church and out to eat on Sunday.

I casually agreed to go.

Oh … I may have failed to mention one small detail. I was *kind of* dating someone else at the time. We were on the four-year roller coaster ride that wasn't going anywhere in particular. And he wasn't interested in going to Bible study with me. We'd been playing the on-again, off-again game for much too long. But still, I began to feel guilty. I tried to tell myself it was okay, Bear was just a friend who was giving me a ride to church … and feeding me afterward. No big deal. I would even tell Bear all about my *kind-of* boyfriend, and just explain to him that he and I could be really good friends.

Sunday morning rolled around. Someone knocked. I opened my door to a pair of enormous blue eyes.

Oh, melt.

In one hand, he held a quart of chocolate milk that he been drinking—straight from the carton.

How cute is that?

In his other hand, he had my morning newspaper—which he handed to me while looking at me with *those eyes!*

I took one look at him and thought: *There is no way I'm telling him anything about anyone else.*

As it turned out, it was the other guy I decided to give the "just friends" speech to instead.

So Bear and I went to church and to the waterfront and to the park and out to eat ... and to the movies ... and canoeing ... and eight months later we got married, and we've lived in absolute bliss ever since. *Except*—we have had a few *tiny* issues over ... animals.

When someone who enjoys catching and eating animals marries someone who likes to rescue animals, it tends to cause a slight bit of friction now and then ... like the time I found five abandoned puppies and brought them all home. On our anniversary. Bear didn't find that real romantic. And the time I got on the mailing list for the animal rights group, and then sobbed every time they sent me infor-mation with rescue photos. And the time I brought home a pet rat because he was on sale for a buck and I couldn't resist a cute animal or a bargain. Bear told me that when you live on a farm you don't need to *buy* a rat.

Over the years, there have been a number of stray pets that have just appeared out of nowhere. There were also a few who disappeared—like Teddy, our teddy bear hamster, who built himself a little condo behind the kitchen stove and didn't come out until he darn well wanted to. Imagine Bear's enthusiasm over Frosty the hamster, who just recently racked up a one-hundred-seventy-five-dollar vet bill ... and died anyway, God rest his soul. And now there's the issue about this elephant orphanage I've been curious about. Have you ever seen a photo of an orphaned baby elephant being rescued?

I mean, how can *anyone* say no to that?

Even as I'm writing this, Bear is hunting for the cat that I snuck inside the house while he was at work (it was really cold outside). Unfortunately, Bear's allergic to cats.

This kind of thing has gone on for over twenty-five years now, and I don't see our *conflict of interests* resolving itself anytime soon. However, we do agree on the most important thing in life—we both love, love, *love* Jesus. And by His grace, I fully expect to stay madly in love with my prince and live happily ever after.

By the way … is anyone still wondering who the character of Danny was based on?

The Fifty Pets You (Hope to) meet in Heaven

Childhood:

Tinkerbelle, the cat

A gazillion pollywogs

Goldie the goldfish, who died on Easter and did not rise, as I prayed during Easter Mass

Bony and Claude, the turtles

Chumley, the collie-shepherd (aka Sailor's mascot)

Luigi, the other collie-shepherd

Mouse rescued from Dorie's cat, who lived in my tree fort in a Tarzan lunch pail

Abigail, the albino hamster living in secret in my closet

Pugsly, the hamster I had Dorie give me for my birthday

Moonie, my Clydesdale draft horse

Maynard, the cat who had five kittens (who we thought was a boy till then)

Rudy, the hamster who I ran away with because my mom said he had to live in the garage

Stray kitten found on our family trip to Hawaii

After leaving home:

The Kid, rescue dog from visiting the dog pound

Sandy, rescue dog from visiting the dog pound

Loser, rescue cat from visiting the pound

Alfie, rescue dog from visiting the dog pound

Birdie, rescue dog from visiting the dog pound

Misha, the mouse

Peanut Butter, the hamster

Jelly, the hamster

Teddy Bear, the hamster

On the farm:

Peach, the half-blind chicken

Butterscotch, the friendly chicken

Elvis, the banty chicken

Mr. and Mrs. White (ducks)

Mama, banty hen who raised a dozen turkey babies

Millie, the cat

Max, the cat

Twig, the stray cat found in a tree

Fred, the cat

Bear, the Great White Pyrenees

Jesse, the other Great White Pyrenees

Curley, the cow

Duke, the horse

Bargain, the rat

Kitty, the stray

Bailey, the abandoned chow with five puppies

Max, pound puppy

Baby Bear, the European black bear hamster

Tiny Tim, the itty-bitty baby dwarf hamster

Frosty, the Chinese dwarf hamster with the one-hundred-seventy-
   five-dollar vet bill

Buster, the baby turtle

References

Research on Orthodox History

The Orthodox Study Bible
Thomas Nelson Publishers
First printing of the Old and New Testaments in English 2008

The Apostolic Fathers: Years 70 AD–135 AD
Including Ignatius, bishop of Antioch, letters to:
> The Ephesians
> The Romans
> The Philadelphians
> Polycarp: early martyr of Christ—mid-second century

Published by Baker Book House 5th printing 1992
First edition published in London by Macmillan and Company in 1891
Reprinted by Baker House 1956

Father Seraphim Rose: His Life and Works
By Hieromonk Damascene
Copyright 2003 by the St. Herman of Alaska Brotherhood, Platina, California

Father Arseny 1893–1973—Priest, Prisoner, Spiritual Father
By Alexander and Vera Bouteneff
St. Vladimir's Seminary Press 1998

In honor of Father Arseny and the many Orthodox believers who lived and died for their faith in Jesus Christ in the Soviet Union during the Stalin years:

> *"Since the fall of the Soviet regime, it has been revealed that six hundred bishops, forty thousand priests, and one hundred twenty thousand monks and nuns were killed during [the Stalin years (1924-1953)]. Many of these died in the harsh conditions of prison or labor camp; others were shot or buried alive. By the end of Stalin's dictatorship, only some two hundred priests remained active in the Soviet Union. The scale of this martyrdom is unprecedented in the history of the Christian Church."*

From Translator's Foreword in the book:
Father Arseny 1893–1973—Priest, Prisoner, Spiritual Father
Translated from Russian to English by Vera Bouteneff 1998
Originally published in Russian as *Otets Arsenii* by St. Tikhon's Orthodox Theological Institute Press, Brotherhood of the All Merciful Savior, Moscow 1993

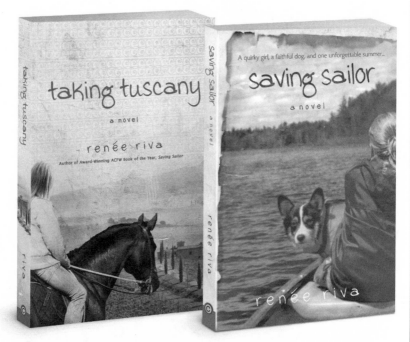